AUGUSTA

The Lost Epic of Rome's Last Days

L.A. Henneke

Augusta: The Lost Epic of Rome's Last Days.
Copyright © 2017 by Logan Henneke.
All rights reserved.

Cover art by Cici Laya.

ISBN: 1976274214
ISBN-13: 978-1976274213

This book is a work of fiction. References to historic figures
and events- combined with the presentation of this story as if
it truly was a historic text- are intended solely for the sake of
adding a sense of immersion and authenticity. All other characters, conversations and occurrences are to be treated as from
the imagination of the author.

ACKNOWLEDGMENTS

I wish to thank CiCi Laya for her fantastic job on the art for the cover. Let me also take this time to acknowledge everyone who has offered me both encouragement and support as I underwent this project. This here's for you.

CONTENTS

INTRODUCTION

If the epic poems of Antiquity were to be arranged in an order narrating the troubles of the Trojan people, with the *Iliad* being the beginning and the *Aeneid* as its continuation, then perhaps *Augusta* might be one day regarded as the conclusion of this cycle. No finer way would there be, perhaps, to finish off this epic narrative cycle than to lead up to the events surrounding the fall of the Western Roman Empire, the end of Antiquity and the beginning of Europe's famed Middle Ages.

If *Augusta* is not a word familiar to those not trained in Latin, at the very least the reader should be able to recognize its masculine counterpart *augustus*. *Augusta* was an honorific title bestowed upon Roman empresses and prestigious women, and Justa Grata Honoria received it as a child in 426, shortly after the ascension of her brother Valentinian III. The poem translated here has long been referred to by this title, albeit transliterated in its syllabic script as *a-u-gu-se-ta*, an appropriate title given that, even though she does not initially appear in the narrative, Honoria is central to the text, both for the historical context in which the story is set and in the events that transpire therein.

If someone told me a few years ago that I would one day translate an epic written in a language nobody knew existed save for those who spoke it, much less that it was still spoken, it should come as no surprise that I would probably have laughed off said remark as if it was some hyperbolic compliment of my potential future. I say that because I think it is important to express, however briefly, that the decision to publish this volume did not come lightly, but as the result of much consideration.

Perhaps one day I shall recount the events leading up to this decision, for they merit their own volume. After all, one could hardly be expected to bear witness to lands roaming with live dinosaurs (and a battle between ancient gods centuries in the making) and stray mum on the matter. Alas, for such a story ought best be reserved for another time.

The story of *Augusta*, however, is certainly one worth looking at, filled with a plethora of epic moments and historic dramas. I hope that you the reader will enjoy the fruits of my long labors and of a journey that would be the envy even of Odysseus and Alexander.

NOTES ON TRANSLITERATION
AND TRANSLATION

Given the fact that I have translated a text written in a language never before encountered by an English-speaking outsider, it is imperative I explain a few of the decisions I made while transcribing this text. I have tried my best to preserve the literal meaning of the words originally used, or at least as literal as a translation can be. In this I have sacrificed both the meter and rhyme of the original text, and I do not deem further detail on that is presently necessary. However, I should at least offer a justification for how I translated a number of terms used throughout the text. This list is surely not comprehensive, but it should at the very least give an idea of the work I have undergone.

Swart Elf

The term 'Swart Elf' is admittedly misleading, but I have chosen to render *Wešekeriatu* (pl. *Wešekeriasi*) as 'Swart Elf' to maintain some sort of mythological familiarity with my primarily English-speaking audience. The origin of this term lies in the Old Norse *svartálfr* (pl. *svartálfar*) meaning 'black elf' or 'dark elf'.

Scholars have noted that these 'swarthy elves' of Germanic legend appear to be synonymous with dwarfs, and the Wešekeriasi characters in *Augusta* serve as obvious historic inspirations for the dwarf figures of later Norse legends. It should be noted that the Swart Elves which appear in this volume are not pointy-eared like the Elves or short like the Dwarves of modern fantasy; their anatomy is more like that of humans, save they are all grey-skinned, generally slender of build, and bear distinctively high cheekbones.

The War-Sky

The god of war worshipped by Attila, the War-Sky is referred to in *Augusta* as *ma-ku-za-ne-pu*, coming from the Swart Elf words *ma-ku-za* ('battle' or 'war') and *a-ne-pu* ('sky'). I decided to fully translate the meaning of the name to preserve a linguistic distinction between the Huns and the Swart Elves, who clearly were not referring to this god by his actual name, but perhaps their own translation of a previously Hunnic title.

Hunnic Names

Archaeological evidence detailing the language of the Huns is virtually nonexistent, consisting almost entirely of proper names. It is thus difficult to confidently classify Hunnic, but I do believe the safest case would consider Hunnic as related in some ways to the Turkic languages. A number of Hunnic names in *Augusta* have not been seen elsewhere in the historical record, and I have so elected to transliterate these names using Proto-Turkic as the basis for their reconstruction. Therefore, my constructions of these names may not be exact, but they should give the reader as good an estimation as one could hope for.

INTRODUCTION

Kolbulut- The famous sword of Attila, Kolbulut is mentioned by Roman historians, though never by a specific name, and it is written in *Augusta* as *ko-le-bu-lu-tu*. Using my aforementioned basis for these transliterations, I chose to render it as *kolbulut*, using the Proto-Turkic words *kol* ('hand') and *bulut* ('cloud'). Assuming this is an accurate rendition, Kolbulut might be translated as something along the lines of 'sword of heaven,' an apt name for a sword belonging to one of Attila's status.

Jalaŋgül- The capital city of the Huns, Jalaŋgül is written in *Augusta* as *ša-la-ne-gu-le*. I have based this rendering off of the Proto-Turkic words *jalaŋ* ('field') and *gül* ('house', dwelling'). Assuming this is correct, Jalaŋgül might be translated as 'settlement of/on the steppe'.

Teŋiŕ- The Hunnic wife of Zerco never mentioned by name in the historical record, she is recorded in *Augusta* as *te-ne-gi-re*. Assuming again that this is a rough transliteration of Hunnic, her name might be similar in appearance to the Proto-Turkic *teŋiŕ*, which means 'sea'.

Biological Nomenclature

A number of animals with descriptions matching extinct taxa pop up in the Swart Elves' so-called 'Land of Dragons', known in their language as Karoputaru ('garden of [the god] Karotu'). After much painstaking research, most of it beyond the bounds of this text itself, I have classified every such creature appearing in *Augusta*.

INTRODUCTION

When these names appeared in the 3rd person narrative of the text, I translated the Wešikeriaya names into their modern equivalents. Therefore, 'Kenateyo' will be read as *Tyrannosaurus,* 'Terikeruša' as *Triceratops, et cetera.* When appearing in internal dialogue, however, these animals will be referred to by their Wešikeriaya names.

Whenever the modern scientific name for an extinct animal appears for the first time, readers may find a footnote at the bottom of the page referring to the creature's Wešikeriaya name. Readers so inclined may also utilize the Swart Elf glossary in the back as a reference.

NOTES ON HISTORICAL CONTEXT

As is typical of the epics from Antiquity, *Augusta* begins *in media res* ('in the middle things'), meaning that much of the expositional backstory is only filled in at later points in the text. The events leading to the tale as narrated in *Augusta* would surely have been known to most of its audience at the time it was written, and it is only in Books Three-Five when we as the readers get much detail on it for ourselves.

While such historical context might have been basic knowledge for *Augusta's* intended audience, it would be safe to assume that the average modern reader knows little, if anything, concerning the affairs of the fifth century. While the events critical to understand are indeed explained or hinted at throughout the text, it seems imperative that I briefly explain them anyway, lest some poor reader jump into the text and feel overwhelmed by obscure historical references.

The story opens up around 450/451, near the end of the Roman Empire as most people know it. Before this point the empire was divided into two halves, one in the East that ruled from Constantinople and another in the West that ruled from Rome, Mediolanum, and then Ravenna. The official date given for the collapse of the Western Roman Empire is placed at 476, while its eastern counterpart would last up until the fifteenth century, ending with the Ottoman conquest of Constantinople in 1453.

INTRODUCTION

In 450, the Western Roman Empire was ruled from Ravenna by Valentinian III, then thirty years of age. His sister was Honoria, who long thought that her brother was a weak and indolent ruler. It is said that she seduced her chamberlain Eugenius, perhaps in an attempt to overthrow her brother, but the affair was soon discovered and thwarted. Afterwards, Honoria was sent away to Constantinople, though there is some disagreement as to whether or not the exile actually happened.

Regardless of the controversy, it is clear that Valentinian wanted to marry off his sister to the senator Bassus Herculanus, a man who would have not likely used his position to supplant Valentinian. Faced then with the advent of an unwanted marriage, Honoria tried to wiggle her way out of this union, sending a plea to none other than Attila the Hun, still on relatively decent terms with the Western Roman Empire.

With this message Honoria sent her ring, perhaps as a sign of authentication, though others would suggest that she proposed to Attila, asking to be married to him instead. Whether one would agree with this latter hypothesis or not, history makes it clear that Attila chose to interpret her message as such, demanding half of the Western Empire from Valentinian in exchange for her hand in marriage.

It should come as no surprise to hear that Valentinian denied the terms. In his anger he was turned against his sister and nearly killed her. It was only by of the intervention of their mother Galla Placidia that Honoria was spared from his rage, though afterwards she disappears entirely from the historical record. Honoria's ultimate fate remains unknown.

But Valentinian's rejection of this marriage offered Attila the pretext he long desired to launch a campaign against the Western Roman Empire. Gathering the nations subjugated by the Huns, he made his way into Roman Gaul, plunging the Roman Empire into its last great war and into some of the most famous events of Late Antiquity after the conversion of Constantine. This would be the beginning of the ancient world's last hurrah before the dawn of the Middle Ages.

Harmonia:
AUGUSTA

BOOK ONE
SAVAGE SIGHTINGS

Let me sing the destinies of she
Who caused the world to burn, yet to it
Offered quenching waters to soothe its pain.
Exiled from Ravenna's heights, by long labors
She traversed the earth's wide expanses
Until she saw a Land of Dragons
Older than human empires and thenceforth went
To contest the Scourge of God,
Met him in hateful contest and laid siege
To citadels beneath the earth, settling there
The strifes of our age. Relate, my Muse,
To posterity the causes of our pain,
And let her legacy live on.
She, though condemned in life as an exile,
May gain her well deserved respect in a future epoch.

There she was, hurled headlong
Into the land of the Franks, a proud people
Established generations earlier as tribes amassed-
The Sicambri, born for battle and marauding,
The Bructeri, allies of old Arminius,
Who shattered the legions of Varus

BOOK ONE

Underneath the shade of German firs,
The Ampsivarii, or at least the few of them
Who joined Arminius in his traitorous advance,
The Chamavi, famed settlers them all,
The Chattuari, turbulent and licentious,
And tribes of Tencteri and Ubii–
Seven nations merged into one,
Still under the shadow of fractured Rome.
A waning empire wounded and weary,
The West limped on broken limbs
Cracked by decades of pressure
From without and within.
Yet one day shall from the Franks
Emerge a mighty kingdom
And among their number shall be named
An emperor of the West,
The first since the fall of high-born Rome.

Yet no heroes or future kings
Did the exile find, wandering Ildico,
Goth by name and Italian by homeland.
Alone through patches of tall grass she crawled,
Watching the wary eyes of Roman pursuers
Like a lion stalking prancing gazelles
Though she was the hunted and not the hunter.
Itching blades scratched against bare skin,
Lashing at their prey with relentless assault,
Yet she did not coil to pain
Nor did she voice her aggravation
For too near were the Romans,
Though even now she held not their attention,
Their eyes fixated on another target
Larger and Stranger,

SAVAGE SIGHTINGS

Wrapped by the mystery of a barbarian land
Oozing with primordial enchantments.
In a slab of stone along the encircling cliff
Appeared a gaping whole
Which had not been there before.

"Almighty Father!" declared Maximinus,
The youngest Roman of the lot,
Untested,
Yet eager now to prove his merit,
"This yonder shadowy cave was not here
Yet moments ago,
And now its opening maw sits ready
To engulf any who stumble within.
What devilish sorceries draw me now
To wander within and see the source
Of vanishing rock with my own eyes.
God has given me many gifts,
Though restraint be not one of them.
I go now to inspect the ensorcelled hollow
And come out again with nary a tall tale."

Down he descended into the gloom,
Trouncing through stagnant pools.
Air immeasurably hot blew against him
And sweat beat at his brow
And stung at his eyes.
The blasting aroma of sulfur
Bombarded his nostrils
As if a blazing conflagration was kindled
Deeper in, yet nothing
Save a single eye could be seen,
Glowing in the dark like a lone torch

BOOK ONE

In the gloom of encroaching twilight.
An evil hiss shook the earth
And tumbled stones from ceiling overhead.
Maximinus turned and fled,
Hastening from the cave as quick
As burning calves could carry him.
The inferno surged forth from the cave mouth
Like rushing water overflowing
From wide-brimmed vessels into libations below,
Meant to sate some ancient god
Worshipped ere Constantine's reforms
Usurped Jupiter's eagle with the cross of Christ.
Then following the trail of flame
Emerged the source of blazing fire,
Galloping over the earth in thunderous advance,
Huge of mass and in color
Orange like the storm it conjured.
Most of its bulk veiled by a cloud of smoke
And flaming pinions of wrath and woe,
Its form was too obscure to be made out
Even by Ildico's hawk-like gaze.

"Alas," the Romans cried in dismay,
"Whatever shall come of us and our kin
Should such a monster be marshaled to war,
Summoned by a myriad barbarians
Or by Attila himself,
Poised to raze to dust
The Eternal City herself,
Brought low from her seven ancient hills?"

They scattered before infernal ire
And Ildico deemed it wise to return

SAVAGE SIGHTINGS

To the cover of dense forest,
And she found within the woodland
High ground near a shimmering pond,
And she crept beneath looming ash trees.
Ceasing her flight, she took respite
Against a maple trunk and looked around
As a flock of quails scampered across forest floor
And an eagle's form soared overhead.
Covering herself with leaves and hide blankets,
Ildico curled up beneath forest canopy,
And some spirit shut her eyelids,
Casting a sweet slumber upon her,
And for a moment she lost all memory of sadness,
Interrupted only by a burst of distant laughter
And the smell of stew wafting through
The cool evening breeze.
And she remembered where she was,
Deep in the country of the Franks,
And knew then these men were of Frankish descent,
Champions of famed Merovech
And brothers in arms.

But one stood out from among the rest,
Golden-haired Sighlut, a head above the others,
Seemed to her to be of giants' descent.
Broad-shouldered, his imposing figure
Hearkened back to the old legends
That he himself was drawn to,
Captivated by heroes in distant ages
Contesting with the monsters of Chaos,
Never shirking from struggle
But marching ever eagerly into battle
With a weapon in hands and a song on the lips.

BOOK ONE

"What kind of woman have I come across,"
Sighlut said, heralding her approach,
"Alone and isolated in the wide woods of the West.
Your name I ask of you, and of your parentage.
From what lands have you come
And what help might I bestow upon you?"

Then Ildico answered, feeling safe
In this contingent of heroes and champions.
"My name is Ildico, a Goth by descent.
And yet my accent is of Italy,
Like that of a Roman accustomed
To a life of luxury and watching chariots
Racing through the hippodrome
In adrenaline-fueled contention.
My father was a mercenary
Employed in the guard of the emperor himself,
Valentinian- the third of such a name.
But the emperor has grown wary of late,
Fearful of betrayal by kith and kin
As he watches for signs of the Huns,
Expecting them to launch their war at any moment.
So his mind was turned against my father-
My mother too- imprisoned in his halls,
And I have fled far into the wild,
Eluding Roman traps until at last.
I stumble here before Frankish arms.
But tell me now who by chance I have graced upon
So we may exchange our own experiences."

So Sighlut smiled and shook her hand.
"As Huns are your foes, so too are they mine.
I hate the Huns, as did my father

SAVAGE SIGHTINGS

And my father's father, and his father too.
I am Sighlut, a champion among Franks
Renowned in the halls of Merovech,
Mentored in speech and arms by Rega.
One of the Swart Elves he is,
Among the few to have left their far-removed lands
Into the world of Rome and Attila,
From a land ruled by dragons
And by creatures older than wandering Wuotan.
You have met me on a joyous day
For in my hand rests keen-edged Gram,
The sword of my father reforged by Rega.
It has tasted Liuvigild's black blood,
Who years ago slew my father
And offered no wergild for his offense.
We hounded his party to these very woods
And learned they too offer Attila their sympathies.
For murder and treason they have been punished,
Routed in a nearby gorge where I slew their leader-
Cruel Liuvigild- and Gram drank up his blood.
Gram's heavy blade clove through the air
And pounded down upon his shoulder,
Crunching through collarbone
As mangled heart oozed profusely.
Coughing up hot blood, he fell limp
And loosened the grip on his spear-shaft,
Joining treasonous brothers in the life to come.
The fight had been quite one-sided,
Loosing two in exchange for their thirty.
Many others were wounded, of course,
Clutching red patches of mail
Or wrapping wounds to stop the bleeding,
But they all shall be well,

Ready to fight again in no time.
But as we went to burn the dead,
We saw before our eyes a sight
Which no mortal could have expected.
We did not fight it, for we knew not this foe.
But it left us unharmed, content to scavenge
Off of bloated corpses left exposed.
Come and see it with your own eyes,
This race of creatures lost to our world,
Forms that may yet hail
From the Swart Elves' distant Land of Dragons
Where creatures old and alien reign supreme."

Gripped by curiosity's iron grasp,
Ildico agreed and answered saying,
"Take me at once, then,
To see these wondrous forms.
Then I may recount to you a tale
Of an awful creature I too beheld.
Fearsome and baleful,
It sent hardened Romans scattering.
Let us away now and see
The beasts of which you speak."

"Come, comrades," Sighlut declared.
"Break into their stores of mead and ale.
You have fought hard and must drink,
So see that your bellies are stuffed
And tankards filled to the brim!
Victory must be answered with jubilation!"

Not one to question his orders,
The Franks eagerly did as commanded.

SAVAGE SIGHTINGS

So they went in jubilation
While Sighlut and Ildico went away
To behold the dead
And those forms feasting upon their flesh.
With leathery wings and fuzzy bodies,
A dozen of them scavenged off the corpses,
Stripping meat from bone
With the toothy tips of long beaks.
As Gaopato the Elves know them,[*]
Safe and secure in Puaita's golden halls
Feasting and reveling, drinking to
Ancient memories and heroic deeds,
Gathered around the throne of Wanaku,
May his kingdom never falter
Even in this tumultuous era!
But now in Gaul the Istiodactylus swarm,
Gorging on the spoils of war
Far from their craggy abode
Opposite Puaita's pristine harbor,
Driven by unknown purpose from their land-
The doings of Attila, perhaps,
Or maybe the machinations of some other force
Wandering through war-ravaged Europe.

"Such strange animals," Ildico remarked,
Marveling at their unknown forms.

"Indeed," Sighlut answered back,
"Of these creatures, it is said they come
From a land far from our own,
Where crafty Rega and his kind dwell-

---

[*] *Istiodactylus latidens*

BOOK ONE

The Land of Dragons-
Karoputaru in their own tongue.
Some say that the Huns themselves
Have gone beyond the walls of our world
And back again with forms strange and savage.
One such creature they brought
Before my illustrious king.
To Merovech they presented
Some fiend like a bird with a long bony tail[*]
And a single claw in place of wings.
I know not its race nor do any among my kind,
And my feeble mind can only imagine
What other forms await discovery."

Ildico answered saying,
"When still I lived in swampy Ravenna
Huns arrived there too bearing strange beasts
Though of a lesser sort than these.
In little boxes they came with ants
Weird and Wondrous.
Their jaws rose like the tusks of boars
And from between the antennae
Arose a horn as if it were
In truth a rhinoceros
Bound in the form of an insect.
But a monster far more terrible
Than ravenous scavengers did I see
Only hours before meeting you.
I could scarcely make out its shape,
As it came wreathed in fire and smoke,
Thundering out of its hollow den

---

[*] Panuko, a.k.a. *Shuvuuia deserti*

Against those poor Romans gathered there
Who did not know such a terror dwelt
So near where they stood."

"Then let us hasten to Tornacum,"
Golden-haired Sighlut declared,
"To the capital of my people
And illustrious Merovech's seat of power.
There we can find counsel in Rega,
Mentor and foster-father,
Who might yet know more of the beasts
Wandering the wilds of Europe
Or marshaled here by Hunnic might.
He has lately gone on a journey
And come back again,
Returned from the heights of craggy peaks
Overlooking glacial vales.
His knowledge might prove true
And offer aid to us
Ignorant of primordial foes."

They were resolved to go,
And as they prepared to depart
On a trek of three weeks' breadth,
The faint silhouette of a rider
Strode through the evening dark.
A bow and arrows were strapped to his back
And in his hand he gripped a mighty spear,
But it was his conical cap
That betrayed his identity.
More of his kin rode silently through the wood,
All of them Huns.
Singing with whistling notes,

BOOK ONE

They vanished one by one into the dark.
What had they been doing here?
Were they scouts,
Harbingers of an inevitable battle?
Even as horseback troops vanished from sight,
The ominous thought could not be erased
From the corridors of the minds
Of those who watched them from afar.
As soon as they came into sight,
The Huns were gone from all eyes.
Yet Ildico and Sighlut knew
This was but a precursor of woes to come.

Many miles away from the monster's den,
Scarcely a league beyond Tornacum's walls,
Rega chanced upon the object of his hunt,
A pursuit begun by the foul stench of death
Carried through the afternoon breeze
To his keen nostrils. A horde of biting insects
Swarmed the corpse he chanced upon,
Hovering over bloated carcass.
A mighty aurochs he saw,
Few finer cattle had there ever been,
Though now its ebony hide ruptured
From a buildup of toxic gases,
The frayed ends of its hide
Engulfed in a sea of maggots.
So awful a stench it was
The grey-skinned Elf could hardly stand,
Covering his nose
With a beard so bejeweled
It gave away his princely origins,
Son of the late king Rhedemaru.

SAVAGE SIGHTINGS

He was eager to be rid of so profane a find.
But he could not leave yet,
For his attention had been caught
By a sight he did not expect.
He took a sip from an Elven rhyton
Fashioned from gold into the form
Of some monster of the ancient seas,
And he walked to the beast's other side,
Its head cocked sideways
And mouth crusted with blood long dried.

As his eyes scanned the white stripe
That ran along the mighty aurochs'
Well-muscled spine,
He eyed the culprit
That did such a fine beast in.
To its hide clung several arrows
Which looked like loose weeds
Creeping up from underneath the earth,
Engulfing life and nutrition
From neighboring plants
As vermin are ought to do.
The goat-horn shafts pierced the lungs,
Whizzing clean through,
Sapping the bull of breath and life soon after.
The shafts were made by Hunnic hands,
This much was clear to Rega.
By why were Huns prowling these parts?
War would soon be coming it seemed.
The Huns must have been scouting these parts
Before falling in a tussle with the aurochs.
They mastered their foe
And fled into the forest,

BOOK ONE

Not waiting for others who heard
Their cacophonous contest
To come along and catch them in sight.

Then came the clattering of hooves
Speeding over dense undergrowth
As horses crashed through swaying branches,
Whinnying they halted before the Elf.
There Rega saw Sighlut
Followed in turn by a woman he did not know,
Tall and dark-haired, haggard and ragged,
Yet in her eyes he saw the blood of kings
Or that of Venus herself
Coursing through her veins.
Regal then she seemed to him
Even as an exile lost in the wild.
What stories she must have had
He wondered, eager to hear them out.
But first came the matter of Sighlut,
Who had so lately gone to avenge his father.

"Well met," Rega hailed them.
"Has justice been made
Against murderous Liuvigild?
Has the wergild been paid in blood
And due punishment enacted?
Come with me back to the halls
Of illustrious Merovech,
Where there we may dine and convene."

Then he went quickly on, followed in turn
By Sighlut and Ildico
Until at last they reached the place where

SAVAGE SIGHTINGS

The king's hall rose above Tornacum,
Abode of Merovech king of Franks,
Seven nations converged into one.
There they found Merovech,
Seated with sons and daughters.
Proud his wearied face seemed,
Comfortably tucked underneath a crown
While pins shaped like golden cicadas
Held fast his encircling cloak.
Servants were busy preparing dinner,
Sticking slabs of meat on spits
While others crowded around the newcomers.
Then Merovech rose from his throne
And offered to each of them
Ox-hides pallets on which they might rest and meet,
Giving them portions of fatty meats
And pouring out wine into their glasses.
Offering a prayer to Wuotan,
He bade them eat and drink
Until they could no more.

"Now," said he, "our guests have had their fill.
We know the names of two among them.
Tell us, mighty Sighlut,
Who is the third member of your company?
Has justice been made
Against Liuvigild, murderer and traitor?
Has the wergild been paid in blood
And due punishment enacted?"

"Indeed it has," Sighlut answered.
"The reforged blade of my father
Has tasted its first fresh drops of blood.

Yet after the kill I met this woman:
Ildico she is called,
A Goth by name and Italian by homeland,
Sent into exile by a paranoid emperor,
Worried that even loyal allies
Might soon betray him
In favor of those wicked Huns,
Gods curse them all!
We saw several of them out in the wild,
Undoubtedly scouts
Preparing for some future war,
And strange creatures too.
Winged shapes like saurian storks
Feasted off of Liuvigild's dead,
And Ildico too beheld a Dragon-
Or so I think it must be-
Hounding after Romans so foolish
To venture near its infernal den
In a valley carved out by olden gods.

Rega frowned, adding to the tale.
"My lord, I too have things to say.
You know I was gone for many days
While Sighlut went off on his quest.
Hearken now, and let me tell the tale
Of that great beast they beheld,
For I deem I may yet know its name
And of its parentage, too.
Its and my own are one and the same.
I must go back,
So Ildico may know the oldest details.
A stranger to our strife,
She has not heard yet the tale.

SAVAGE SIGHTINGS

Once I was a prince among my people.
With brothers Oturu and Fanefiru
We dwelled in the halls of father Rhedemaru,
But Dola the Trickster,
God of traps and deceits, slew brother Oturu,
Mistaking him for a beast of the wild.
So compelled, he offered wergild
To my father as payment for this homicide.
The price offered was a great hoard,
The vast stores of Anadavara,
Whose cursed ring Anadavarenu
Day by day adds to the wealth
Through magics long lost to the world.
All this you have already heard, Sighlut,
Though the rest will be new to you."
Rega paused, waiting to build up the strength
To recall those bitter memories
That were still too fresh,
Wounds so lately opened
Merely speaking of them caused him pain.

But as his audience encouraged him,
So he continued saying,
"Then all became dark
Once horseback Huns approached
Father's splendid halls
In Newa Sikeria's cavernous crags
Where his line has ruled uncounted ages
Since the doom of our old world.
Much to my shame and remorse,
Father Rhedemaru consented to their terms,
Ready to establish an awful alliance
Between Elf and Hun.

BOOK ONE

To honor the terms,
He offered Attila a portion
Of Anadavara's vast hoard,
That he might fund his armies
And ceaseless far-flung campaigns.
Down into the depths of the mountains
Our descent led us ever onward
To that abode where no light dwells
In the forlorn crack between your world
And the primordial Land of Dragons
Where my kind dwell,
Kept in check by a hoard of beasts
Older than any god I can recall.
In these caves we went until at last
We beheld Gold Tor itself,
The mountain of accumulated gold
Conjured up by Anadavara's tricks.

"Seated upon a pedestal of ivory and bone
Was the great ring Anadavarenu.
No finer band have I beheld,
Nor more ominous indeed, bejeweled,
Around its length extends the form
Of some ancient serpent
Rising from the deeps of the sea
And prepared to engulf any mortal
That dares trod its path.
But Fanefiru, strong-willed though he was,
Could not resist the ring's allure.
Gripped by ravenous greed,
He seized it for itself
And then the cursed band
Unleashed the full measure of its power.

Fanefiru's form was changed,
No longer a regal prince of Elves
But rather a hideous creature,
A huge monster of fire and smoke.
The flap of his wings
Sends storms hurling in their wake.
A Dragon unlike any other,
At once he slew our father
And seized Gold Tor for himself.
But crafty Attila was undaunted,
Eager to make the most of this opportunity.
At once he parleyed with the Dragon,
My late brother,
Offering him the one price that in splendor
Could rival Anadavara's vast hoard-
The Eternal City-
High-borne Rome seated on seven hills.
Though the Dragon has not yet emerged,
Eager for battle, already I rue that day!
Then shall the Western Empire fall
And a new one rise in its ashes,
An unholy alliance
Between cruel Hun and dread Dragon,
One surely to last through the ages.
But here am I,
Living beneath Merovech's shadow,
Once the next in line
For my kingdom's wondrous throne.
I know not the fate of this succession,
Instead plotting to avert calamity
While others fight for father's throne."

At this news, Ildico stood still,

Gripped by mournful silence.
Exile though she was,
She had it not in her heart
To wish for such a fate against Italy,
The land of her birth,
Where she had spent long years
Walking down Ravenna's regal streets
And strolling past the harbor
As dark ships sailed in
From the heights of Constantinople,
Well-walled and splendid.
Then she spoke saying,
"How can we hope to avert
Such a wicked fate?
Are there any means by which
This alliance may yet be thwarted?"

"Fear not!" Rega answered.
"There is one yet who may aid us,
He who opened the door to Gold Tor.
His name is Evoric, a Goth like you.
Young as he may be,
There are few more accustomed
To life in the desolate wild
Nor more learned of ancient lore."

"I know that name!" Sighlut declared.
"I met him once near the shores of the sea,
Opposite Gautar's far-distant beaches
Watching pods of speeding dolphins
Breach the surface and ride
Down along the foaming waves."

Rega nodded and spoke back.
"That Evoric is the same as mine.
He is of an order native to my land,
Conceived when the first of the Elves
Came into the Land of Dragons.
Wardens they are, these Forest-Walkers,
Ever watching for signs of evil
And hoping to thwart calamity
Whenever it rears its ugly head.
But he is held now by the Huns
Among Attila's own retinue
As the Scourge of God prepares
To plunge Europe into war.
Seek him out, if you will,
And Evoric will yet aid you."

"How long then," asked Merovech,
"Shall it be before Attila makes a move?"

"It will not be long," answered Ildico,
"Given Italy's dire situation.
He claims Honoria, sister to the emperor,
As a new bride among his many.
He sought her in exchange for half the empire-
That was the dowry demanded,
Withheld from him by Valentinian.
Under this pretext does Attila march,
Eager to send his hordes to war."

"So we have heard," Merovech spoke.
"May she perish for leading him on thus,
Spurning him to battle
With lustful desires to lay against

BOOK ONE

The bosom of yet another woman,
One among many,
Added to his myriad wives.
In time shall Flavius Aetius,
Famed general of Rome,
Send word to this place in Tornacum,
Marshaling us to come to the aid
Of Valentinian's empire.
Whisked to a war not of our making
We shall all of us be.
Still we will fight, though bear no love for it,
Save those among us eager and ready
To prove their merit and seal their place
In the annals of history."

"Wuotan preserve us," Sighlut declared,
Raising his glass as he spoke,
"I will be among those showing their worth
Running Huns through on Gram's keen edge.
Wuotan preserve Honoria too,
Or otherwise condemn her.
Either judgement is just
For one who prostitutes herself
Before Pannonia's vile king!
But come now, it is no time for curses.
I shall march on to find the Hunnic horde
And deliver Evoric from his prison.
Ildico I shall bring with me,
And merit I will earn through my feats
Both against the Huns and their alliance
With dread Fanefiru."

Ildico spoke little but gave her consent,

34

Hesitant though she was.
"I am new to your struggle,
But the Huns are my foes too.
My foe's foes may be counted as allies."

"Yes you must go," Merovech agreed.
"Find Evoric and learn from him
All knowledge that can be learned
Concerning Dragons and their kind.
But then, Sighlut, you must return to me,
As the time for war is near at hand.
Then you will prove yourself in hot battle
And win a name for yourself
That your sons' sons' shall yet recall
To their sons' sons' beside the hearth.
But save this journey for tomorrow,
For night is coming fast. Rest,
And tomorrow you may start at once."

Soon after the sun set,
And darkness came upon the land.

BOOK TWO
DAUGHTER OF ROME

These were days of change for the world.
The growing might of the Huns' empire
Had decades earlier so compelled
Thousands of Goths to try their hand
At settling beyond the Danube
And within the Eastern Roman Empire.
Emperor Valens had allowed this,
But the dishonesty of local commanders
And other hardships manifold
Urged migrating Goths to revolt
And win a decisive victory
Against the Romans who mistreated them.*
The stage had been set at last,
And countless other nations continued
To settle the empires of East and West.
In a matter of decades,
The once mighty Rome had been stripped
Of Britannia, Africa, Hispania, and Gaul.
Even the heights of Rome herself

---

* The Battle of Adrianople; August 9, 378

DAUGHTER OF ROME

Could not be counted as invulnerable,
A lesson sorely learned but four decades
Before Attila launched his own campaigns.[*]
Rome no longer yielded the might
Possessed by her ancient rulers,
Hardly a recent realization for those
Who still lived in Italy,
But always with each passing decade
Did this reality become more apparent.

It was to this Italy past her prime
That Honoria returned, stepping
Foot in Ravenna's port at marshy Classe.
She took one look back at the vessel which
Bore her from well-walled Constantinople,
Its lateen sails rippling in the gushing wind
As crewmen worked hard at the rigging.
Oh, how good it felt to see her returned!
She remembered all the sights: great houses,
The arched gates and the paved courts,
Bubbling fountains and folk hustling to-and-fro.
There by the docks she awaited
The coming of her brother the emperor,
And dressed up for the occasion she was,
A single belt wrapped around her stola
Just underneath the breasts, as is
The ancient custom. A violet palla
Hung ever loosely from her shoulders.

Dark-haired and tall, the light of her face
Shone in the rising sun, or so it seemed to

---

[*] The Visigoths under Alaric sacked Rome in August, 410.

BOOK TWO

Many of those admirers who passed her way,
And though the palla with modesty
Concealed her figure,
Ever they admired her from afar
As if Venus Victrix walked in her place.

Then he came, Valentinian
Followed in turn by a royal entourage.
Honoria had heard him call her out
Even amid the clamor of laborers
And the harsh cawing of gulls.
He too wore the attire of one his rank,
Though he lacked the cunning and the ambition
Worthy of one bearing such prominence.
Better would it be if he was named emperor
During the days of Trajan or Hadrian,
When Roman supremacy was unchallenged.
At least then he could indulge his pursuits
And so in hypocrisy call his sister a harlot
Without the pressures of holding together
And empire wounded and weary.
In this day and age, however,
The stakes were simply too high.

So Honoria thought, even now
As he approached her with a hug.
"Look who has come at last
From well-walled Constantinople.
I trust that Theodosius treated
You well in the confines of his court."

"Yes," Honoria stammered.
"Now about Eugenius-"

DAUGHTER OF ROME

"It is done," he said. 'I don't want
Any more trouble between us two.
I want a sister, not a heated rivalry.
Can we so agree to move on?"

"Yes," Honoria said. "I'd like that."
Despite her contempt, she meant it.
As they stood beneath squawking gulls,
She embraced him with sincerity.
She felt like she was loved, not caught
Up in politics or manipulative schemes,
But accepted simply as a sister.
So in that moment was a heart
Hardened like stone made soft.

Valentinian led his sister from that place
Onto the walls of Ravenna proper,
Down which they proceeded to walk
As wandering eyes peered out upon
The lands around the city.
A swampy expanse stretched outward,
And beyond it rich farmlands.
Along the banks sat moss grown mounds.
Reeds hissed as the winds brush against them,
And in this place the smell of nearby pines
Gave way to that salty sea spray.
As they looked out on all this, Honoria
Asked her brother how running Rome
Had gone in her absence, and so
He turned and answered her.

"Management of this far-founded empire's
Been well enough so far, though Attila

Has not made things easy. Forgetting
His past campaigns against the East,
He seems interested in meddling with Gaul
And the affairs of the valiant Franks.
But our alliance is still hale, and I
Do not know how to stop this
Without hurting our relations."

"I understand," Honoria said, resting
Up against the parapets. "You want
To ensure all parties are satisfied."

And Valentinian answered her saying
"As long as Constantinople does not
Think me a turncoat and Attila keeps
His eyes away from our lands, I
Will count myself satisfied. But how
Should I achieve this end? I have
No answer that would offer justice."

"But Attila's eastern campaign is over,"
Honoria answered. "In Pannonia they
Have settled as per Aetius' agreement,
And the Huns seem more set on Visigoths
And on Franks than the Romans. Perhaps
Things will be well so long as you make no
Aggressive move against his riders."

"Your mind is clear,' Valentinian
Praised her. 'So you know what is just,
But do you know what's truly unjust?
The fact that you are thirty-two years
Of age and yet still unmarried."

DAUGHTER OF ROME

"Well," Honoria answered him, "it was
You that committed me to celibacy."

"A crime I must amend," he said,
Stroking his clean-shaven chin
As if he was deep in thought.
"In fact, I think I may have found a man
Who'd make a great match for you:
The senator Bassus Herculanus.
He's of good character, and you
Can have your *fun* without getting
Into any further trouble."

And then Valentinian
Paused and raised his clenched fist,
Lowering and raising it again
With a boyish smirk on his face.
Honoria got the hint, although
She did not like it. Herculanus
Was ancient, soft-spoken and mild.
He had not the vitality or the charisma
One thought would be needed
To match the ambition of Honoria.

Honoria voiced her concern, saying
She was unsure the match would work.
But to her Valentinian answered, "I
Understand you're not proud of your deeds,
And Herculanus lacks that sort of dirt
Underneath his fingernails. Do not worry;
He does not condemn you and neither do I.
After all, everyone deserves a second chance."

BOOK TWO

So frowning, Honoria returned to
Her palace which long ago she called home
To think and ponder over all these things,
Wondering if her brother wielded
Other motives in his heart
For setting up such a match.
Before a door of polished metal
She stood. It opened, and in her palace
She saw a roof held aloft by towering pillars,
A great chamber lit by tall windows built
Into deep aisles on both ends. Brilliant
Mosaics of Christ and his apostles lined
The walls with gold and purple and luminous red,
And among those holy ones were previous
Emperors which could also be seen.
Alone, Honoria passed the inner courtyard
Down winding ancient halls, eyeing
Before the Caesars ruled the world.
At last she neared her own bedchambers-
A welcome sight indeed!

Here in this silent tranquility sheltered
By remote alcoves had she always
Felt most at home, and here she saw
Her mother Galla Placidia seated,
Watching intently a curious ant
Hustle across her hand. It bore jaws
Like the tusks of the Calydonian boar,
And a great bulbous horn arose
From between its antennae. Nukera*
Is the name which the Swart Elves give it.

---

* *Ceratomyrmex ellenbergeri*

DAUGHTER OF ROME

"Hello, mother," Honoria sighed.

"Well there's a genuine greeting
If ever I saw one," Placidia remarked.
She said nothing else, her mind
Distracted by the horned ant.

"Thanks for the warm welcome,"
Honoria folded her arms.

"I apologize," Placidia answered,
"But you must take a look at this."

"What plague has struck that ant?"
Honoria asked, awed by its form.

"This is no pestilence," Placidia answered,
"For truly this is its natural form.
Emissaries from the Huns came to us
And brought odd insects like this,
But they are not from distant Pannonia
And the seat of Attila's empire.
They've seen an ancient land-
Or so they say-
A land in which dragons and ancient serpents
Have long established their abode.
The Land of Dragons they called it,
A realm that cannot be located
On any map of ours, but one
Which can be accessed through doors
Scattered across the wide earth.
I had heard tales of other such passages
Found near the heights of Aksum

By folk under the rule of King Ebana,
But I cannot confirm such tidings.
Nor can I confirm that of the Huns,
But the bug itself intrigues me.
But speak to me, daughter.
Something troubles you,
If your countenance I can trust.
Valentinian did not so soon reveal
The aims he had for you, did he?"

After gawking at the odd insect,
Honoria spoke to her mother concerning
Valentinian's proposed match for her.
"Let me be frank," she said, "after
That whole affair with Eugenius,
I do not think I am yet ready to be
Tied down in marriage to a man,
Much less an old senator like Herculanus."

When she said *old* Placidia nodded,
And when she finished her mother spoke.
"I should not tell you this, but I will.
Learn in and hear what I have to say.
That's why he was paired with you,
You see. He may be a decent man,
And that's why he was chosen. After all,
He is old and tame. He will not exploit
His newfound rank in the imperial family
Or cause any trouble like you did
With Eugenius but a few months ago."

Honoria frowned and continued,
"Now it all makes sense to me.

DAUGHTER OF ROME

Here I was, actually thinking my brother
Wanted to make peace with me,
To make amends and put the past behind us.
What a stupid girl I have been, falling
For these emotionally charged tricks.
He thinks he can shut me up,
Clean and simple. How sorely mistaken
My brother is. I would have given no trouble,
If simply he let me be. Yet instead he thinks
To bind me to a loveless marriage.
I will yet escape these bonds."

Honoria's eyes wandered toward the box
Which held that horned ant.
The fearsome beasts and maritime monsters
Etched into flanks of ashen wood
Told her of a newly risen empire, one
Powerful enough to explore Karoputaru
Yet also amicable enough to send
These strange forms as gifts to Ravenna.
"I cannot appeal to any Roman,"
Honoria spoke, "for he would
Be underneath my brother's grip.
But an outsider? An outsider
On decent enough terms with us
Yet deadly enough to cause us trouble?
An outsider capable enough of venturing
To far-flung lands and harvesting
Creatures weird and wild? Therein
Lies the hope of my escape."

"A poor choice I think this will be,"
Placidia answered her. "It's risky, for sure.

But I've done no worse than you have.
I will not praise your decision,
But neither will I hinder it."

Honoria hatched her plan and made her appeal.
She penned a letter detailing her plight
To none other than Attila himself, asking
Him to bend her brother's arm and so
Deliver him from unwanted matrimony.
In this way she sought to free herself
From these binds, sending a eunuch,
Hyacinthus of name, to Attila's stronghold
Upon the Pannonian plains, dread Jalaŋgül.

To see her will done she sent Hyacinthus,
A eunuch whose testicles were crushed
When he was but a youth. Emasculation
And its pains were but a distant memory,
And it was this position that offered him
A chance to travel far and wide
To see the remote land of the Huns,
An island in a sea of open plains.
As he neared the palisades of Jalaŋgül,
He watched Hunnic riders pass him by.
Over their tunics were elaborate sets
Of armor made of small rectangular plates
Sewn skillfully together. Barbarians though
They may have been, there was intricacy
To their art, and he could see it.

Forsaking his armed escort, Hyacinthus
Continued on into Jalaŋgül, watching
As spinners wove fine fabrics

DAUGHTER OF ROME

And artisans crafted bows from goat horns.
Though he saw a land which he deemed
Far from Rome's pristine standards
Of civilized life, he could not disregard
The rich abundant found here,
Heaps of goods won through conquest
And through the art of trade.
But Hyacinthus saw also another side
As through Jalaŋgül he went.
Rich though the settlement was,
Its poverty was also clear.
There were no stores of timber
To finish the construction of dwellings
That had already begun.
Flocks of horned sheep ambled by,
But it did not seem enough to Hyacinthus
To feed the growing population.
The empty expanse of Pannonia
Offered little in the way of resources.
It was obvious to the eunuch
That soon the Huns would be dependent
Upon trade and conquest to obtain
Even the most basic goods deemed essential
For life in the civilized world.
On he went through the settlement,
Making note of these grim details
Until at last he neared Attila's royal hut
And saw seated there the king of the Huns.

His brow was high and sloped
From the binding inflicted on Hunnic youths,
And his hair was tied back in a ponytail.
Behind him sat an assemblage of guards

BOOK TWO

From all across the bounds of his empire:
Choice warriors from the nations of
The Alans, Saxons, Goths, Burgundians,
Thuringians, Franks, Sarmatians, and more,
Their fealty bought either with fine gifts
Accrued through Roman tribute
Or through feats of conquest.
None among the Huns would dare
To look Attila in the eye, for such
Was the dread with which he ruled.
When he returned from long journeys,
Always he was met with singing, and
He managed to establish through murder
A rule without any rival.
On campaign, his commands were never questioned,
Nor did any openly challenge him.
Such absolute power to his name
Was a far cry indeed from
The fragmentary hold of the Romans
In these troubling times.

But Attila was no monster, and
He spoke with no hostility
In his voice when with those he trusted
Discussed with him important matters.
"The time to act is near," he said.
"We cannot wait much longer
If we're to make a new advance."

"I understand," spoke Ellac,
Son and heir to Attila's throne.
"But you've no cause to fight, and
Any such incursions will be unprovoked.

DAUGHTER OF ROME

If nothing else, it would certainly
Strain relations between you
And the emperor of the Romans."

Attila frowned and answered Ellac,
"My empire has grown vast,
But a myriad nomads on the Pannonian plain?
We cannot sustain ourselves on the steppe.
How shall we build without sufficient timber
Or go without drinking the rivers dry
And starving our herds to extinction?
My people cannot sustain themselves,
So we feed off the Goths like parasites.
But we are not parasites,
And this is more than gathering resources.
The War-Sky has shown me the way.
It is my charge to usher in a new age."

"I understand," his son spoke,
"But perhaps it would be prudent
To evaluate the circumstances more thoroughly
Ere the hurl ourselves into a war
That will cost us heavily."

Attila frowned but said nothing,
His attention turned towards a herald
Of his announcing the coming of a foreigner.
Attila beckoned Hyacinthus to approach his throne.
"Come here," he said, "and reveal
To me your name and your purpose."

"I am Hyacinthus," the eunuch bowed,
"And I serve in the court of Valentinian.

I come before you with payment
And a message- not from the emperor-
But rather from his sister."

Hyacinthus reached for a lumpy sack
Filled with gold strapped to his saddle,
And he revealed the letter penned by Honoria.
A mounted attendant approached him
And conveyed both offerings to Attila,
Who frowned and confessed
He could not read Latin.
But another near Attila could,
A Goth clothed in robes
And kept as a prisoner
Always by Attila's side.

So this Evoric took the letter
And read the words within:
"Honoria, sister of Valentinian
The leader of the Romans,
Says greetings to Attila.
My brother wishes to bind me
In marriage to the senator Bassus Herculanus,
But I do not want to marry him!
Yet I am a woman and cannot convince
My brother to cancel the wedding.
Send a messenger to Ravenna
And ask him to end it with haste.
I send you my ring to demonstrate
That this letter truly is from me.
Do this, and I will be a friend to you.
Farewell."

DAUGHTER OF ROME

Hyacinthus then pulled from his satchel
The ring offered by Honoria,
A golden band adorned with a set
Of blood-red hardstones. Turning the ring
Over and over again in his fingers,
Attila eyed its every detail.
This was a fine band indeed, truly one
From the hand of the emperor's sister.
After a moment, he turned his gaze
Back toward the eunuch and said,
"Away with you, Roman. Rest for a while
And make off toward Ravenna's heights.
You may give your mistress my answer.
Say nothing to her save that- by the War-Sky-
I will deliver her from this evil.
To Valentinian will I send my own riders
Once I've weighed all my options."

"And what options would those be?"
Asked Hyacinthus. All eyes turned
Toward Attila, wondering how
The Scourge of God would answer.
Finally, he broke the silence.
"The price of an acceptable dowry."

And Attila smiled.

BOOK THREE
HARBINGER OF STRIFE

Rosy-fingered Dawn peered over the horizon
And trumpets blasted throughout the camp.
Seated on an ebony throne Attila watched,
German forests to his back
And the Danube just ahead,
As all around stood amassed his host
Resting in tents that numbered tens of thousands.

A hundred tribes stood before him,
The Rugii, the folk who eat rye,
Marching into battle behind round shields;
Heruli who once dwelled along the Black Sea
Though now linger here
Along the shores of the winding Danube;
The long-haired Burgundians, a crowd of giants
Who smell of garlic and overindulged onions;
The Scirii, fair of face,
Who deem themselves purer than other peoples,;
Thuringii, heirs to the Hermundiri,
A people who like all others in this host
Joined Attila when his nation engulfed theirs.
These were not the only peoples

HARBINGER OF STRIFE

Arrayed before the bends of the Danube,
A hundred subjugated nations came now
Behind the Scourge of God to war.
The cloudless sky grew tainted with dust
Kicked up by tens of thousands of stamping boots.
All the earth trembled underfoot
And the hills shivered beneath Hunnic advance.

From the formless mass a horn blasted,
Its cries carried through the German countryside
As from this assemblage of nations came the kings
And the chieftains of those subjugated peoples
To meet before the lord of this vast host.
There came Ardaric of the Gepids
And the three famed Ostrogothic brothers
Valamir, Thiudimir, and Vidimer.
Also among them was the Frank Childeric,
Whom Attila had accepted
Upon exile by his father, Merovech himself.
Yet Childeric counted himself unconcerned,
Deeming that this exile was merely on account
Of Frankish unhappiness with private affairs.
The Huns did not seem to care,
And among them he would remain
Until that eventual homecoming,
Leading Frank against Frank
In this great war of the ages.
There too was Attila's secretary,
Steel-eyed Orestes, a Roman
By heritage and opportunist at heart,
Whose future son would one day
By ill fate he counted as

BOOK THREE

The last emperor of the West.[*]
Then came cheery Laudaricus,
Chieftain among the Huns and by blood
A kinsman to Attila himself, brought
Not for counsel but for his company.

Among this league of nations,
No host was more numerous
Than that of Attila himself,
Who even far from battlefields
Stank with the reek of death.
All around the German countryside
Patrolled the ever-watchful Huns,
Spears held upright
And bows slung onto their backs.
From the saddles on which they sat
Oozed blood trickling down
Their horses' flanks from slabs of meat
Tucked underneath,
Protecting steeds from saddle sores
And tenderizing food.
Over their tunics Huns were donned
With sets of elaborate armor
Of small rectangular plates sewn together.
Conical helmets shielded their heads
From stray arrow shafts
And from the bitter winds
Of their homeland on the steppe.

"Rise up," Attila hailed Laudaricus,
Passing him a bottle of wine

---

[*]Romulus Augustus, a.k.a Augustulus ('Little Augustus')

HARBINGER OF STRIFE

Imported from well-walled Constantinople.
Attila took a sip from his own bottle
And Laudaricus did the same.
Then Attila's gaze was turned towards
The others gathered round his seat.

"Oh of course," he declared,
"You too must be thirsty.
Come, my attendants,
And bring for them wine
That their bellies too may be full."

Then he sat and he waited,
Expecting the arrival of one more
To join this gathering.
At last came the Goth, wandering Evoric,
Mailing clinking beneath his brown rode
As he came with staff in hand,
Fashioned in form like a shepherd's crook.
A prisoner he was,
Yet free to wander the war-stead
So long as he made no attempt
To cast this place aside
And try to make it on his own.

"Allow me to apologize," said Evoric
"For my lack of punctuality.
Last night was a long one,
And I had only just awoken
When the rest of this assembly had gone,
And it surely was not because
I had too many bottles from your stores
Of that excellent Persian wine

You offered me last night."
He hiccuped and retracted this claim.

"All is well," answered Attila,
 His arms gesturing out toward the host.
"Harken now, you sons of the West, and
Behold! This is history in the making.
Centuries on scholars will discuss these affairs
While the common folk recall our names
In idle conversation,
Regardless of victory or defeat.
All of Europe shall be invested
In the outcome of this war
And the scars we leave behind
Will carry on through the nations.
So the dread War-Sky has decreed."

He raised aloft his sword
Forged from meteoric iron
That came to him the first night
He slept as sole king of the Huns.
So it happened that an old farmer
Was tending to his herd.
He heard a tumultuous crash
Booming through the sky,
Which followed a blazing light
Blinding all who looked skyward.
Cast down from heaven was a great stone,
The likes of which the War-Sky,
Dread battle god of the Huns,
Is wont to hurl against the earth.
No finer portent could there be!
At once a keen blade was forged

HARBINGER OF STRIFE

From the innards of this divine omen
And presented before Attila,
For a weapon forged from such a source
Could only be wielded by a lord of war.
Who else ought to carry a weapon
Forged from those things sent down
By the true Lord of War himself?
The seers confirmed that the stone
And the sword therein, called Kolbulut,
Were both a gift from divinity.
The message was clear:
Attila was to lead the Huns
Into a new era of battle.
So all eyes looked up into the air,
Gazing in awe at such a weapon,
Held aloft like a scepter
Raised toward the clouds
Where the forms of birds flew overhead.

An eagle greater than the rest
Swooped upon the other birds,
Talons bared as it tore them through.
Flapping its huge wings,
The eagle tore apart those lesser birds,
Shredding frail wings with piercing claws.
Attila and the rest beheld the aerial fight.
Flapping great wings the eagle took off,
Limp prize held firmly
Within the grasp of clutching talons.
With a raucous cry, so passed the eagle
From the eyes of all.
The other birds were scattered
As chaff in the wind,

And the flock dissipated to oblivion.
Gesturing toward heaven, Attila spoke.
"Tell me, Evoric, one so skilled
In the tongues of beasts
And the ways of the wild,
Well-versed in ancient tradition,
What omen do you see above?"

Evoric peered at the parting clouds
And gave his answer saying,
"Many shall flock to war-
Kings, chieftains, champions of legend-
None shall be exempt!
Only one, however, will outlast them all.
But this one too will then depart,
Lost to obscurity,
Forever a memory among the rest,
Though this one's presence
Will have been felt by all."

With these words he moved Attila's heart.
"Of course it will," he said smiling.
"I knew this sign could mean nothing else.
But come now! I have heard word
That some among you saw a sight
Just last night. Tell me what you can,
For I was hunting boars when other eyes
Met the form of this portent."

Then spoke Ardaric, famed
For his loyalty and his wisdom,
Prized above all other chieftains
Alongside Valamir,

King in the Pannonian countryside.
"It was a great flying shadow
Shaped like an immense bird
With wings of fire and smoke.
It passed over the southern bank
Of the winding Danube.
My Gepids were the first to behold it,
And straightway their hearts
Were seized by terror.
Its sheer size blocked out the sun's
Waning light from their eyes
As it passed over the Black Forest.
Only ten minutes later it emerged again
Conveying a horse in its claws,
And off it went into the West."

"My troops saw the same," said Thiudimir,
"I bade my host of Ostrogoths
Not to assemble in the fields while it was out,
Instead spending their time in the tents,
I did not want to draw its attention,
For I feared it was a Dragon,
One of the dread Fire-Waurms
I heard tales of as a child.

But Attila knew well to allay their fears.
"Come Evoric," he beckoned,
"Prepare the libations, so we may speak
With my most potent ally."

Evoric nodded and brought forth the items
Needed for the ritual. Out came three jars,
One filled with milk and honey,

The second with sweet wine,
And the third with brackish water.
A Hunnic youth drove a pair of bollocks
Dragging behind a cart filled with wood
Which was heaped down into an altar
Upon which Evoric emptied out the libations,
Pouring out each jar in the order
By which it was brought forth.
Then a torch was brought to the altar
And Evoric slammed the earth with his staff.
Upward the flames roared
As smoke drowned the assembly,
Cloaking them in a foggy veil.

The world around seemed to give way,
The tents and trees around the war-stead
Replaced by looming cave walls
And figures carved from great standing-stones,
Huge and ancient,
Sculpted in the likeness of primordial titans.
Some were worn from the passing of time
With little remaining
Save drooping eyes and chipped beards.
Others still bore every scar and blemish-
Downcast faces-
Their somber eyes looked upon
The meager assembly gathered below.
The earth shook beneath their feet,
The grass and soil on which they stood
Now usurped by a sea of gold,
Hundreds of tiny coins drifting downward
Each time someone shifted his feet.
Thick smoke drown out all light,

HARBINGER OF STRIFE

And in the gloom a lone eye flickered,
Casting down its glaring gaze.

"Thieves and intruders," a voice grumbled,
Its dread echoes chilling the souls
Of those who had not heard it before.
"Why have you come to disturb me
At this hour of war and of fortune?"

Attila answered him saying,
"You gave my men a good frighten
Last night, so I wished to calm their fears
And reveal our alliance to their fold."

"Our deal is still alive," said Fanefiru,
"Breathing like all who are marked to die.
Offer me a chance at seizing Rome,
And I shall join your horde.
But you are not yet prepared
To invade old Italy, are you?"

"No," answered Attila. "Gaul comes first.
We must make a mess of that land
Before moving southward.
Once this campaign is done, however,
You shall taste the sweetness of battle."

Fanefiru growled, "Your ambition is childish,
But for the time being I will continue
To play along with this game.
If there is nothing else
You wish to bore me with,
I will slumber in peace, stopping only

To snatch a horse or other prey
When hunger so compels me."

Attila assured the mighty Dragon.
"That is all I wanted, great Fanefiru,
To proclaim our alliance to this lot.
We will leave at once.
Whisk us away, wandering Evoric,
So we may leave Fanefiru in peace."

Evoric waved his hand over the space
Entwined by the crook of his staff,
Blowing two breaths on its end
And whispering words indecipherable.
At once the cave began to fade away,
Gold Tor vanishing from beneath their feet.
The assembly once more stood within
A sea of tents, the war-stead of Attila,
Gathered before the great ebony throne.

"You may return to your tents,"
Attila assured the chieftains.
"Be sure to reassure your men,
Let them know they have naught to fear
From the great Ōtebren.
If push does come to shove,
The Dragon shall be on our side
Rather than the enemy's.
We shall wait here for one more day
While the last few bands of allies come.
Tomorrow, we march to war
And to the ending of this present age."

But Childeric said, "What of your men
Who have gone into the Land of Dragons?
Will they too be joining us, or have you
Spared them for yet another fight?"

"They march under the lead of my sons,"
Attila answered him thus.
"Their host shall join us later in this war,
I suspect when we have passed by
The walls of Aurelianum,
Perhaps when we have taken the city itself.
Then shall they come with their reinforcements,
Great beasts from the Land of Dragons
Trained and eager for battle, for
Evoric is not the only living mortal
Who speaks to and controls these beasts."

"Perhaps," Evoric answered, "but you
Of all living folk should know
The relationship binding me with them
Can never be matched by your underlings.
They are dangerous creatures,
And you cannot hope to wield
Absolute dominion over their will."

"And if I wanted you," Attila said
"To tame that beastly lot,
I would have bade you do thus.
But then again that would have given you
The opportunity to turn them against me
And lead a host of monsters against
My horseback horde."

Laudaricus laughed, loud and mirthful.
"Thank the gods that is not a fight
We will have to endure.
Let us hope it remains that way."

"Remember though," Attila added,
"That dear allies may be turned against you."
He gestured to the standard to his left,
Upon the pole stood a brazen eagle,
Its wings still proudly outstretched
Despite centuries of rust and decay.
"Once there was an age
When the mighty eagle
Flew out before the Roman host.
The eagles have flown away
From the seven hills of high-born Rome,
Who has abandoned their ancestral god,
Mars, lord of battle, and Jupiter too,
To a god who professes peace.
Yet they do not truly serve him.
Tell me, Evoric, whom does Rome serve?"

"Rome serves Rome," answered Evoric,
"And the emperors serve the emperors.
For if they served the one who commanded
To care for the poor
And to love the enemy,
The empire would certainly have
A very different face, would it not?"

"And so," declared Attila,
"I shall unveil their pious façade.
When I come bearing my full wrath,

HARBINGER OF STRIFE

They will return to the ways of war
That first made their empire strong,
But they will not find the eagles
Before them to guide their steps.
The birds have taken flight,
Resting now upon my shoulders.
A new god of war has struck the land,
And the eagles turn on their former masters."

"But why the theatrics?" asked Evoric.
"Why march to war if on good terms
You were before Valentinian denied you
The hand of his sister Honoria?"

"Honoria was merely my justification,"
Attila answered, "a pretext for my cause.
In the eyes of Rome, I march now
To claim my Helen robbed from me.
But when we march, Rome will see
Far more than a lover scorned.
Rome is obsolete, a relic of days
That long have come and gone.
The emperors bear no ambition,
And so a new emperor must rise
And fill the void left in their absence.
My wars shall but hasten the inevitable.
The ways of the prosperous steppe
Shall usurp the hapless politicians."

Attila looked up toward the sky.
The shrieking of that eagle they earlier saw
Once more pierced the rippling clouds.
Soon the sound was drowned out

BOOK THREE

By the host of crackling campfires,
And as the eagle's calls were silenced,
Attila rose from where he sat,
Casting an evil gaze toward the South.
"The eagle has spoken, you ancient Caesars,
And with gleeful anticipation shall I watch
The ending of your world."
Then Attila poured out drinks
And continued the day feasting
And drinking to his heart's delight,
Eager for evening to come
And morning to follow,
Signaling the dawn of his campaign.

The first city that should succumb
To the full weight of his wrath
Was ill-fated Argentoratum.
History as of late
Had not shown any benevolence
Toward this place.
All the land had lately been ravaged
By Alemanni incursions
Only mere decades earlier,
And no cities here or nearby
Could muster up a suitable defense
To ward off warmongering Huns.

Still a fair distant away, Sighlut and Ildico
Heard the clamor rising from the streets.
They heard the incessant pounding
As stones hurled from newly-made catapults
Crashed against frail battlements.
Machines were loaded, launching missiles

HARBINGER OF STRIFE

Over the walls, tumbling into packed streets.
Pitiless yells cried out with harsh voices,
Carrying Attila's malice in their breaths.
Like vultures swarming about a carcass,
Unending foes surged through the gates,
Drowning the city in a deluge of blood.

For two weeks, Sighlut and Ildico
Had their eyes on Attila's advance,
And their observations proved true.
Just as they suspected, the Franks of Childeric
Would march through Argentoratum's
Southernmost end while Attila's Huns
Came from the North, Goths and Gepids
From the East and all other tribes from the West.
So it was now, and directly behind distant kin
Sighlut stood, watching as they carried out
The will of the Scourge of God
With brandished spears and hate on their lips.

Attila was never one to keep his prisoner-
Wandering Evoric- locked away
From the thick of the fray,
Preferring instead to hold this single captive
At the front lines of it all,
Beholding the slaughter with his own eyes
As if Attila enjoyed his company
Or otherwise did not trust him
To stay put if kept in the back,
Perhaps trying to slip out unnoticed.
Sighlut a Frank and *Ildico* a Goth,
It seemed not at all unlikely
That they could slip through enemy ranks,

Probing enemy lines
To break through to their quarry.
A tall order it seemed,
And Ildico was unsure it would work,
But Sighlut was confident
And would not hear out her concerns.

"What use is there in arguing?"
She told herself. "Better to stay united
Now than divided over petty issues
Caught behind enemy lines.
Swallow my pride. Swallow my pride."
And with a sigh she followed Sighlut,
Passing beneath Argentoratum's crumbling gate.

A storm of fire blazing like Dragon's breath
And carried by torched houses
Went rushing through packed streets,
And on the same breeze
That carried the on-rushing tide of fire
Followed afterward orphans' piercing wails.
The calls of snarling war-hounds rang above
And bared teeth tore flesh from bone.
House by house, all those who called
Doomed Argentoratum their home
Were skewered upon bristling spear shafts.
All throughout the chaos of this holocaust
Rose up wailing lamentations.
Then Ildico saw from afar
A sight she hated most dreadfully.
A short distance off stood two Franks
Who held a local man to the ground,
Pressing his head against a small box.

HARBINGER OF STRIFE

Behind him another Frank held his battered wife,
Sobbing promises that soon they would be
Forever joined in the halls of the life to come.
Before them stood a child, eight years of age,
Watching in horror amid the rising smoke.
"Julian," cried out the father, his tears mingled
With blood that flowed down
From a dash left in his left cheek.
"Go! Run away! I'm done for! I-"
The Germanic blade had done its work,
Its keen edge punching through vertebrae,
Cleaving neck from shoulders.

Ildico stomped with protest and
Clasped the hilt of her sword,
Ready to rush in and save the others.
But Sighlut halted her advance,
Pulling her aside and speaking with a whisper.
"The city is already doomed as it is.
We must maintain this illusion
If we're to find Evoric. Saving a couple souls
All to cleanse our misguided conscience
Will do us no good. Whatever it takes, Ildico.
We must do whatever it takes."

Ildico stepped backward.
Hating this as much as she did,
She knew his mind could not be swayed.
As the wife was forced upon
That awful chopping block,
Ildico turned away. Wanting never to see
The grisly murder of this family.
She darted away, forcing a path

Through a labyrinth of tightly-packed Franks.
The smoke began to seep in eyes
Already dripping with fresh tears.
The pain was stinging,
And she struggled to see through it,
But still she continued to run,
Stopping only when she found herself
Exposed on the Frankish front lines,
Deep in the heart of the smoldering city.
Just ahead sat Huns perched on horses,
Spears tipped in blood and quivers emptied.

Behind them sat a looming amphitheater
And before them rode a single Hun,
One whose head bore a crown
And whose hand bore a standard,
An eagle old and rusted,
Battered from grueling fights
And long treks through German woods.
Horror swarmed about his visage-
A herald of strife,
A harbinger of death.
"Gentlemen!" Attila cried with a shout.
"Let it be declared that on this day
The last of Varus' lost eagles
Has emerged once more,
Recovered by barbarian hands.
The Eagle returns to Rome
Not as the symbol of her own gods,
But of a new god, the true Lord of War,
Poised to end a fractured empire
And reclaim the bride robbed from me!"

HARBINGER OF STRIFE

Jubilant cries rose from among the Huns
And the joy of battle came upon them,
Loosing what few arrows they had left
Upon the last remaining civilians.
Ildico stood back in shock,
Amazed that the eagle Varus had lost
Four centuries earlier was found,
But even more terrible than that,
She finally saw the very man
Who inspired so many dread rumors
Crying out in bloodthirsty rage,
Piercing terror in his eyes
And hate on his lips.
And yet Ildico perceived something else.
In this act of returning
An ancient symbol of Rome
As a herald of its destruction,
She thought that maybe it was all an act.
Perhaps there was something else at work
Within the heart of the Scourge of God.

But she saw another figure among the Huns.
While his brown hood cloaked
Much of his bearded face,
It was clear enough he was no Hun.
He bore a staff in his hand,
And at once Ildico knew who he was,
Wandering Evoric, face of the Forest-Walkers.
Evoric looked out at the Frankish lines
And his gaze met hers.
Ildico raised her brows and gestured to him.
And at once he knew her purpose,
That she planned to break him out,

BOOK THREE

But for what purpose he could not surmise.
Yet in his heart he knew
The wisdom in joining her.

"Dear Attila," Evoric spoke,
"It has been a pleasure,
But my time in your company is done."

At once, the form of his body was lost,
Consumed in a cloud of winged shapes
Like those very Istiodactylus
Ildico earlier saw feasting upon
The spoils of Sighlut's honor-kill.
The swarm of flying beasts
Passed over Ildico's head,
Flocking past the city's southern end.
So Ildico followed after them,
Weaving through the gore and carnage
She left the city the way she came in
Until at last she found herself
Safely within the forest outside a city
Ablaze with fire and with death.
"He will return," Attila laughed.
"I'll even leave a seat reserved for you.
I'll spare some wine, too!"
But to this Laudaricus replied,
"Does it not concern at all
That your prisoner has escaped?"

Attila smiled and answered back,
"I never had control of him to begin with.
His power is ancient and immense,
Greater than you or I shall ever know."

"And yet you treated him like a friend,"
Laudaricus replied, "telling him your plans.
I do think that perhaps you have him
Too great an insight to your ploys.."

Then Attila frowned, realizing his error.
"Then I'll leave him a little *less* wine."

In a distant grove, Ildico stood
Surrounded by looming trees,
Tucked safely away from the awful clamor
Of Argentoratum's grim demise,
Faint moonlight creeping through
The leafy canopy overhead.
From the cover of the trees Evoric appeared
No longer a cloud of swarming beasts
But in his true human form.
In the distance he seemed grand and mysterious
Yet he was modest of appearance
And unassuming of demeanor.
Like her must have seemed tiny
Standing against Sighlut's massive frame.
Yet through his veins coursed a power
Predating any empire, old as the eldest spirits
Long revered as primordial gods
And the bones of the earth.
An avenger of the wild he was,
And the power to his name was feral.

Evoric broke the silence saying
"That was your first taste of battle, was it?
In your eyes could I perceive this."

BOOK THREE

Impressed, Ildico asked of him,
"Do you ever get used to it,
To the blood and slaughter of innocents?"

Gravely, Evoric answered her
"I try not to, lest I become blind
To the hurts war leaves behind. Apologies,
I do not think I got your name.
Mine is Evoric, as I assume you knew.

"And mine is Ildico," she answered,
"Goth by name and Italian by homeland,
Hence the accent. Before we continue,
I have a question, odd though it may be,
I so desire to know its answer:
When you change forms
Into that cloud of swarming beasts,
What happens should one of them be shot?"

Evoric paused for a second and laughed.
"It seems that my sleight of hand worked.
I did not turn into those creatures.
They are my eyes and ears,
Prowling the land for news I may find.
And they make a fine distraction, too,
Attracting the attention of a whole army
And keeping it diverted from us."

At last came Sighlut, drenched
In the blood of the slain, fists clenched
With anger at Ildico.
"How can you hope to make any progress
In our fight against Attila,

Slinking away at blood's first sight?"

Baffled, Ildico answered and said,
"They murdered an innocent family!
Was I to blindly cheer them on
As they clove a father's head
Before his own wife and child?
If I could not save them,
Then I could do nothing but retreat."

Sighlut sighed and answered back,
"You must be willing to endure such sights,
Unflinching before fire and murder.
If you truly hope to stop this evil,
You must do whatever it takes
To throw of such monstrous shackles.
Keep that in mind, for this is not
The foulest deed that shall come
From this fight. That said,
You have done well finding Evoric.
You may yet prove yourself."
"Thank you, but we did not free him.
He broke out by his own volition.
It seems he wanted to be a prisoner
At least for a while."
"Why do this?" asked Sighlut.
"Why spend all your days
In the company of Attila the Hun?"

Evoric began, "If you so wish
To defeat or convert your foe
You must first get to know them.
Know how they work- what motivates them,

The things that set them off.
Of course, you would not think that,
For the very moment you see a Hun
You want to severe his or her head.
My weapon, however, is far more potent
Than any keened sword, be it Gram
Or Attila's own Kolbulut: understanding.
I get all the information I want
Out of Attila. I see the intricacies
And the complexities of his ambition.
I've played the fool upwards of a year
To get whatever information I could,
And by God's grace did I get plenty!
Despite his reputation as God's own rod,
He's really amicable once you get to know him,
Babbling on all the day long,
Telling you his favorite stories.
You'd find it hard to believe,
For you hear the name of Attila and
All you think of is bravado
And an uncultured barbarian who wants
To see the world burn in fire.
He is a man of turmoil and conflict,
Both internal and external.
According to the stories,
The very god of the Huns has decreed
Attila go to war. Everything about Attila-
From birth to ascension- has been declared
The will of the War-Sky since his infancy.
If you were told by the king of your worldview
That slaughter was the greatest commandment,
How could you refuse it?

Though deemed the barbarian's barbarian,
I do think Attila shall yet prove himself
A man of honor before the end."

"That we shall see," said Sighlut,
"Though I doubt there is honor to his name.
I prefer simply to drive my sword
Through a Hun. That's the surest way
To make an end of you foe.
There is another matter, though,
The matter of why we sought to free you
From Hunnic hands.
I'm sure you are curious.
Have you heard of the alliance
Between Attila and Fanefiru,
The dread Fire-Waurms?
Tell us what you may,
And how we might thwart it."

"That is not a fear," Evoric answered,
"That will soon be realized.
Yes, there is indeed an alliance,
But the Dragon shall only stir
Once Attila marches on Italy.
Thus are the terms, and a good way off
Is Attila's campaign into Italy.
More pressing is the campaign underway,
Stripping Gaul from Rome and her allies.
I have a plan to hinder the Hun,
But I must return to the land I know best,
Karoputaru, the Land of Dragons.
Perhaps you have heard rumors of it.
I must spend some time there

Among the ancient beasts of that place
And come out again.
Only after that shall Fanefiru pose a threat,
Many months from now. If you so wish,
You are welcome to join me
As I prowl the primordial domain
And see for yourself
A world older than our own,
Taking in what peace and awe you can
Until you are thrust again
Into the ending of this age."

"Would that I could," answered Sighlut,
"But by the will of my good king
I am called to return
To illustrious Merovech's halls.
I wish you good fortunes,
Wherever you may find them.
Perhaps your path and mine
Will cross again ere Fanefiru stirs."

"I will go," declared Ildico.
Afraid to voice her concerns out loud,
She no longer felt safe around Sighlut.
The execution, or rather his apparent
Lack of sympathy sapped her resolve.
But another force compelled her so,
Curiosity to see these far-off lands
And to have legends at once realized.
"I wish to see these far off lands
With my own two eyes,
To walk the world of ancient creatures
And the halls of the Swart Elves."

"Excellent," answered Evoric.
"Now the hour is late, And the sun
Has long sunk behind the horizon's edge.
I do think it is time to sleep,
Then tomorrow we may part ways."

"But how" asked Ildico,
Ignorant of the road ahead,
"Shall we reach the Land of Dragons?
What road shall we take
To reach the land that cannot be reached?"

"There is a way," answered Evoric.
"I know its path well,
Though few morals ever could.
We shall need no guide
To reach the Wall Between the Worlds,
The World Tree: ageless and undying,
Shielded from the eyes of unwanted mortals.
Artaru it is called-
The Tree of the King of Heaven.
We will beseech the wardens of the Tree,
None older walk this earth than they.
The way will be opened to us,
The thin wall dividing all realms torn
For but a brief moment,
And in this tear in the cosmos
Shall we plunge ever onward,
Hurled from this world into another
But down into the deep must we go
Ere we reach Artaru's roots."

Ildico knew not how to answer.

She did not fear the road ahead,
For her guide seemed trustworthy.
Yet the idea was nonetheless daunting
To take a road few ever have trod.

"Very well," she consented. "That way
Shall I go, following your lead.
Wish us good luck, Sighlut, as
We trod this Wall Between the Worlds."

Sighlut nodded and pointed westward.
"Our tents are located this way,
Just a few hundred paces yonder.
The hour is late, and I must be off
Tomorrow, to rejoin Merovech's retinue
And thus prepare for your eventual return.
We should be safe, for I doubt the Huns
Shall emerge so soon from newly-won walls."

BOOK FOUR
FAMILY FEUD

I sing now of the day Valentinian,
First received those fateful demands
Sent to him by the Scourge of God,
Called away from the thrill of the races
To confer with the Huns he hated.
Few thrills could match the euphoria
Offered by the chariot races-
The crescendo of whistling cheers,
The whinnying of horses whizzing
Like stones hurled from Balearic slings,
The ground screeching under the weight
Of the carts and the choking of the air
With rising dust and the stench of manure-
Oh how Valentinian loved it all!
The air smelled with the punching stench
Of manure carried through
Rising dust clouds,
But the riders did not slow down
To shield their noses from this assault.
None could afford to, lest some rival seize
The opportunity to pass them by.

BOOK FOUR

Amid the startled whinnying and the clamorous
Turning of wheels, the charioteers guided
Their horses through each lap, taking extra care
Whenever the teams flooded congested turns.

In this way they went around once,
Then twice, thrice, even four and five times.
Each time a favored rider in reckless haste
Passed a foe, the crowd burst in cheers
Only to watch him get passed up again.
Although the chariot races
And the enthusiasm of the crowds
Here in Ravenna do not match in scale
And spectacle to their counterparts
Off in well-walled Constantinople,
The ruckus here still made
For thrilling rounds of entertainment,
As the emperor himself would have noted.
And Valentinian was watching all of this,
Sitting on the edge of his seat in hopeful anticipation
For the triumph of his favored charioteer.
It was normal to see the emperor so enthralled
By the chariot races, for it was no secret
That his bravery, martial prowess, and skills
As an administrator in no way compared
To those of his many matchless predecessors.
He very much preferred to spend his time
Watching athletic competitions or in the company
Of magicians and entertainers, and it was this
Same love for idle pleasure that had earned him
Honoria's contempt so many years ago,
Though his love of leisure showed no signs
So dying down in any coming days.

FAMILY FEUD

But none of that mattered to Valentinian.
He had competent men capable of that
Risky business of maintaining empires,
Especially the *Magister Militum* Flavius Aetius,
Who was certainly an accomplished general
Competent in any deadly endeavor.
If anything went wrong or an invader
Stood poised to wrestle for control of Italy,
Aetius would be more than capable of driving
Such hostile forces far away from Roman lands.
Why did Valentinian need to worry so much
About running the empire anyway
When he had allies like Aetius
That could do the dirty work?
He could be the face for Western Empire,
The one the masses could look up to
As a symbol instead of one dulled with labor.
After all, the lives of his predecessors were risky.
How many emperors before him were killed
While in office? The list was too long
To count. Caesar, Nero, Caracalla,
Constantine's immediate successors,
And even a previous Valentinian were only some
Among the many cut down before their time.
It was dangerous business being an emperor.
Perhaps he was entitled to his share of pleasure.

In this way he justified his hedonism
To himself, not that many other people
Were ever convinced of it. He felt good
About himself, and that was all he cared about.
He would only have one life on this earth,
He might as well enjoy it. And what better way

BOOK FOUR

To do that was there than to take in the sights
And sounds of one of Rome's oldest games?
Assuming our stories are true, then it is
A sport that Roman tradition has carried on
For over a thousand wars, going back to when
Tarquinius Priscus built the Circus Maximus
Between Rome's Aventine and Palatine hills.
The oldest, longest-lived spectacle of our history,
Few thrills could challenge the euphoria of the races.
But Valentinian was called from the race,
Even as his favored driver claimed the lead.
That was an annoyance enough for him,
But the news he received only made it
Sting all the worse, hearing that Attila
Expected half an empire be handed over
Because of the stupidity of his sister.

Those negotiations went poorly, of course,
And Valentinian did little less than threaten
Open war with the empire of the Huns.
The Hunnic emissary warned him to cool
His temper, but Valentinian drove him off,
Saying Attila could have his empire if only
He pried it from his cold, dead hands.
The Huns rode away, and as they did
Valentinian heard a single overtone whistle
Carried by the wind. He first heard that sound
From Actius, who learned to sing like the Huns
When he lived among them many years back.
Piercing eerie silence, the whistle rang loud
And clear, an ominous herald of woes to come.
Valentinian was chilled by both the song
And by its implication: that the anthem

FAMILY FEUD

Of the Huns might soon rule Roman land.

For perhaps the first time in all his years
As emperor over the West, Valentinian
Acted with a swiftness that surprised
Even himself. He wasted no time
In seizing Hyacinthus, accomplice
To scheming Honoria's machinations,
And now over the eunuch's battered body
He stood, stretching it out bare
Across the rack, his body torn open
By the jagged edges of the scourge.
Hyacinthus' body continued to quiver
With every movement that was made.
Streams of gushing blood poured out
From the fresh gashes in his flesh,
And the popping of cartilage as his limbs
Were stretched beyond their limits echoed
Throughout the dimly-lit chambers.
It would not be long now before his body
Was utterly broken and he himself dumped out
As meat for dogs and carrion birds.

Looming overhead was Valentinian himself,
Ominously imposing in the growing gloom.
His whole apparel was stained with the blood
Of that poor tortured eunuch he personally beat.
With each lash the emperor delivered,
The raging light of his eyes piercing darkness.
With each lash and pull, Hyacinthus wailed,
And with each blow Valentinian's taunts
Simply grew all the sharper,
And in bitterness he there declared,

"You were once a eunuch of high standing
But justice knows every man's number.
So draws the hour of your unmaking."

Valentinian released his grip on the scourge,
Letting it fall into a puddle of blood inching
Across the cold stone floor, creeping into every
Crack and crevice in its way. Hyacinthus groaned,
Though the pitiful sight of his trembling body
And quivering lips were given no sympathy.
"What more do you want, my lord? Already
Have I told you everything I know.
All I did was deliver a message! I had no plans
To conspire against you and usurp your position
Or help Attila claim your empire as his own!"

"Yet you left me in the dark." Valentinian ran
His fingers along one of those many gashes,
Pushing down as more blood seeped out.
"You let me wait until the hated nomads
Sent their barbaric envoys to me."

Hyacinthus winced at the pressure, and yet
It did not overcome him. Now he felt bolder
Than he had been a minute ago, or even
At any other moment of his brief life. Perhaps
It was because he knew his end was near
And no longer feared its coming,
Or years of broiling resentment bottled up
Against the emperor were finally let loose,
As what had happened with Honoria.
Either way, he spoke now amid his gasping
And coughing up of his own blood

FAMILY FEUD

With a confidence he had never felt before.
"I am sorry that hindsight is always clearer
Than the wisdom of the moment.
You're going to kill me over some folly
When your sister would have sent
Any other fool to do the same job.
Idiot! No wonder you have to rely
So heavily on the likes of Aetius
And all your other toadies to see
What semblance you have of a will done."

The emperor turned his back to the eunuch.
There stood in the deepening gloom
Magister Militum Flavius Aetius himself,
Clad in a coat of armor shimmering
Even in the depths of this darkness.
A crimson cloak fell from his shoulders,
And he bore no helmet on his head, exposing
The wearied countenance ever present
On the fifty-nine year-old general's face.
His age did not sit so heavily on his shoulders
As one might have expected, but still his face
Was marked by the creaks and wrinkles
So often left by a long and laborious life.
At once Valentinian commanded him to gather
Armed troops and make for Honoria's palace.
Aetius nodded and offered wretched Hyacinthus
One last sympathetic glance before leaving.
It was said he thought the eunuch innocent,
Or at least not-deserving such a punishment.
Perhaps he might have saved the man
If it did not mean going up against
None other than the emperor himself.

BOOK FOUR

But Aetius did as commanded and left.
The eunuch's body was forcefully bent over
So that he was forced to watch his blood
Leave rippling drops in the red puddle
His trembles hands splashed as he fell.
Suddenly, he felt the cold tap
Of a blade's keen edge rest upon his nape.
Then the chill left departed his neck
As Valentinian's sword was raised.
The next time he felt it,
The biting tap came much quicker,
As Hyacinthus felt the fierce
Sting of steel cleave deep into his neck,
Crunching through his vertebrae
As the eunuch's head crashed
Down into his own blood
On the ground, separate from his body.

The night deepened, and there was little sound
Amid Ravenna's dark streets save clinking mail
And the pattering of feet on the pavement.
Like a troop of wraiths creeping over the ground,
Valentinian and Aetius with a dozen soldiers
Sped through on toward Honoria's palace,
The glint of their drawn swords piercing the gloom.
Sentries parted from their posts whenever
The emperor barked at them, and otherwise
Honoria's palace was completely silent.
Through great metal doors the entourage hastened,
Passing by the most vibrant tapestries
And by the glittering of lamps.
Saints looked overhead from their mosaics
As the intruders sped silently through marble halls,

FAMILY FEUD

Prepared to put down any goon of Honoria's
That had been stationed to oppose them.
There were none of those sorts, however,
Allowing the Valentinian and Aetius unhindered
Passage to the most dangerous women alive.

Pushing tables and chairs aside, Valentinian
Broke into his sister's bedchambers,
Cursing profusely at her. Honoria jumped
From her sheets, surprised to be awoken
By her screaming brother. She sat upright,
Holding her blanket close to her body as
A dozen armed figures surrounded her bed.
Her pulse quickened and sweat began
To seep down her brow. Honoria heard rumors
That a Hun was seen outside the city.
Perhaps he brought Attila's demands.
But even if that was the case, why would
Valentinian be coming at her with armed troops?
All she wanted was not to be married
Off to that old senator Herculanus.
Was it seriously that important to her brother
That she be married off to the old senator?

"Why have you come to my bedchambers?"
She asked, her voice raised with concern.

"How dare you speak to me like that
After all the evil you've done!" screamed
Her brother as he stamped his feet.
"From your weasel of a eunuch
Have I uncovered your machinations.
Ere I released his burdensome head

From those miserable shoulders,
He told me of your proposal to Attila
And of the price demanded by your groom."

"I offered no such marriage," Honoria said.
Her widened eyes and raised brow revealed
Her inner disgust. "Why should I ever want
To be married off to Attila the Hun?
I've no desire to be made a wife
In his goat-herding harem. This is bad."

"Oh, this is quite bad," Valentinian answered.
"I cannot accept this *bargain*, nor can I
simply refuse Attila. You know he's dangerous;
Any excuse could be taken as pretext enough
To begin some ill-intended conquest.
I've already killed one dog today."
Valentinian looked down at his sword,
Still red and wet with Hyacinthus' blood.
"What harm is there in ending another?"

"If I may so intervene," Aetius spoke,
"This is a poor time to act rashly.
Heed my wisdom as long you have,
Killing her now would be poor timing."

"Indeed you may be prudent at times,"
Valentinian raised his sword up, brandishing
And pointing it towards his sister,
"But it's my judgment that reigns supreme."

"Fine," Placidia's voice boomed from afar.
The emperor's mother stormed through

FAMILY FEUD

And came into the room. "End the wretch.
Let's see how Attila responds to you
Killing his proposed bride-to-be."

Valentinian kept his blade up
For a while longer, breathing heavily.
Honoria's grip on her blanket tightened,
But otherwise she did not move.
If she was to die tonight, then
She would have to accept her lot.
Disgraced twice now, what else did she have
To live for? But Valentinian's arm dropped.
His blade fell from his hand
And clanged carelessly on the floor.
"You're right, mother. He will see
This newly-commuted affront as reason
To avenge her death. Leave us, Aetius."

Aetius did as commanded and went
Away with his armed troops, leaving
The dysfunctional family to quarrel alone.
When they were gone, Aetius again spoke.
"I know not what I shall do, but know
That you may have just brought war
Upon Europe and on all her peoples."

Honoria shook her head as tears
Already left wet trails down her cheeks.
"This is not what I wanted. I'm sorry, brother."

"Do not call me that!" Valentinian answered.
"Rot in here for all I care. You will not find
A brother in me anymore, you siren."

He stormed out of Honoria's bedchambers,
With Placidia following closely behind.
Honoria was left to weep alone, knowing
That her actions may have sealed the fate
For an empire already wearied by long decades
From troubles in war and politics.
Those first couple weeks following
The murder of Hyacinthus were nothing
It not torturous for Honoria. Her mother-
The one person she thought she might
Be able to confide with- would not
Lend her a listening ear. Eunuchs
And court attendants looked on
At Honoria with nothing more than contempt,
Fully aware that it was her failed ploys
That threatened to bring the Roman Empire
Into bitter war with the might of the Huns.
Priests prayed more fervently whenever
They passed her by, worried that she might
Try to seduce them or otherwise entice
Them into another wicked scheme.
Honoria lost count just how many times
Some clergyman made the sign of the Cross
On his chest after accidentally
Meeting her eyes with his own.

But none of that compared to what
Valentinian had done. Honoria always
Was a strong woman; rejection she could handle.
Her brother, though, offered more than rejection.
He had become aggressive towards her,
Occasionally storming her bedchambers
Consumed by a raging frenzy. At first

FAMILY FEUD

He did little more than land a few flailing punches,
But things got worse once their mother fell ill.
Galla Placidia was now stretched out across
What was very likely her deathbed,
The once strong woman of Rome reduced
To little more than a haggard shell clinging tightly
Onto the bucket that would catch the vomit
Surging from her reeking mouth.

Honoria stood by her mother's bedside,
Counting each of the bruises that ran across
Her own arms. She felt the soreness in her legs,
Knowing well how bruised up they had been.
Her stomach was tight and her loins ached.
Even now, though, she could not speak
To her mother of their fighting.
She knew that Placidia had in her heart longed
To see the day that she and Valentinian
Would cease their rivalrous quarreling.
To the rages of her brother would surely
Be too much for their mother to take.

No, Honoria told herself that it was better
To keep it in for now, to enjoy whatever
Few moments she had left with her mother.
What she would do after that, still she did not know.
Galla Placidia's rhetoric was the only reason
She still held her head on her shoulders,
And she certainly was the only person who might
Have been at least willing to listen to her,
Even if her patience was lost after this latest scandal.
Honoria understood that she was truly alone,
A shamed girl left to fend for herself

In this city of scornful men.
Yes, she had done something stupid-
Very stupid, actually.
But did she deserve this? She was not sure.
Even if it was warranted, these burdens
Hung too heavily on her shoulders.
Surely her days of sanity here were numbered.
She could no longer stand being met
With scornful glances whenever she went about.
She could no longer stand being a piece
Of idle gossip on the tongues of sanctimonious
Rumor-mongers. She could no longer stand
The abuse hurled her way by the her brother.
No more.

Honoria had only one option left to her.
It was by no means pleasant, nor would
It be easy, but Honoria knew that was
The only chance she could take.
If she was to find any more meaningful days
In this life, she had to do it.
She could not wait until Placidia had passed.
She would act now, hoping and praying
That Placidia would eventually recover,
As unlikely as that wishful thinking seemed.

"My sister is a dangerous woman,"
Valentinian said to Aetius, standing before
Honoria's palace with several dozen soldiers
Mustered all about their flanks. "Surely
You can see the injury done to me."
Valentinian pointed to his right eye.
It was quite swollen, blackened from

FAMILY FEUD

Subcutaneous bleeding. Honoria had landed
That blow on him the night before in self defense,
Though clearly it failed to dissuade her brother
Either then or now. If anything, it gave him
An excuse to attempt this next stunt.

"I see nothing," Aetius answered,
Faking the confused look on his face.
Valentinian was in no mood for jokes
And mouthed curses under his breath.
"She dealt me this blow last night."

Aetius leaned in, examining closely
The emperor's stricken eye. "So I see
That she did, and a mighty blow it was.
Was this strike landed without warrant?"

"What do you think?!" Valentinian stomped
His foot in a fit of anger. "Of course she did!
She struck me out of the pure hatred
That has long brewed within her black heart!
She has assaulted the emperor himself!
Now justice must be dealt and my sister
Punished at last for many heinous misdeeds."

But Aetius was no fool, and he understood
Perfectly the truth of what had happened,
Or so those who witnessed this exchange said,
And none of it sat well with him.
Valentinian, although married, had a history
Af such activity. He was no conquerer
Of far-flung provinces like the Caesars
Of days long past or like Alexander,

But he certainly matched their prowess
When it came to another domain.
He had excused his own sins as quickly
And thoughtlessly as he condemned
Honoria's night with Eugenius.
Today was hardly any different,
Although it was clear to all
That Valentinian had decided to take out
Those frustrations he had bottled up
Directly on his sister herself.
But regardless of what
Honoria had done, this was too far.
So Aetius told himself,
That the deeds Valentinian had done
Could hardly befit a Christian emperor.

Then again, did Valentinian really care about
What was Christian? Had Aetius cared?
Did anyone care? Among those Romans in power,
It certainly seemed like Christian morals
Only mattered when it was convenient,
When it gave Valentinian someone
At which he could point his little fingers
And divert negative attention from himself.
But Valentinian was not the only one.
Far from it! This was normal for emperors.
It was normal for leaders in the church.
It was normal for politicians and commanders.
When the church came to power,
Christians went from being persecuted
To inflicting the persecution,
Certainly not an easy thing to reconcile
With the commandment to love one's enemies.

FAMILY FEUD

But Aetius wrestled with all this in his mind.
He was convinced that any attempt to bring
Honoria to justice would be murder meant
To hide Valentinian's own crimes. Never!
Aetius then said to himself that he would go in
And lead his men through her palace,
But he would not kill Honoria.
There would be no justice done in that.
If he had to, he would confront that weasel
Of an emperor that stood before him.
Maybe that was the right thing to do.

At once Valentinian's escort stormed
Through the palace. As before, the guards
Within offered no resistance, ignorant
Of the dire machinations at work.
Ready to put his sister down once and for all,
Valentinian led the charge himself,
Recklessly overturning tables and statues
As he proceeded down the halls,
Letting them shatter into a thousand shards
Upon the richly inlaid floors.
The troops examined every room they passed,
Hoping not to miss Honoria wherever she was.
One by one, the rooms proved empty,
But Valentinian showed no signs of stopping.
The armed contingent broke through the door
To his sister's bedchambers,
And everything within seemed to be in order.
The covers were tidy, and all
Was wherever it was meant to be.
Except for one thing, that is.

Valentinian scowled, scanning the room
With the utmost attention to detail.
This was the one room of the palace
That had not yet been checked,
But still there was no sign of Honoria.
His sister was nowhere to be found.
It was obvious then that she had fled.
If she did a good job, she would likely never
Be found again. From a hidden place she saw
Valentinian storm her palace, and in silence
She left, hidden from all unfriendly eyes.
"God be with you," Aetius mouthed,
His prayers unheard by the emperor.

Outside the city, Honoria led her horse on.
Walking on foot, she turned around to give
Ravenna one last glance. The Adriatic Sea
To its left and the swampy expanse to its right,
She took in the smell of pine needles
And the sound of waves crashing on shores.
Gulls cawed overhead as the sun began
To dip behind the looming pine forest.
The sister of the emperor traded regal garb
For simple brown robes. She raised up a hood,
Resting it on the top of her head.
The tawny horse was loaded with supplies-
Food, money, gear for setting up camp
And provisions for cooking food.
She had enough to hold out on her own
For a while, but she knew she could not
Survive indefinitely alone in the wild.
Honoria would have to figure out something.
She might even have to leave the bounds

FAMILY FEUD

Of the Roman Empire that had long housed her.
Maybe she would have to learn a new language.
How difficult would be it be learn Gothic?

Whatever her final destination was,
Honoria knew she had a fighting chance.
She would be free from her brother
And perhaps be allowed to start over.
That now was her only ambition.
If it failed, then perhaps she deserved to die
Lost in obscurity. She was prepared for that.
Even that would be better than spending
Another day in swampy Ravenna,
Where the painful memories simply ran
Too deep for her to bear any longer.
Honoria had no happiness in leaving Ravenna.
She barely even had hope for this future life.
What she did have, though, was relief-
Relief to be away from Valentinian.
And that would have to be enough for now.

BOOK FIVE
INTO WORLDS BELOW

When at last came rosy-fingered Dawn,
Lighting the earth with her elegant touch,
Sighlut took off, packing possessions
And riding back to Tornacum's walls.
Ildico and Evoric prepared for their trek,
Loading a pair of horses with their provisions,
Weapons too, should any foe assail them.
In the wild they went, upon a road
I dare not detail in full, lest any ears
Willing ill should learn the path
And corrupt its purpose.
Beyond the North Wind their road led them
Through a land that cannot be found
By any mortal save one who already knew
How to find it- Hyperborea-
Far removed from toil and war,
Where never there is lack of muses
Caught in jubilant chorus
And the sun never sets,
A joyous land- though bitterly cold
It may be- a land of giants too,

INTO WORLDS BELOW

Dark-haired and ten feet tall.
They herded great creatures
That ages past walked the earth
When it was colder place,
The land shaped by huge glaciers,
Preserving them here long past
The hour of their extinction
Elsewhere on the earth.
In the hidden vale of Pajwajuk they stayed,
Where Ketjin served as chieftain,
Receiving wares and stores of mead.

Yet this was not their destination,
For deep within the remote crags
Of Hyperborea's mountains
Did their road continue on,
Through a path none knew
Save for Evoric and others
Of his order, elusive Forest-Walkers.
Unpacking steadfast horses
And leaving them behind,
Never to trod beneath the earth,
Through sinuous tunnels they delved
Deep into the earth.
Rarely they spoke and only in whispers,
Not wanting to awake whatever
Fiends dwelled deep within,
Down in the Heart of the World.
Yet Evoric raised his staff aloft,
Whispering gentle incantations,
And a light surged forth,
Chasing shadows into the recesses.
Before them stretched a sea of cities

BOOK FIVE

Abandoned in an earlier age,
Sprawled across subterranean mountains
For miles onward in all directions.
"Here is Toratanatu," said Evoric,
"Famed in the legends of the Elves.
It is said that the sprawling Under-City
Was built by their gods long ago,
Ages before history began,
In the midst of the God-Strife,
Primordial battle between deities.
Can we truly say this place dates back
To a mythic war before the dawn of our world?
I do not know, but it is nonetheless ancient.
It is said that those who dwelled within
Were allied with the older generation,
And so when ancient Karotu fell,
Dewo cursed them with eternal undeath."

On they went through crumbled marketplaces
And collapsed palaces
Until they came across a true lost relic
Not seen in any city today.
Through adamantine halls they went,
Flanked on both sides by unending rows
Of glass vials holding blood.
Above each vial was etched an image,
Depictions of ancient creatures,
Forms both weird and wild.
Ildico saw titanic brutes and sail-backed predators,
Hideous sharks and huge marine monsters,
And other assortments of alien beasts
Unknown to human civilization.

INTO WORLDS BELOW

Aghast, Ildico spoke. "Have they stored
The blood of ancient animals
Deep within these forlorn halls?"

"Through the Blood-Halls I have gone before,"
Answered Evoric, ever leading the way.
"Toratanatu was not simply a fortress
For ancient gods, But a center
For an art most profane-
Necromancy.
Those who lived here dabbled
In a strange spell-craft, harvesting
The blood of slain creatures so that
They might be reborn in ages to come.
Yet all this was not magic,
Or so far-removed descendants
Are wont to profess.
Everything was physical, bound
By the laws of the natural world.
These vials are all worthless now.
One day, perhaps, they might again
Be worth more than a few small coins."

All throughout the city,
The bones of men and women
Perished long ago were strewn about.
Huge boulders hurled by siege engines
Or launched by titanic monsters
Flattened buildings and overturned markets.
Overabundant was the debris,
And the air was thick with foul decay,
For here lingered the spirits
Of those long dead,

BOOK FIVE

Cursed by the gods of the Elves
For their part in this prehistoric war,
Armor still smeared with blood,
Bearing the injuries they suffered
All those ages ago.
They posed no threat,
Eternally caught in idle wandering.
Ever somber they went on,
Heads sunk with shame and remorse,
Bound here as they have been
Since before human empires.
Perhaps one day they shall be released,
Free to enjoy their afterlife,
But such an occasion has not yet come,
And few thought it ever would.

Then along the outer skirts
Of the age-old battlements,
They saw in mountainous walls
A door of marble and obsidian
Molded into a single form-
White and black, light and dark.
Etched upon the door was
A cruel battle between grotesque forms,
Central among them a looming beast
Engulfed by a hundred sinuous limbs.

"We will not go that way," said Evoric,
"For there lies the prison of Aegaeon,
Famed among the Hecatoncheires.
The titans of a hundred hands fought
With those shades against the younger gods,
And for his crimes and deeds of war

INTO WORLDS BELOW

Has Aegaeon been so condemned,
Chained as a prisoner and a door-warden
To the realm beyond his cell,
The kingdom of Zaršu-Mot.
Among the deities of the Elves
He is the most feared, for he holds
In his halls phantoms of the dead.
Even gods fear to pass by
The prison of Aegaeon, and even I
Would only go at direst need."

On Ildico and Evoric continued
Until at last they reached the library.
Its volumes long decayed,
The tomes remained,
Though never again could they be read.
So they wandered through,
Eyes running up-and-down imposing shelves.
Oh, how much knowledge had been lost
Simply from the span of time
Between the binding of these tomes
And the arrival of human eyes
To behold their decayed forms!
Yet even here could no peace be found.
Distant nails scratched against stone
As clawed feet pattered in the gloom.
Guttural clicks echoed throughout,
And a pair of eyes shone in the dark.
From the shadows emerged a creature
Over two cubits high at the hips.
Though its neck was bald,
Its body was covered in black feathers.
Its toothy snout nipped at the air

BOOK FIVE

As it continued its clicking calls.
At once, Evoric knew its form.
Mena the Elves call it,*
Or Meša when they are many.
Karoputaru was once their home,
And like the other creatures of that place,
They heeded the Forest-Walkers' voice.
And yet there came a time
When they were led astray,
Summoned by a voice with great power.
Was it a rogue perhaps,
Who once counted himself as Torapaï
And left their order for some other purpose?
None knew for sure,
But one thing was certain.
Where there is one Tawa,
Many more are sure to be found.

And indeed there were.
From a shelf above, another leapt down,
Clamping dozens of small teeth
Upon Evoric's left shoulder,
Barreling him to the ground
And clawing at his flesh.
The first of the pair
Entered the assault,
With his jaws seizing Evoric's hand
And forcing him to drop his staff.
The hot breath of the Tawa beat down,
Mild venom mingling with Gothic blood.
Dizzying was the pain,

---

* *Tawa hallae*

INTO WORLDS BELOW

And Evoric's mind swirled
As he succumbed to the creature's bite.
But Ildico dove into the fray,
Shoving aside the Tawa
That had tackled her companion
And driving her sword into its neck.
Rising to her feet, she saw the animal
Lying on its side, mouth agape
And flapping spastically
As lethal wound oozed with blood.
Recovering from the sudden assault,
Evoric unsheathed his own blade
And drove it in the first Tawa's eye.
The animal screamed with pain
As it loosened its grip on his hand,
Its limp body slinking backwards
As Evoric returned to his feet,
The cries of the dying carried throughout
The vastness of Toratanatu,
Calling kin to avenge themselves
Upon these fools prowling their domain.

At once the two knew their peril,
And in haste they fled the library,
Headed towards the Under-City's outskirts.
Houses hewn from the flanks of cliffs
Loomed perilously overhead,
And directly before them stood an amphitheater.
They passed through an arched doorway,
Flanked upon both ends
By some devilish ghoul
As they made their way into the arena.
From their left leapt another Tawa,

Filthy claws extended bare,
Leaving a loathsome stench in its wake.
For the suddenness of its attack
And for the ferocity thereof,
It might have succeeded at latching one
Of the intruders or maybe the other,
But Ildico struck it in the middle of the neck,
Sword cleaving through sinew and vertebrae,
So that its head fell rolling
And tumbling through the dust
Even as it still squawked.
The two went onwards surrounded,
Surrounded by the stench of blood
And the odor of the pack.
Upon a sandy field they now stood,
Surrounded by lines of benches
Arranged in tiered rows of withered stone.

But in these seats was an audience
Neither human nor elven,
Instead was here amassed a legion of Tawa,
For this was their breeding ground.
Then crashed down the full swarm
Like foaming waves upon the shore.
Thrice Ildico and Evoric cried out
And met the horde in hot contest
Set furiously upon the Tawa.
Ildico drove her blade onward,
Punching through opened maw
Right into the nape of the neck.
Evoric smote another across its chest,
And hot bowels went pouring out,
Kicking up a cloud of dust

INTO WORLDS BELOW

As they hit the earth, leaving
In their wake a mangled mess of gore.
Evoric sent his sword toward another
Screening through where the neck
Met the collarbone, and at the neck Ildico struck
Yet another savage Tawa,
Cleaving through the bones
So that the neck dangled loosely,
Severed on one side
And flapping precariously on the other.

And as the bodies of mangled dead
Began to pile high with reeking stench,
The animals soon recoiled,
Called back by the approach
Of their dread lord now returned,
He who first drove them
Away from Karoputaru's lush forests
And to this hollowed city
Forgotten by the rest of the world.
A veil of blinding fire
Overcame the two intruders.
At the heart of the flames could be seen
A thick mass of rising smoke huge and ominous,
And from this shroud rose a figure.

A helmet sat upon his head,
And the fires of his face were kindled
As ashen tendrils lashed from the cloud.
With a swing of his staff,
Evoric sent forth a sphere of light
To ward off the assault
Arrayed by this unknown foe.

BOOK FIVE

More serpentine tendrils came their way,
And each advance was driven back.
Ildico did not move, awed by the terror at work
And by the power summoned
To drive off its bombastic attacks.
"What are you?" Evoric called out,
Speaking with a loud voice. "Speak!"

But the mass, rude and unformed,
Gave to its foe no answer.
Fire and smoke surged forth,
And Evoric stood firm.

"You will not hinder us," he declared.
"Begone now, whatever you may be,
And fly back whence you came!"

With a loud shriek, the formless mass
Withdrew its dread assault.
The flaming radiance surrounding it
Pulsated rapidly, like an overworked heart
Pumping blood through the arteries
And fueling the body
Until at last it suddenly vanished,
Taking with it the unknown assailant.
Then thick silence sank down
Upon the arena, for swarming scavengers
And ancient spirits were both long gone.

Evoric winced as he sat on the earth,
And Ildico saw the many bleeding marks
Imprinted in the arm. "Evoric,"
She declared, "this venture of ours

Shall be the death of you."

But Evoric reassured her and said,
"Take heart, for these wounds are shallow
And I was not struck near
Any vital parts. Yet still it hurts,
The pain earlier dulled by the venom
Lacing pointed fangs, that and the thrill
That so often follows the rush of battle.
And yet my leg has so received
Gruesome wounds left by the Meša.
Let us rest here a while,
Putting no pressure on my torn limb."

And Ildico answered, "I trust then
That the severity of these wounds
Is as you say. But even so
They must be tended to.
Perhaps those who guard the Tree
May yet offer herbs to relieve your pain."
She reached into the leather satchel
Hanging alongside her waste,
Pulling out several gauzes
And wrapping them around Evoric's wounds.

"I'm sorry to put you through
All these troubles," Ildico said.
"Just looking at this mess
Has me wanting a few rounds."

"Don't apologize," he said.
"This is the most excitement
I've had in months. Cuts and bruises

Are all part of the job."

"What fiend was that," she asked,
"That led the assault against us?
Ancient it must be, and powerful
To muster the weapons it wielded
Against lone wanderers in the wild."

"I do not know," Evoric said with a wince.
"Some ancient spirit perhaps,
Imprisoned forever deep within
The desolate Heart of the World.
I know not its origins
Nor can I repeat its name.
Even I am ignorant of its kind.
Perhaps he once was like us,
A member of my ancient order
Compelled by ambition to go forth
And so corrupt his ordained purpose.
He held command over the Meša
So perhaps I speak true of him."

She took his arm around her shoulder
And hoisted him up,
One arm holding his back
And the other his staff.
"Is it safe if I hold this?" she asked.
"It is your tool, but to walk comfortably
It is better I hold it instead.
I will not throw the world into chaos
Should I hold this ancient rod, shall I?"

"Do not worry," Evoric answered.

INTO WORLDS BELOW

"The world is already a mess as it is.
You can inflict no more grave a wound
Upon its gaping side."

"Yet already have I done so," she said,
Yet only in a soft whisper
Unheard by her companion,
Who with an arm draping her shoulder
Hobbled on one unharmed leg,
And they hastened as quick as they could,
Not wishing to lure with the smell of blood
More fearsome scavengers eager
To pick off the spoils of battle.

So they went from the amphitheater,
Passing through what little remained
Of the winding corridors and decayed streets
Of this city interred beneath the earth.
For several hours their procession continued,
Ceasing only for the injured to catch
But a moment for a quick breath.
Down through the deep their road led on
Until at last they reached the end
And there came upon the roots
Of the World Tree,
The Wall Between the Worlds.
Up ahead the cavern opened
And a vertical tunnel stood before them.
Huge roots that seemed like stone
Crept their way slowly down
From worn crevices in a rippling ceiling
That twinkled with orbs like starlight.
Up the tunnel drifted blue lights,

Ethereal orbs bound to their course
And passing through the web
Of colossal roots overhead.

Out came the warden of the Tree,
She who kept fast the thin veil
Separating world from world.
She had only to shout, it was said,
And mountains would break before her,
Though she was not wont to venture out
And rend the earth beneath her strides.
It was said that gods sought her aid
In their primordial kin-strife,
To turn the aid and win victory
For one side or the other,
Though even they could not
Sway her to their feeble causes.

In no human form did she go
Nor that of any elf,
But in like an ancient reptile
From time immemorial.
Like a barrel her body
Wrapped in plated scutes was shaped,
Nearly the size of an elephant's.
And from her broad head
Rose cheeks of bone from
Underneath those ageless eyes
With which she looked on
As wandering humans ambled in,
Knowing full well Ildico stood
Perplexed by the oddity of
Her armored hide and horned head.

INTO WORLDS BELOW

"I am as the All-Father made me,"
She spoke, "as are you.
Nildahgiiv I am called,
And I bid you welcome
To the roots of the World Tree Artaru-
Ageless and immortal.
It is good to see you again, Evoric,
And Ildico too,
Though we have not yet met."

Aghast, Ildico stepped back.
"How can you know my name,
Though never have we met?
My homeland is leagues away,
Separated by waters and by wilderness."

And Nildahgiiv answered saying,
"I know your name and your deeds,
Or are those the deeds to be done?
Time is much more fluid here
At the doorway between worlds.
I have seen epochs come and go,
Empires rise and fall,
Cults rise and religions die.
Among many you are but one star,
A single thread in the tapestry
Of the celestial sphere.
But I reckon you have not here come
To listen to a decrepit serpent
Drone without cease on the nature of time.
In Evoric's company you have come,
And thus I surmise your road
Leads ever on to the lush jungles

Of distant Karoputaru."

"That was our plan," Evoric said,
"To hinder there the ambitions
Of Attila, lord of the Huns."

"But you shall not enter," Nildahgiiv declared,
"Bloody and bruised as you are.
Come Tosarkhaan, from your perch
Must you descend and tend to guests."

From crevices overhead crept
Yet another serpent, though smaller in size
With hooked claws on his forelimbs.
A claw adorned his prehensile tail,
Wrapped tightly around the roots
As he slinked ever downward.
Tosarkhaan has he long been called
And his charge it is
To scale the carven ash Artaru
Bearing news from Veydaalfar above,
Who sits upon the crested brow
Of regal Pahkvaas,
Whose blazing crests cuts through clouds
Whenever wings bear him aloft.
To Nildahgiiv down below
Does the climber convey these tidings,
And so has he always done
Since before the God-Strife
Forever changed the face of the earth,
Though rather would he
Spend his days in idle leisure.

INTO WORLDS BELOW

"Why do you disturb me?
You've caught me at a time
Most inopportune. There's
A keg out back calling my name."

"Your debauchery can wait," Nildahgiiv replied.
"You must ascend the tree's heights.
Give Veydaalfar the word
So off shall he fly and thus
Harvest for us salves of elf-make,
So that wandering Evoric here
Shall be in fighting condition
In only but a day or two."

With a grunt, Tosarkhaan consented
And hoisted himself back up,
Scaling further into the crevices
As he mumbled curses under his breath,
Though off trailed his voice
Once he had passed out of sight.

"If I may be so bold," spoke Ildico,
Caught by curiosity's iron grasp,
"By what power are you able
To perceive me from afar?"

Nildahgiiv gave Ildico her answer,
Speaking with a proud and booming voice.
"Indeed as I have already said,
My abode sits upon the precipice
Overlooking the gap between all worlds,
Not simply your own realm
And that of the Land of Dragons,

BOOK FIVE

But other places as well,
Just as ancient and wondrous.
From the crossroads of reality
I see the affairs of mortal kingdoms
Unfold, disasters as my kin
Were once held in check by.
The currents of Time fray here,
And I may see past, present, and future,
Though its beginning and its end
Are lost to my eyes.
Even I, ancient and ageless as I may be,
Am not without my barring limitations.

"And are there more like you?"
Ildico continued her investigation,
Eager to hear what Nildahgiiv would say.
So she spoke in response:

"*Grovaar,*" she said in her own tongue,[*]
Older even than that of the Swart Elves.
"But little more than savage beasts
Are they counted now, trudging
Through thick forests and rocky scrublands
Before calamity overtook the old world
Now little more than idle playthings
Held in the hands of Fate are they.
Yet in that regard are we alike, I suppose,
Though I in my own unique way.
Time flows ever on, my child.
Soon you and Evoric will be lost

---

[*] Transcribed in *Augusta* as *ge-ro-va-a-re*, *grovaar* is an affirmative
particle in Arhkvun. Refer to page 385.

INTO WORLDS BELOW

To memory, and on shall I linger
Here in the gloom of my forlorn abode."
"But the others," Ildico continued.
"If you had it in your power,
Would you help your distant kin
Aquire the consciousness you bear?"

Nildahgiiv growled and answered,
"I have asked myself that question
For countless mortal lifetimes.
I am alone: no thing older than I
Walks this earth. I saw those gods
Of the Swart Elves when they were conceived,
And generations uncounted
Of my own kind have come and gone.
And yet in a way I envy their lot.
Since time immemorial they have gone
Eating and sleeping, unfettered
By the concerns and the philosophies
That have seized this one's mind.
Would I do to them a favor
By giving them an awareness
Of all things evil in the world,
Or would they be happier drowned
In stupid ignorance? I do not know.
But the hour has gone late.
In my nest shall I take respite now.
I enjoy your questions, though.
Throw more of them my way
If you so desire."

Now in her nest Nildahgiiv slept soundly
While elf-make medicines

Were sent on their way
To relieve Evoric of his injuries
And offer him newfound strength
To trod dense Karoputaru.
Yet the guests were still awake,
For Evoric slept little
And an evil dream kept Ildico up.
So she rose from her bedding
And found Evoric sitting there
Upon a gentle slope.
She placed herself to his side,
And so he spoke to her.

"What keeps you awake?" asked Evoric.
"Surely you've had a long day."

Ildico nodded and gave her answer.
"It has been, yes.
But the dreams of my past
Have barred sleep from my mind."

"I am sorry," said Evoric.
"You grew up in Ravenna, yes?
I wonder how things fare
Down in Rome's latest capital.
Word has come to me that Aetius
Will soon march northward,
Ready to face Attila in combat."

"How came you by such news?"
Asked Ildico, eager for an answer.

"Scouts came to Attila," Evoric said,

"And to him they told everything.
The emperor gets more and more anxious,
And not simply because of his sister.
Their mother, Galla Placidia,
At last her sickness took her.
I cannot imagine the pain
That must have seized her family.
For decades has she been
A vital part of the imperial household.
The weight of all the world
Now bares down upon their shoulders.
They have my prayers."

All this he said, but by this news
Was Ildico suddenly overcome.
Bitterly she wept,
Like a mother who lost her son,
Having marched out to the perils of battle
All in the name of glory,
Yet only returned carried on the back
Of his father's shield. So now she wept
And struggled to wipe the tears
From her overflowing eyes,
Though Evoric did not know why.

Evoric sat in the silence
Until at last he spoke again.
"I take it, then, that you were close
To this family, counted a friend perhaps,
Before Attila's war began."

"More than that," Ildico answered.
"I was not simply close to Honoria,

Nor counted among her closest friends.
Her struggle was my own. I was, I am…"
Again she stopped, choking on her tears,
And at last Evoric understood.
She did not weep for a distant friend
But for her mother. Ildico, Honoria-
They were one and the same.
Honoria wept again and her head sank,
Shoulders drooped with the weight of remorse.

"What- by God- is wrong with me?
I was *Augusta*, but one step removed
From the title of emperor.
Why do I weep like this? I know.
The campaign now underway,
The thousands that shall be slain
All because of Attila's ambition
And quest to reclaim a stolen bride,
That weighs upon my shoulders.
Half the world wants me dead,
And it's right to do so.
All this rests upon me
And the pain of my burden
Shall soon be too much to bear.
How can I go on
When all the world hates me so?"

"Not all," Evoric answered,
Revealing his scarring wounds,
Still fresh, yet slowly healing.
"Were it not for your part
These wounds would be worse,
And myself a meal caught within

A hundred separate stomachs."

"But," Honoria spoke again,
Skeptical that one good deed
Could undo the thousand pains
Her actions would soon inflict.
"All that was only something
That any decent person would do."

"Precisely," Evoric nodded,
Leaving her to her thoughts,
Hoping she would realize then,
Regardless of the faults she had done,
There was more to her tale than a single story
Or a handful of misdeeds.

It was but a short while later
When Evoric took her by the hands
And looked her in the eyes.
"How then can I help you, your highness?
Is it respite you need, or perhaps
An escape from these calamities?
I can delay my quest for some time,
Take a few weeks off from my labors
If that is what you need.
I do not know what your brother did,
Blinded by fits of rage,
But here with me you are safe:
That much I can promise.
Should you continue with me,
We shall go to a place
Where respite may yet be found
Beneath the shadow of wondrous forms

Lost to this war-wearied world,
Safe from the struggles of our war.
Or would you rather be left to yourself,
Free to process all that has happened,
Unbothered by outside meddling?"

Honoria shook her head, wiping more tears
As she gave her answer. "No."
Then in her eyes flickered a fire
That was not there before.
Honoria's voice was stern,
Hardened by a newfound resolve,
As if the night of bitter weeping
Awoke a slumbering giant within her.
"Still I continue on with you,"
She said, rising to her feet.
"Do not count me as a refugee
Hiding from the strife of my past,
In futility hoping for reconciliation
With a brother whose rage
Can never be sated."

"How then shall I count you," asked Evoric,
"If not as a refugee from strife?"

"We shall see," answered she.
"The events of the future shall yet
Determine the course of my path."
Sweet sleep came and went,
And when light crept back
Upon the surface world whence
It hid beyond the horizon,
Tosarkhaan returned from lands elsewhere

With salves bitter and potent.
At once Evoric drank them
And life returned to his limbs,
Dried wounds were sealed
And sapped energy renewed.
Then at last the moment came
To leave this world behind
And plunge into the Land of Dragons.
One following after the other,
Honoria and Evoric made the leap,
Bounding from over the ledge
And down into the pit,
Though Fate had not marked them out
To plummet to the Heart of the World.
The draw of the World Tree
Hoisted them up through the air.
Drifting ever upwards,
They passed the wardens of Artaru,
Past carven roots slinking down,
And through the stone ceiling overhead.

Through the trunk of a tree of light
They spiraled at break-neck speed,
Hurled aloft through the vastness
Of the expansive cosmos,
And all the realms of the universe
Were laid out before them,
From the desolate glacial fields
Where mighty Giants roam,
Fishing for their colossal prey,
Spearing great shelled squids
As they pass beneath ice-floats,
To the gloomy mist-crags

BOOK FIVE

Of the deep Nether-Places
Ruled by dreadful Zaršu-Mot,
Most feared among Swart Elf gods
And who holds the phantoms
Of those who have died so lately.
In that place they also beheld
The great shadows left by he
Who was long imprisoned
In this place- Aegaeon,
Greatest of the Hecatoncheires,
And even at his shadow they trembled.

Seas of fire they also beheld,
Churned up by volcanic ire
Amid crags of black obsidian,
And the gloom of Chaos itself,
Rude and unformed since ancient days
When the world was young
And gods afraid of monsters.
But among these was another realm,
A land of jungles and floodplains,
Of pristine coasts and open plains,
Lorded over by Swart Elves
And by primordial creatures
Long forgotten by other worlds.
And so they passed into
The Land of Dragons.

BOOK SIX
SWART ELVES AND PRIMAL BEASTS

Within a small alcove tucked inside
Looming mountain flanks
Honoria and Evoric now stood,
A hidden passage said to be
Sacred to immortal gods
Long ago worshipped by the Elves,
To Karotu whose name was first given
To the vast expanse of Karoputaru,
Though long has his cult been lost,
Forgotten by the decay of time,
And Karotu himself now but a vessel
For tales of other gods, those that usurped him
And threw down his power
In ancient days, long before
The empires of Elves and Romans.

The stiff cave air was long gone,
Usurped by the cool breeze
Of a world beneath the sky.
"Look now at this wide expanse yonder,"
Evoric said, gesturing to the land

BOOK SIX

Outside this craggy recess,
"Your highness, I bid you welcome
To this, the Land of Dragons.
Welcome to Karoputaru."

Before them stretched a sea of trees,
Slender-trunked monkey puzzles,
Flanked on their southern and western ends
By a phalanx of snowy peaks.
To the north a canyon cut
Straight through the heart of the wood
Until at last it reached the pristine sea.
Bands of orange and purple
Poured across the azure sky,
And no sun hovered over the land,
Instead forever illuminated
By the light of the twinkling stars,
And nebulae scattered like clouds
All across the heavens.

Above the distant Shadowdells hovered
Temekuš, that huge stone raised up
From the land below by Karotu's commands,
Who grew within its hollowed shell
A fount to offer nourishment
To these lands in his absence.
Like waterfalls ran streams
Out from within Temekuš, fueling
All of the Land of Dragons,
And now for aeons has it hovered,
Its crags a home for winged residents,
For monks and sorcerers who delved
Hallowed refuges from its crags,

SWART ELVES AND PRIMAL BEASTS

Far closer to the land than that moon
Which gives light to Roman nights.

Honoria turned her eyes to the northeast,
Where monkey puzzles huddled close together,
Encircled by shorter ginkgoes.
Long and hard she watched
Towering trunks sway in the wind,
And at this distance one of them was moving,
Not a sway in the wind,
But the shifting of a gargantuan neck.
A dozen winged shapes took off
As it brushed through forest canopy.
No birds were they,
And strange crests from their heads
Rose like the unfurled sails of a ship.
Off they hastened as swirling trunk
Let out its trumpeting song,
Reverberating all throughout the land.
Its anthem was answered in return
By a chorus of other voices
As colossal shapes lumbered
Onto the plain underneath caught between
Mountain crags and monkey puzzle forest.

Eagerly, Honoria scrambled down
Precariously narrow steps lining
The mountain's looming side.
Evoric followed after her,
Watching as a herd of beasts
Joined the melodious titans.
Smaller in size they were,
Though no less magnificent,

Heads adorned with menacing horns
And necks covered by bony shields.
They joined their giant neighbors
Browsing among dense plant-life,
Shaking the earth beneath thunderous advance.
And Honoria lingered beneath their shadow,
Taken aback, Laughing,
Her knees faltered beneath her,
So awed was she by the sight,
Yet she had no words for such an occasion.

"The first time I came down here,"
Evoric said, standing by her side,
"I wept. So overcome with joy I was,
And wonder too." And Honoria snickered,
No bigger smile had been seen on her face
For uncounted years, and she knew it, too.
Yet even now Evoric wasted no time,
Eager to show the sites and sounds
Of this strange land.
As joyous as her first impression
Might have been, his second
Was even more so. Fewer things
Delighted him more
Than sharing this beauty with others,
Especially one so in need
Of a break from the turbulence
And clamors of the world,
However brief it may be.

Then Evoric tapped the earth with staff,
Crying out with a whistling overtone.
Clear and piercing, the song carried

SWART ELVES AND PRIMAL BEASTS

Through the gentle breeze as it
Echoed across the open landscape.
One among the horned Triceratops*
Came trotting up towards them,
Tail wagging happily as she advanced,
The matriarch of the herd.
As Sophia she was known to Evoric,
His companion on many long treks.
Through wilderness and through war
Has she been by his side,
When he fought with daemons of the deep
And turbulent spirits from crags above.
With a soft whisper he spoke to her,
Rubbing his hand gently upon her snout.
Located in a hut nearby,
Which Evoric was wont to visit,
Rested a saddle built for Sophia's kind,
Made by Swart Elf hands,
Suitable for one rider and a second
To roam across the fens
And through labyrinthine forests.

Rosy-fingered Dawn crept through
The dense canopy of gingko leaves
And at once the air was filled
With the melodious chirping
And the whooping of ribbon-tailed birds.†
Lizards soared from tree to tree,
Carried aloft by membranous wings

---

* In Wešikeriaya: Terikeruša

† Likely Duworekoro, a.k.a *Changchengornis hengdaoziensis*

Extended from gangly hind limbs.
Scores of Sharovipteryx bounded,[*]
Leaping overhead noisome birds
And lumbering Desmatosuchus,[†]
Which happily ambled along
Through dense undergrowth,
Shielded by a carapace of armor
And lances on their shoulders,
Content instead to gorge themselves
Upon the fresh spoils of forest greenery.
All these forms and many more
Have called Karoputaru their home
For uncounted ages,
Long before the Elves came here
And erected strongholds along the coast
And within craggy peaks.

Alone and in peace elsewhere
Among turbulent foaming waves,
A winged reptile perched on craggy rocks.
Foaming waves crashed against stone,
Sending up blasts of salty sea water.
The Pteranodon[‡] ran his long beak through
The fuzzy coat covering his body and
From the fibers plucked out a lone bug.
Then he stretched his neck out, gazing
Across the pristine sea at the nebulous skies.
Bands of orange and purple streaks

---

[*] In Wešikeriaya: Paotopuga

[†] In Wešikeriaya: Toraku

[‡] In Wešikeriaya: Gaotalu

SWART ELVES AND PRIMAL BEASTS

Were strewn all across the alien sky,
And at last the Pteranodon took to the wing.
Over crystal clear waters he made his flight,
Stopping only to dive beneath the surface
And snatch up a single herring
From shimmering bait balls.

In murky depths beneath a monster stirred,
Its gaze focused on the diving Pteranodon,
A gaping maw opened wide as a the beast
Sped without effort through watery dark;
Its giant fore-flippers kept its body cruising
Through azure deeps as powerful hind-limbs
Braced to accelerate its immense mass
Ever upwards toward its unaware prey.
Yet the Pteranodon caught wind of this terror
As it approached from far beneath.
In a flash he clutched his beak around
The flanks of a herring before
Thrusting with great force his body up.
Breaking the surface of the water,
He took off into the open air
As a massive pliosaur* breached the waves,
Clamping huge jaws down upon thin air.
Free from this menace, the Pteranodon resumed
His continuous journey over the deep.
Riding the wind and the waves, here he
Was unfettered by the bounds of terrestrial life.
Here he and the rest of his kind were free,
Rare icons of natural freedom
In an age marked by the dominance

---

*In Wešikeriaya: Talhuit

BOOK SIX

Of human empires and Elven states.
This much was clear when the winged traveller
Came once more near the pearly white shores.
Upon a ship's mast he made his perch,
Allowing a vessel driven by deep magics
To push him towards his final destination.
The sails unfurled with the wind to their backs,
The sailors making their way across the sea
Until at last they reached their port of call.
Pristine waters drifted onto a shoreline of sand
Nearly as white as snow-capped mountains,
And palms like towers rose from the earth.
Hundreds of sea birds with toothy mouths
And stunted wings flocked about the shores,
Their incessant squawks ringing loud and clear.

Further down these shores bustling with life,
Between cliffs of rising limestone
And treacherous crags home to the Istiodactylus,
From within this cliff-flanked strait
And out toward the open expanse of sea
Sat a city upon the roaring waves.
A city of twelve stepped pyramids, each of them
As large as an average town, rose there
Upon foundations built beneath the water.
Two further foundations could be seen,
And hard at work were Elves constructing
The lofty heights that would rise from them.
Bridges painted purple spanned the watery gaps
Between one district and the other,
And on the faces of tripled-tiered pyramids
Were laid the houses, markets, and other
Amenities that so befit a city of such splendor.

SWART ELVES AND PRIMAL BEASTS

Here was Puaita, the newest of Swart Elf cities
And no doubt worthy to be counted among them.
Few finer cities would there be
In all the vast regions of Karoputaru.

Through the wilds of this realm
Honoria and Evoric continued their travels
Seated atop their mighty horned steed,
For weeks wandering and exploring
Until they passed into pristine Puaita,
Where Elves leap over Diabloceratops,*
Clutching charging brutes by their horns
And vaulting over imposing frames.
The feats of courage and agility
Honoria watched with Evoric,
Taking a seat within an arena
Built upon a pyramid's sloping edge,
Where thousands others flocked about
To see these feats performed.
Nearly opposite the arena from where
Honoria and Evoric sat, they could see
Poliwu, Puaita's First-Elder seated
And draped in robes of violet
Imbued with bands of sacred gold.
With him were his attendants, who brought
To Poliwu and his guests favored wine
Which was shared by all he invited.
Among them were men of Ethiopia,
Envoys of king Ebana who like the Huns
Stumbled upon doorways that led
Into this ancient Land of Dragons,

---

* In Wešikeriaya: Orokeruša

BOOK SIX

A kingdom lorded over by the Elves.
They exchanged their goods and enjoyed
The arts and games so loved by their host.
About their ranks stood Poliwu's guard,
Who on their faces wore bronze masks
Topped with crests of crimson plumes
Swaying to-and-fro in the cool breeze.

Upon a sandy floor within the arena
Stood the beast, a mighty Diabloceratops
Wagging about a frilled head crowned
With a pair of lethal curved horns..
Naked attendants goaded it on,
Gently prodding it with their staves.
Before the beast stood the jumpers,
Swart Elf women who for years
Were trained for this deadly sport,
A leap over death-dealing horns.
They were hardly clothed, save
For a single tunic of light linen,
Exposed to the thrill and the danger.
With no arms or armor to stave off
The advances of raging ferocity,
A single misstep could spell their doom.

Oil was poured over their bodies,
Oil which was mixed with urinal traces
Of the Diabloceratops' wild predators.
So diluted was the mixture that those
Who donned the scent could not smell it,
But the Diabloceratops could, confused
Yet enraged by the mingled odor.
It hissed and growled in agitation

SWART ELVES AND PRIMAL BEASTS

Before letting out blaring honks,
Cries of battle and impending doom.
The attendants leapt aside, lest
They too should be gored
Or barreled into their own blood.
On it stampeded, barreling through
The clouds of rising dust as on
Toward the jumper it charged.
But she was prepared- trained Aïšti-
Long had she harnessed her skills,
And many times had she leapt
Over the beast and landed unscathed.
Still her heart thumped in her chest
As always it did when she jumped.
It had to, she thought, for the jump
She made without fear would surely
Be the final leap she took,
Overcome by reckless pride.

The Diabloceratops drew closer, thundering
Across the earth with hateful rage.
Aïšti stretched out her arms, and
With a single move latched upon
Its lethal brow horns, pushing up
And somersaulting through the air
Above those keratinous stakes.
The horned beast continued its run,
Passing underneath the leaping Elf
Who safely landed behind its tail.
With arms stretched out Aïšti bowed
While attendants hurried with their staves,
Prepared to ward off the beast and
Signal a second jumper for her leap.

BOOK SIX

But Aïšti dusted her hands and went off,
Content with her day's work and so
Scrubbed off the dirt of the arena
And the residue of slick oils.

But as the Diabloceratops raged about,
Huffing and puffing as with
Cacophonous anthems it cried,
Honoria gazed into its eyes
Which shone like glossy marble.
And as she stared she could see
Its ire slowly begin to cool.
Its cries grew silent and its
Roaming was driven to a halt.
The beast would surely be stirred again
For the second of the jumpers,
But for a moment it was calm,
And Honoria was gripped by
Its beautifully colored frill and
By the splendor of such a creature
So often used to dance with death.
These things she contemplated as
Athlete after athlete made the jump,
Some leaping as Aïšti did
And others vaulted with great staves,
As one Diabloceratops was replaced
By another and a third after that.

These feats and many more Honoria saw
As through Puaita's heights she went,
And by a grove set up within the city
She spoke with the Swart Elves
And learned their ways from them.

SWART ELVES AND PRIMAL BEASTS

There she came upon the great temple
Built for Ara- consort to Dewo
And most wrathful of the goddesses.
Honoria approached the temple,
Its vast doors flanked by images
Of those famed Diabloceratops,
And inside she saw the gifts
Laid out before Ara's altar.
But in this place she saw a frieze
Which told the long story of the Elves
From when their ancient island sank
Until they settled wondrous Karoputaru.
Honoria saw before her an island
From which the Elves ruled
Before this place was deemed their own,
When their people lived on the sea
As the furthermost of all races,
Whose mastery of the sail was unmatched
By all kingdoms under heaven.
Yet it was not their lot to forever claim
Mastery over the wind and waves.
Honoria saw on their shores
A refugee driven to them from afar,
Clinging to safety from the ire of their baleful god.

So came Oruseu, battered and bruised
From years of riding the waves
And battling ancient monsters.
Him they gave refuge, treasure too,
And all these goods were laid out
In his ship for Honoria to see
Along with safe passage back home.
But he had angered a god,

BOOK SIX

Posedawone- lord of waters,
Whose strides shake the earth itself.
Ruthless and unforgiving,
He tore asunder the isle of Sikeria,
Ancient homeland to sea-faring Elves.
An earthquake rent their land in two
And surging tsunamis drowned their cities.
In the chaos of cataclysm,
The Elves thought they could sate him,
And offer as wergild he who first
Offered Oruseu his boons, none other
Than King Arikenou himself.
So the king was slain, his throat slit
And body thrown upon a pyre
In the frieze as it was in history.
His murder achieved no end,
For baleful Posedawone in all his rage
Was not one to forgive them
Their hospitality so soon.
Those who outlasted the doom
That befell the island fled,
Scattered as chaff in the wind.

Some took to raiding, aligning themselves
With a host of tribes who ushered in
The end of empires uncounted
Before they too were scattered,
And before them went the army
Of a king armed with bow and chariot,
Joined by ancient folk of Evoric's order
And by those few scattered remnants
Of those empires the renegades destroyed.
This coalition drove those Elves

SWART ELVES AND PRIMAL BEASTS

Into a full rout, and never again
Would they see cities built
By the hands of Swart Elf artisans.
Those Elves who sought not war
Searched for new land on uncharted shores,
Journeying far and wide,
Across leagues of arid deserts
And weaving through treacherous rifts
Until they found for themselves
A place lush unlike any other.
And so they called it Karoputaru,
For the ancient god Karotu
Who ruled the earth long ago
When it was wild and untamed,
Savage yet beautiful,
All was plenty and war unheard of.
Laodame, son of Arikenou,
Ushered in a new age for the Swart Elves,
One of growth and prosperity,
And ever since has his line ruled
Unbroken for sixteen hundred years,
For every king who usurped another
From that point unto this day
Was still a descendent of his fruitful line.

These ancient stories were all laid out
Upon the walls of that marvelous temple,
And looking closely Honoria heeded
Every detail that she could, though
Hardly could she remember all she saw,
For many were Puaita's sights and sounds.
So impressed, Honoria went with Evoric
Away from the city once their short visit

BOOK SIX

Of four days' length came to an end.
Once more they went into the wild,
Wondering if they might chance upon
Those Huns which Attila long boasted
Had been sent into these lands
To harvest the creatures.
And unleash them upon Europe.

Some hours had passed
Before they departed from atop
Their lance-armed steed, standing before
What seemed like a barrow-mound,
Its stone door engraved with
The forms of alien sea creatures
Honoria had not before seen.
Only a short distance off
The vast expanse of azure sea
Unfurled before them, lingering
Where it has for uncounted ages.
Parahu-Ku this mound was called,
Or rather does that name go to
The facility beneath the hill.
Visitors were wont to come by day
To stand within its observatory
And gaze out into the deep beyond,
Where great creatures sleep
Underneath the foaming waves.
Here fell the mighty warlord Akeru,
Firstborn from gods of the deep
And resting down beneath ocean-floor,
And this mound commemorates
Those warriors whom he called companions
Now wandering gloomy mist-crags

SWART ELVES AND PRIMAL BEASTS

Until the end of days.

Through the door they went
And down finely-carved stairs
Until again their path opened,
And feet again met level ground.
Before them stretched an open chamber
And on the far end were laid bare
The seas, blocked from the humans
By no barrier, yet they felt no water,
The doings of the forge-workers of Kunasa,
Master artisans, whose predecessors
Once were trained by Apatiyo,
The Master Artificer,
Who in volcanic forges labored long,
Making enchanted designs unmatched
By all other arms. So these Elves
Continue his legacy, spreading his skills
Through the deep wilds of Karoputaru,
Leaving their mark on an untamed world,
Carving out a view of the sea that transformed
Its likeness into that of cloudy skies.

Faint sounds echoed in that clouded expanse,
Deep moans followed by high-pitched upsweeps.
Even before it came into view
Its calls shook the ground with tremors
More ominous than its ringing song.
Then at last the sea-beast appeared,
Its body the size of a whale's,
Cruising through on four flippers.
And Honoria, alarmed by its size,
Gripped her sword, but Evoric

BOOK SIX

Raised his hand and bade she lower hers.
Curiously it eyed the meager humans,
Truly a gentle giant if ever there was one,
Content to let its melody carry out
In wishful hopes that it might be answered.

In turn they were, a loud whistle
Followed by repetitive clicks.
Then came second whistle
Followed by bellowing groans
As a female emerged from the vastness.
Even larger was she than her counterpart,
He whose summons she answered,
And in their courtship
The Salorana continued their melodies.
She accepted his advances,
And gracefully their enormous forms
Slid together through the waters,
Cruising effortlessly through the deep,
Caught in their chorus
And in the art of romantic embrace.
Few ever have seen the Salorana
When they are caught in courtship,
And long has it been said
None can leave such an occasion unchanged,
Two of nature's greatest musicians
Lost in their art labor seamlessly
To beget posterity.
No finer testimony is there
Of the splendor that divinity
Has placed on this good earth.
Then sea-giants vanished into the deep,
Carrying the next generation with them.

SWART ELVES AND PRIMAL BEASTS

"Oh what my eyes have seen,"
Declared Honoria, gripped by awe.
"The cares and the afflictions
That once seized my wretched heart
Have fled from my mind, now
Directed toward the sights before me.
Are there even words to describe
The sensations I have beheld?
Words are potent, but even they
When at their most eloquent
Can do little to do justice
To the beauty of experience."

"Then do not struggle in vain,"
Evoric answered, "to put to words
Expressions that cannot be penned.
Simply enjoy the awe and wonder.
Embrace your own frailty
Tucked beneath the shadow
Of such colossal titans."

"Why do all this?" Honoria asked.
"Why take the time from your charge
To take me sight-seeing?
Is there some far grander purpose
Which you have planned in store,
Or do you simply want of me
To behold the same wonders
That have gripped your heart
And share in this with you?

Evoric answered her. "My aims for you
Were nothing beyond doing

What I thought I should. Here,
There is no agenda, though always
An agenda you have had. Whether in conspiring
To free yourself from Valentinian's ambitions
Or to seek refuge out in the wild.
Then there came Sighlut
And the ghastly sack of Argentoratum.
Indeed you may have faltered
When you thought that Attila
Might have offered you
The escape that you needed,
But that hardly means there should
Be no ladder to hoist you up
When you fall into a ditch.
I know full well what it's like
To live completely on your own,
And I would wish that on no one,
Even if all the world blames you
For the war to come."

Then Honoria answered back saying,
"If but a single word could entail
My life these past few months,
It would surely be *displacement*.
Though it may not be the same level
Experienced by Goths and other nations
Under the yoke of horseback Huns,
But it has been upheaval nonetheless.
I've never been settled since my exile
To the heights of well-walled Constantinople
And that brief return to swampy Ravenna,
Resolved against a loveless marriage.
I do not think I am the same

SWART ELVES AND PRIMAL BEASTS

As when I first fled Ravenna,
The same who plotted with Eugenius
And appealed to Attila, though how precisely
I cannot yet put into words."

"I do not know. I can say little except
That perhaps all this is but a part
Of learning from experience,
More skilled than any tutor
At correcting our veering paths
And shifting our focus on greater things.
I do think that this is so,
And history will prove me right.
But also well I know that one
Cannot thrive compelled by guilt alone.
Your shame has already been paid for."

"Your confidence is assuring,"
Honoria remarked, turning her gaze
And looking back out through the glass.
"Let us stay here a while longer.
I enjoy watching the forms
That glide through this enchanted sea."

There they stood in silent contentment,
Entranced by the mystic expanse
Laid bare before peering eyes.
Here there was no politics,
No war stratagem or petty affairs.
There was only wonder,
Wonder for a beauty
Forgotten by a world filled with hate.

BOOK SEVEN
THE HOST OF DRAGONS

Across rolling hills and through floodplains
Their winding road led them on,
Guiding them through dense jungles
Until they came unto a ravine
Cutting through the heart of dense woodland.
In fleeing from the clamor of war
That now consumed Europe in flames,
Honoria came across the final clash
That would see Huns expulsed from Elf lands.
Several hundred feet below looming cliff face
Marched a host of men clothed
In the leathery armor and conical caps
Huns were so often seen in,
Marching both on horseback and on foot.
Warily they proceeded, battered
From uncounted clashes already.
Long had they labored to harvest the creatures
Of this realm and lead them away,
Summoning tooth and claw
Against the Romans and their allies,
A hundred nations turned on each other

THE HOST OF DRAGONS

In bitter contest. A horn!
Its bombastic blasts echoed
All throughout the gorge, followed
By whizzing arrows fired into Hunnic ranks.
Missiles were thick in the air,
Sending Huns crashing to the dust
Filled with Elven darts.
Then from a cage near the end of the pass,

The Elves unleashed their weapon,
Kenateyo they called him,
But to the Huns trembling there
His dread kind was Ulug-beliŋ,
The Great Terror,
A predator unlike any that prowled
The wide wastes of mortal lands.*
Draped with a sparse, rufous coat,
He opened wide his scaled snout
As he screamed profusely,
Crashing from the swaying trees
And bounding into the ravine.
Arrows harmlessly snapped off his hide
As he thundered in with awful wrath,
Two-fingered hands tucked underneath
That massive body bounding through
The ranks of Huns and Akatziri.

Men and horses fled before him,
Gripped with panic and terror,
And many were trampled beneath his feet.
As the rampage went on,

---

* *Tyrannosaurus rex*

Countless Huns ripped apart by cruel fangs.
Honoria's eyes turned to one of their number,
The leader of the host,
More finely dressed than the others-
Ellac, son of Attila
And chief over the Akatziri tribes
Settled along the shores of the Black Sea.
All around, the prince watched in horror
As grey-skinned Elves sprang
From the rocks and from the trees,
Clothed in sheets of bronze
And helms lined with crocodilian teeth,
Butchering hundreds of his soldiers,
Fighting more like beasts than people.

Weaving through a labyrinth of corpses
And ducking beneath dying comrades,
Ellac fought for a while to save his comrades,
Piercing the Elf Demodoko with his spear,
Landing its point between the shoulders
And clean through the chest,
Armor rattling as he fell to the ground.
Akareu he slew, driving his spear
Through the nape of his neck
Before turning on battle-hardened Tuwinono,
And blood came spurting out
From the hole Ellac drove
Through the Elf's rent body.

But elsewhere the fighting went ill,
And countless Huns were lost.
Some thought to retreat from carnage,
And Ellac too succumbed to this fear.

THE HOST OF DRAGONS

He fled from the scene, vanishing into the forest
And watching with horror and remorse
As fellow Huns around him were slain,
Brought down by whizzing darts,
Skewered upon shimmering spear shafts,
Or trampled underneath the Great Terror.
Honoria watched on, and then she saw
The Elves turning back into the trees,
Resolved not to spend the time
Or exert the effort to recapture
The beast they had unleashed,
Clutching their arms and vanishing
Back to the carven halls whence they came.
Some stayed behind the finish the Huns,
To slay them as they scattered
Beneath the shadow of the Ulug-beliŋ.

But as they fled from the scene,
Honoria was drawn to it,
Compelled by some unknown force
To stand before the looming threat
And meet him amid the carnage.
And so she left Evoric behind,
Who for reasons he could not explain
Did not halt or hinder her.
Compelled by instinct to trust her gut
Even as she approached gaping maw.
From a distance Evoric followed,
With Sophia trotting alongside.
Through the clamor Honoria walked,
Huns and Elves parting as she went.
Some continued their fighting
As the dying rolled in the dirt,

Clutching rent armor
And holding in hot bowels
With arms wrapped around stomachs.
The screams continued,
One after another cut short
As those who wailed were run through,
Impaled on shafts and hewn by blades.
But she continued, eyes fixed upon
The Tyrannosaur looming over a field of gore.

The mighty creature saw Sophia,
Whose kind has long been deemed
A bitter rival to his own.
At her approach his snarling increased,
His heart fueled for further fighting.
Few ever have beheld a fight
Between his kind and hers,
Between Tyrannosaurus and Triceratops,
But even the epic scale
Of mere rumors alone
Would have been deemed fit
To sit beside the cosmologies
Or in the songs of the bards.
The Elves even have a word
For such fights- Taumazo.*
Such is the renowned legacy
Instilled by these rumors.

But Honoria continued on,
Even though Evoric had told her well
Of these rumors as they travelled

---

* 'Dread War'

THE HOST OF DRAGONS

All throughout Karoputaru.
The beast stopped where it stood,
Growling as she approached
With arm extended, speaking out
To the beast with a stern voice,
Questioning in her mind why she spoke
Yet allowing the internal current
To guide her on regardless.
"Come to me, you herald of terror,
Clutched away from your home
And ordained by Elves to fight.
Hear my voice and withdraw your ire.
Temper your rage,
For it is not your purpose to inflict
Uncounted woes upon the afraid.
A protector I shall count you as.
You serve to defend the beleaguered world
Rather than as a mere dealer of slaughter."

To her awe the animal calmed,
Dropping rufous back and
Lowering his dagger-filled maw
As she came closer, reaching up
And stroking his snout.
His eyes rolled back with contentment,
Soothed by the Roman's calming touch.
Elves and Huns rose together,
Amazed by the feat they just beheld.
Evoric, too, came up to her side,
And she spoke to him saying,
"I do not know what power compelled me,
Nor what kept you behind,
But I felt a draw, an irresistible allure

BOOK SEVEN

To approach this creature
And speak to him, as if my words
Bore in themselves the power
To quench at once his baleful anger,
As would your words when spoken
To the creatures of this place."

Then Evoric answered her saying,
"Long have I been suspicious,
Though reluctant was I to speak,
Lest I prove myself the fool.
You have the gift, as do I
And others of my order- Torapaï,
Forest-Walkers in your own tongue.
Treat that knowledge as you may;
I shall not coerce you into joining us,
But know the power in your grasp
And the likeness between us both."

Honoria smiled and continued
Stroking the Tyrannosaurus' snout,
Grumbling like a great cat might purr
When left in sheer contentment.
His tail shook from side to side,
Happily wagging as she scratched.
"Jiggles* I shall call you,
Watching your tail wag as such.
An odd name for a giant perhaps,
But you are no monster,

---

* Written in Wešikeriaya as *Šabasu*, a participle form of the verb
ba-si meaning 'to shake lightly'. Jiggles seemed an appropriately
cute translation.

So I shall not call you a terror
But rather address you endearingly."

Then at last fearful Ellac emerged
From where he hid in the undergrowth.
Passing through battered Huns
And through awestruck Elves,
He knelt down and asked of them
If he could stroke the Tyrannosaurus,
Even if only for a brief moment.
His request was straightway granted,
And he spoke to them saying,
"Small odds indeed, that I should see
Evoric here after the shattering of my host.
A woman, too, whom I have not met,
Though clearly she is skilled
In taming the beasts of this land
Like Evoric beside her."

"I am Ildico," Honoria answered,
Still using the name of her alias,
Lest word of her true identity
And thus her survival in the wild
Reach Valentinian's ears before their time.
"A Goth by name, you can tell,
Though as a hostage in Italy was I raised
Before coming here to this gorge
At the end of your own expedition."

Then Ellac spoke again saying,
"Indeed this is the end of my long road.
Long has father Attila thought
That we could tame these beasts like horses,

BOOK SEVEN

Even against my better judgement,
For horses were tamed over generations
Uncounted while we only knew these creatures
Over the span of a few short years.
A waste of resources this campaign has been,
A waste of lives too. Now if I had your power,
Then perhaps we Huns could muster an army,
The very same which you might need.
Father Attila has marched to war.
I am ordered to return homeward
After this failed expedition is ended.
But my brothers Ernak and Dengizich,
They have been charged with a host
That shall meet his and crush Aetius
Wherever the Romans might oppose us."

Then Honoria addressed Evoric.
"Has the thought occurred to you,
To array a host of creatures
Such as those by our side
And lead them to Rome's aid?
Such a sight would be a relief
To the eyes of Romans and allies alike,
For at the coming of their host
Would Attila be forced to flee in fear."

"Indeed I had these aims in mind,"
Evoric answered, though unwilling.
"But to wield such an army
Upon the tips of my own fingers.
Such power is too dangerous.
Yet all along has this been my plan,
To summon their might against Attila

156

THE HOST OF DRAGONS

And call short his campaigns.
Rome is dying, and the empire
Runs now on her last reserves.
To avert his wrath I see no alternative.
So still I shall pursue our cause,
This charge to save beleaguered Europe,
And I'll pursue it to whatever end."

"If I may interject," Ellac added,
"You say that Rome is dying,
But the Huns too are in great peril.
Long have I warned my father
That this war would destroy us.
We ought to consolidate, not
Expand our powers. Should ever you come
To our stronghold in Pannonia,
You would see the truth in my words.
Take these animals, lead them to battle,
And send my people fleeing back.
Perhaps by cutting short this invasion
Can salvation be won for both sides."

"A dramatic turn," Evoric remarked
"For a man who moments ago
Led an army through these lands."

"I have learned my lesson," Ellac answered.
"And you have seen what happens
When I blindly follow my father.
Perhaps history will brand me a traitor
For my part in all of this,
But I will go on with it nonetheless.
At least my conscience will be clear."

"And you want to go through with this?"
Honoria asked of him. "Truly
You wish to allow our ambitions
And to take part in our conspiracy
Against Attila's ambitions?"

"I've not been more certain," he answered.
"I could see in your eyes your pain
As you implored Evoric for Roman relief.
You must have loved ones there,
Perhaps some stories, fond memories,
And a whole lot of regrets.
In my arms I held a friend today
As he coughed up his last breaths,
Bowels slipping into my hands as he died.
All around were others like him,
And folk uncounted await their return
Back home, yet never shall they come.
So too it is with Rome.
Go with my blessing,
Rally a host to your side,
And harass the Huns for a while
Before meeting them head on.
Surely then their nerves shall be stolen
And they shall break ere
Too many lives are lost.
But I must go. If I hasten,
I may yet reach my camp ere night falls,
Gathering what provisions I can
Before leaving this place for good."

"God be with you," Evoric said.
"I will see to it you are left unharried."

THE HOST OF DRAGONS

"You have my thanks," Ellac answered.
"Now are there any words I should give
To my father from your mouths
Once again we meet with Jalaŋgül
Or shall I stay mum upon our reunion
And say nothing of this meeting?"

"You may give him my regards,"
Evoric answered, "if you so wish.
I'm sure your father will be pleased
To know that I am still well."

"Give him a warning," Honoria added.
"Tell him not to let down his guard,
For one day shall his bride come to him."

Ellac stood motionless, mouth agape.
Then he spoke. "It cannot be. Are you-"

"Indeed," Honoria answered,
Nodding her head. "I am she,
And I share in her strife and her fate."

"That explains far more than my mind
Could have imagined," Ellac remarked.
"Very well, now I shall be off.
I reckon the site of Oretera lies
Not too far off, perhaps a couple days.
I know you know that, Evoric,
But no finer place could there be
To call together a Host of Dragons."

Down the course of winding Kupasiyo

BOOK SEVEN

Their ambitions led their course,
Marching beside giant companions
As the river guided them
Toward the fringes of the forest.
None dared to assail them
In the company of such dangerous allies,
Sophia the horned Triceratops,
And Jiggles the dagger-jawed Tyrannosaurus,
And along the river they went,
Free from threat and from danger
As they watched local fauna
Wading through the coursing river.
Down in swampy water, the Deinocheirus* fed,
Breaking the water's surface
With keratinous beaks,
Plucking up aquatic plants
To fuel their massive bodies and humped backs.
Honoria and Evoric left them alone,
Watching in silence until at last
They had left the animals behind,
Emerging now from the shadows cast
By looming forest canopy.

Upon a grassless plain they now stood,
Its ground covered instead
By rushes and tree ferns,
And the occasional gingko
Rose up from among the other plants.
Even now a herd of striped Ouranosaurus†

---

* In Wešikeriaya: Makarosola

† In Wešikeriaya: Gamaru

THE HOST OF DRAGONS

Bombarded the temperate air
With an orchestra of blaring honks,
The striped sail-backs so densely packed
One among the other that to
Distinguish one from the rest
Was no simple labor.
But in the midst of their herd
Sat the ruins of old Oretera,
The ancient spire twirling upward
From the center of a ring
Of standing stones erected ages before
The tower itself was built,
Predating the arrival of the Elves
And dating to a forgotten epoch
When nymphs danced alongside streams
And the colossal denizens of this place
First took their steps in Karoputaru.
It was here that the Forest-Walkers
Rallied the creatures of the Land of Dragons
Against the primeval gods
Conspiring ill against their lot.
More myth than history, Evoric thought,
But even he could confess
That myths such as this may yet
Wield some glimmer of truth to them.
So it was that if ever one
Of Evoric's order planned to summon
A new Host of Dragons from the glades,
This was where it ought be done.

As she stood beneath the withering spire,
Honoria spoke, "Let us hope
The others of your order allow this.

Do you think they might hinder us,
Or will they go along with our ambition,
Seeing the dire position Europe is in?"

Some may not like it," Evoric answered,
"But the head of us all-
She has a soft spot in her heart
For me and for the plans I make.
They will not oppose her,
That much is certain."

First came Ezana, tall and lean,
An Ethiopian of origin
From the Kingdom of Aksum,
Kin to Evoric not by blood
But by the ancient rites.
With a curved shotel to his waist
And a red tunic clinging to his chest,
He hailed Evoric with a smile.
"I see you have brought a friend,
Have you come to do what I think?"
Evoric nodded at once,
His eyes shut and his lips moved,
Though Honoria heard nothing
And neither could she read their movements,
Whispering some obscure language
Lost on her Roman ears.

Then at last they were summoned,
The phantoms of Evoric's peers.
Then came the Swart Elf twins,
Brother and sister,
Araksadra and Kuanipou,

THE HOST OF DRAGONS

She wearing the scaled armor
Common among the Elves of the coast
While he still wore the raggedy tunic
He had slept in the night before.
So they came, and Kuanipou complained
That Evoric did not wait another half hour
To call them to this place.
Then came Shirin, hailing from Ctesiphon,
And at once she remarked,
"I see you've gone to Oretera,
Hallowed among our order.
It is clear enough to me
Why you have summoned us
To gather round the withered spire."

"Indeed," Araksadra nodded. "I see too,
But do you not think this might be
Just the slightest bit presumptuous?
The Huns are beaten back from this land,
Unless, as I suspect, you wish to march along
And lead a host against Attila himself."
Evoric said nothing, but his silence
Spoke loud and clear.
Then Kuanipou rent the silence
As a dagger cleaving through a veil.
"You know the situation better than we,
Though we shall see if the boss objects."

"You know she will not refuse him,"
Araksadra answered openly.
"After all, this is Evoric
Who's making this request of her.
Can you recall but a single time

She has rejected his ambitions?"
The others nodded, knowing well
The truth in these words.
And after she spoke came the others,
Nildahgiiv and Tosarkhaan,
Wardens of the age-old Tree.
Tosarkhaan cursed under his breath,
As if the two were caught in a tussle
But moments before,
Their temper resolved now,
Knowing the business of war
Had come upon them.

Then at last she came,
The appointed leader of Forest-Walkers.
One of the Valkyrya she was,
The Light Elves, distant kin
To grey-skinned cousins settled
Along Karoputaru's woods and coasts.
Like a god she appeared in stature,
Adjusting the violet flower
Perched in her golden hair
Before turning radiant gaze to Evoric,
Humbly kneeling before her.

"Always so formal!" she declared.
"Rise up, dear Evoric. No need is there
To kneel before a comrade such as I."

"I apologize," Evoric said,
Rising up on his legs.
"I suppose I've been set in my ways,
Bound by old habits and practices."

THE HOST OF DRAGONS

"Yet they could not have been that old,"
Brynhad answered, "you who
Have been a part of this assembly
Nearly as long as I have.
Long has it been since we last saw you,
At least a year, I reckon,
And it is good to see you again."

"Likewise," Evoric said,
"And here is my friend-"

"Honoria," the Roman interrupted,
Deciding to go by her true name,
The title bestowed upon her birth.
These were not the folk, she reckoned,
To shield her identity from.

"Like us she has the gift," Evoric answered,
"Pure, raw talent. I saw her tame
A Kenateyo, the same one to our backs,
With but a whisper as we would do."

"I bid you welcome," Brynhad said,
"Not many are blessed as you are.
I take it, though, you have not come
To count yourself among us.
I will not pressure you, for I can see
Some other cause compels you,
A Roman seeking safety for her people.
So Evoric has led you here
To Oretera's withered spire,
That you might call a Host of Dragons
And chase Hunnic invaders

BOOK SEVEN

Away from fractured Rome."

"All this is true," Honoria said.
"You know my name, so perhaps
You know the burden I bear,
For I am the same Honoria
For whom Attila claims to march,
Seeking the empire as dowry
For one hated by all,
Romans and barbarians alike.
Two armies march on the West,
One led by dour Attila,
Another by Ernak and Dengizich,
Renowned among his sons
Born from countless brides.
I seek your aid. Will you grant me a chance
To redeem my name and deliver Rome
From the shadow of the Scourge of God?"

"That I will do," Brynhad answered.
"If you had come alone,
Or Evoric had done the same,
I would still have granted this request.
I trust him well, and your plight
Stirs my spirit, for well I know
The trials you have long endured.
Go with my blessing, and so
Deliver Europe from Pannonia's wrath."

Then Nildahgiiv spoke saying
"You may go with our blessing,
But know the war will not end
Once the Gallic campaign is stopped.

THE HOST OF DRAGONS

Far more pains are there to be endured
Until at last peace comes to Europe.
I fear you may yet bargain with gods
Or else be compelled to contest them.
The phantoms of ancient kings
Call with a warning even now,
Saying, 'Go thenceforth to war
And remain undefiled by our foe.'"

Then the others slowly began to fade,
Summoned phantoms vanishing from sight
Until at last Brynhad's was all that remained.
Then Evoric spoke again saying,
"There is another matter. For as we walked
Through the depths of gloomy Toratanatu.
Some dread spirit assailed us,
Wielding control of the rogue creatures
That call the Under-City home.
I know not what it was,
Perhaps some forgotten deity, or maybe
Yet a fallen member of our own order
Lost to the passing of the ages.
I bid you keep your eyes open,
In case more signs of such a being
Reveal themselves to be seen.
This is not the last that we shall see
Of this dread foe."

"I will do as you say," Brynhad answered.
"You and Honoria are not alone
In your struggles against
The uncounted evils of this age.
I bid you good fortunes.

BOOK SEVEN

May you yet prevail in your strife
With the Scourge of God."

Then she too was gone,
Leaving Honoria and Evoric with Ezana,
Who at once spoke to them saying,
"Your strife is my own, brother,
Sister too, if so I may call you."

They wasted no time, and at once
Evoric began the rites.
Raising his staff into the air,
He flicked his wrists and turned it downward,
Striking the earth with the curve on its end.
The rod was reduced to ash,
Its hardened shaft shattered like glass
As from its shards came vibrant bands,
Light in shades of gold, violet, blue and orange.
Whizzing through the air, they went
Into the chest of he who shattered the crook
And of his companion, granting them command
Over the Host they had summoned
Evoric claimed for himself a replacement crook
And waited amid the following silence.

"They come," Evoric said,
Gesturing toward distant shapes
Stirring from afar. "An army
For the *Augusta*, your highness."

Into the air, Sophia and Jiggles
Raised their snouts as countless shapes stirred
Across the horizon. Herds of Ouranosaurus

THE HOST OF DRAGONS

Formed a ring around the ruins,
And a herd of long-necked Patagotitan,*
Whose massive forms awed Honoria
The moment she first entered Karoputaru,
Lumbered slowly into view.
In their wake came many forms
Weird and wondrous alike.
Tribes of agile predators preened their feathers
As they weaved through a labyrinth of bodies.
Brutes with clubs on their tails or
Rows of spikes stretched across their backs
Eagerly ambled toward Oretera,
And all the skies were darkened
As winged creatures with beaks like pikes
Soared in from luminous heights.
Species uncounted stirred as all
The Land of Dragons marshaled for war.
The clamor of their cries rose and fell,
And then there was silence;
Nothing now could be heard save
For the swaying of bodies
And the scuttling of a few pairs of feet.
Then came the Guanlong,†
Appointed heralds for this Host of Dragons.
Nine of them there were, each of them
Named by Ezana for the Muses.
Calliope, Clio, Euterpe, Erato
Melpomene, Polyhymnia, Terpsichore,
Thalia and fleet-footed Urania.

---

* In Wešikeriaya: Suiayo

† In Wešikeriaya: Tiwokeru

BOOK SEVEN

Nine waist-high bodies eagerly clustered
Around the triumvirate,
Who gently stroked their mottled plumage.
On each of their snouts sat a crest
Made of hollowed bone and vibrantly colored,
The trumpets of the heralds.
Honoria climbed aboard Jiggles
Evoric onto Sophia, and Ezana
Upon Azaba the crested Parasaurolophus.*
And so Ezana called out,
"Let your songs be heard, my Muses!
Let all the armies of Attila hear our advance
And tremble as the Host of Dragons
Marches off to war. To war!
And to the ending of this age!"

Nine Gualong hastened ahead of the host,
Honking as they scrambled over ruins
And leapt from one tree to another.
Behind them went a host unlike any other,
Hundreds of massive animals
Joyously singing anthems of war
As they passed over hills and through vales.
Honoria laughed; her eyes turned to Evoric's.
They were solemn but without remorse,
And in them was kindled a light
She had not seen before, a light that grew
As the flames of his machinations rose.
The war-anthem of the Host of Dragons
Rose to a crescendo and Evoric proclaimed
"Twilight falls upon the Scourge of God!"

---

* In Wešikeriaya: Zamaro

BOOK EIGHT
SIEGE OF EUROPE

Europe was sick, stripped bare
By a plague of swarming locusts.
The sun sank down on the Western Empire
As a new light joined the host of mournful stars
And the fires of Nemesis ravaged
A hundred ill-fated cities.
Argentoratum was but the first of many.
So fell Borbetomagus and Mogontiacum,
Their riches plundered and their people
Dragged away to populate foreign lands.
Turning westward, Attila followed the Rhine
And down the bends of the Mosella.
Augusta Treverorum and Divodorum
Were lost, and the bishop Nicasius
Hindered the Huns at Durocortorum,
Biding time for others to escape.
"My soul is attached onto dust,"
He in piety recited the Psalms
As his neck was hewn and head severed.
"Revive me, Lord, with your words."
His city too was consumed by torch-fire.

BOOK EIGHT

Red the sun rose the next day,
The heaviness in the air growing.
Attila's eyes went further west,
Turned toward Lutetia Parisiorum.
Birds flew ahead of his host, eager
To fatten themselves on the spoils
Of war dragged on. An ashen canopy
Rose as villages were torched
And farmsteads put to the flame.
No time was spent looting these places,
For Attila's campaign was one of haste.

Already the folk of doomed Lutetia
Prepared to leave their city,
But the lady Genoveva intervened,
Imploring them to linger and to pray,
Surely a lost cause if ever there one.
But then the remarkable happened;
Attila did not attack.
Some say the prayers stayed his hand,
And others would suggest Lutetia was
Simply was not worth the effort to take.
Whatever the case, Attila was gone,
His eyes turned instead to Aurelianum,
Setting a siege against Sangiban,
King of the golden-haired Alans,
Equal to the Huns in battle
Yet alone and outnumbered, without hope
It seemed, to stay Attila's bloodstained hand.

Sangiban gave thought to surrender,
But instead closed shut the city gates.
Hot June rain beat down on Hunnic yurts

SIEGE OF EUROPE

As the thousand tribes rallied by Attila
Assailed beleaguered Aurelianum.
Alans on the walls watched without rest
While a sea of foes set up the siege works.
The fourth day came and finally the Huns
Went upon the city, hurling from catapults
Limp corpses against the battlements,
Hewn bodies and marred faces of those slain
Resisting Attila's advance- fine warriors,
Starved children, or lowly peasant wives.
None were exempt from the cruelty
With which their corpses were ravaged.
Such despair fell upon Aurelianum,
Echoed in turn by Attila's ringing laughter.

Alans stationed on the walls scattered,
Arrows whistling and clanking
Against the battlements as they fled.
No answering shot was fired,
And flames leapt up as rams
Were pushed across the muddy fields.
Horsemen trampled over the dead,
Singing in whistling overtones
As they let their missiles fly.
Past the gates Attila rode,
A shroud of despair going before him,
And he cut down the Alans' defense.
Yells and screams broke out
As ominous thunder rolled in.
Through the city Sangiban rode,
Trying in earnest to rally those
In flight to his side. But even now
His resolve began to wane.

BOOK EIGHT

What honor could be won
In meeting a death with no gain?

But to the relief of all the West,
Attila did not continue the advance.
In the thick of the fray,
Just when it seemed he had prevailed,
The Huns pulled back.
Horns sounded as they gathered
All they had brought and turned tail.
Just moments away from victory,
Attila had received the tidings
He dreaded the more than any other.
Aetius was near. Rome had come.
The Romans marched to meet him,
So he withdrew many miles away,
Stationing his force upon an open plain,
As the Romans of Flavius Aetius
And the Visigoths under Theodoric
Followed in hot pursuit.

Others had joined this coalition,
Among them Merovech's own Franks,
And Sighlut went among them.
Eager for battle and to prove his worth.
So he went, and met opposed Gepids
But a short distance away
From the great gathering of armies.
A fine victory he had won,
And mounds of slain Gepids
Were heaped up beneath looming firs.
Those that survived gave themselves up,
Afraid to present themselves to Attila

SIEGE OF EUROPE

After suffering their first defeat
In all this ghastly campaign

Up came Theodamar, a fellow Frank,
Who greeted Sighlut with a hug
And pointed to the axe-dent in his helm.
"I fine swing I was dealt," he said,
"But not fine enough, thank Wuotan for that!
What a victory you have won, dear Sighlut.
How many of our foes lie dead?"

"Fifteen hundred," Sighlut answered,
"And our fight has only just begun.
Come, let us speak with our captives,
Learn what we may of Attila's plans,
His strategies perhaps, or of troubles
Already plaguing his far-flung horde."

So they proceeded, and found a Gepid
With a swollen black eye, but otherwise
Untouched by the horrors of battle,
A boon many of his kinsmen
Were not so fortunate to receive.
Giesmus was his name, and so he said
When asked for his identity,
And afterwards Sighlut asked of him,
"Already do the spies of Aetius
Know well the make-up of Attila's force.
No soldiers remain in his host
That shall surprise us in battle.
But for Attila to speed through Europe
Alone as he has is a dangerous gamble.
Thus I am left to ask you this,

Answer it fully and off you shall go,
Free to be alongside your comrades,
As generous an offer I can give.
Is there another force on its way,
Poised to assault us with sudden surprise?"

"Another comes this way," Giesmus answered.
"Ernak and Dengizich lead its advance.
Already have they plundered many cities.
Caesaromagus, Tornacum, the city of your king
Stripped while you marched off to war,
Though its walls and people were spared.
After them came Samarobriva and then
That one with the absurdly long name,
Colonia Claudia Ara Agrippinensium-
Or so I think that is its name.
Did the Romans really think it necessary
To bestow such an awfully long title?
Nevertheless, those Huns are coming,
Their host nearly as large as our own,
But we have heard of another power
Prowling among them, harassing their ranks
Even as they proceed onward."

"And what power is this?" Sighlut asked.
"What tribe assails them thus?"

"It is no tribe," Giesmus answered.
"At least, it is no human tribe,
Or so the soothsayers have spoken.
Awful creatures of a sort none have seen
Are picking off the outliers, sending
Whispers of fear throughout the army.

SIEGE OF EUROPE

So the messengers have reported,
And though I do not know
What terror has been stirred
In the heart of Europe, my gut tells me
It is no ally to either side."

Sighlut nodded gravely, then let
Giesmus free just as he promised.
The other Gepids were set loose, too,
And off they went into the wild,
Far away from Attila's clutches.
But Sighlut took note of what Giesmus said,
Resolved to report these rumors
To Merovech himself, and to those
Kings and warlords allied with him
In this struggle against Attila,
All the while wondering what host indeed
Now harassed the Huns as they marched.

Nor had twilight come too soon,
For battle was near at hand.
Slowly Sighlut walked through
The sea of tents raised by this coalition,
Following behind illustrious Merovech.
How many soldiers were arrayed here
On just their side alone!
There was certainly at least forty,
Perhaps even fifty thousand spears,
Each one of them fiercely desperate
To defend beleaguered homelands.
Seeing them all from afar,
Sighlut followed his king's procession
And came into a fine tent,

BOOK EIGHT

That of steel-eyed Aetius himself,
Where he saw an assembly
Gathered around a table.

Next to grave Aetius stood Theodoric,
King of the Visigoths, whose silver beard
Fell like snow upon his chest,
And on his brow a golden circlet rested.
To his right stood Thorismund,
Thick muscled in frame, young and strong.
Also there was the wiry Sangiban,
Who so lately survived the siege
Set by Attila against Aurelianum,
And there stood burly Gundioc,
Thick-bearded king of Burgundy.
Here was a gathering of kings
And of conquerers, yet among them
Sighlut was allowed to stand,
Surely an honor to his heart,
And more honor he hoped
To win for himself that day,
Once the trumpets had sounded
And armies crashed against each other.

As he entered, Merovech hailed Aetius,
Humbly lowering his head,
And Sighlut did the same,
And to the Roman they both spoke
"Hail, *Magister Militum* Flavius Aetius."

"Welcome," Aetius answered back,
Pouring out wine for them both.
"It is good you have come,

For now I understand in what way
I shall arrange our marshaled host.
Rising between our men and
Those of Attila is a ridge,
And to its crest we must be first.
Sangiban and battle-hardened Alans
Shall hold our center, with Franks
To his left and Burgundians to his right.
Myself and Theodoric shall hold
Those farther flanks, Rome on the left
And the Visigoths opposite me.
For the thinner center Attila will push,
And thus we shall engulf him,
Surrounding him on both ends."

"Like the Greeks at Marathon,"
Sighlut spoke, "but this time we
Come crashing downward against him."

"Indeed," Aetius answered. "And
Thus have we come to it at last,
Brought together by an alliance of need
To the great battle of this age.
How many thousands will yet fall
Ere the sun sets, God only knows,
So let us pray then that those thousands
Are those of Attila's horseback horde.
A toast then, to the end of an age."

"To the end of an age," the others said,
Raising their glasses in the air
And tapping them against his.
Then they drank a somber drink

BOOK EIGHT

Unlike those revelries to which
Sighlut had long been accustomed.
As he drank his heart skipped a beat.
Of all the fights he had endured,
None bore with them the weight
Bearing down on the Catalaunian Plains.
He saw those same solemn thoughts
Etched upon the wearied faces
Of all those gathered around him.
Even Aetius, glimmering beacon
Of the glories of Rome long lost,
Even he had not the foresight
To see how such a contest would end.

Other cares pulled at Aetius' heart,
And even now they could not be swayed,
Grim thoughts dancing in his mind
As if planted there by dread whispers.
As earlier he said, this alliance here
Was uneasy at its strongest,
Forged by necessity alone. If the Huns
Were broken now, never to emerge again,
The others might band together
And turn their spears against Rome.
Aetius knew Attila needed to loose.
None could argue that!
But perhaps he could retreat,
Call off the campaign upon defeat
And so let his looming shadow linger.

Theodoric then spoke to Thorismund,
"Call out the heralds, my son,
And marshal our spears. Now we shall

SIEGE OF EUROPE

Assemble our host. I feel the warmth
Beating down from the rising sun,
And with that dawn comes the morning."

Aetius and all the rest left as well,
Each marshaling legions and comrades.
Seizing a horn, he let out a blast,
And at its ringing all Roman horns
Sounded a great thunderous anthem,
Like the rolling of a fearsome storm
Across placid meadows. "Arise now!"
He proclaimed. "Arise for war,
And for the breaking of an empire!"

Fifty thousands formed up their positions,
Unopposed by their Hunnic counterparts.
Tall and proud Aetius must have seemed
To those legions under his command.
Rising in his saddle, he rode along the ranks,
Seated upon a pitch-black steed before
A glimmering wall of lifted shields
Emblazoned with the the Chi-Rho
With a song on his lips he quoted Homer,
"'A day will come when sacred Troy shall perish
And Priam and his people shall be slain.'
So too shall the empire of the Huns
Be now lowered into oblivion!"

In the distance, the faint image
Of a rusted eagle was lifted up,
And the lost standard of Varus
Mockingly went before the full mass
Of Attila's army, vast beyond measure.

Cloudless the sky may have been,
Though already its light was choked
By a haze of dust kicked upward.
Continuously it grew thicker
And swirled ever up as Huns approached.
The green earth itself quivered
As countless thousands of feet trampled
Ceaselessly across its surface.
To Romans and their allies alike,
The Hunnic hordes were foes fowler
Than even the curses of some ancient god.
Such was the might and reputation
Of Attila, Lord of the Hun.

Hateful fear tugged at the hearts
Of those who stood arrayed against him,
And already they shook in their boots.
Attila's renown went before him,
And that alone was a weapon greater
Than any sword forged by human hands.
But these were Romans, and with them
Allies to high-born Rome.
Though those days of glory
Have long been lost to the Empire,
Aetius had not given up on her just yet,
And neither did mail-clad soldiers
Marching underneath her standards.
Though yet this would be
The last great battle for the Empire
In the West, she would not go
Quietly to oblivion.

From the formless mass opposite them

SIEGE OF EUROPE

Blasted a horn, its cries echoing
Throughout the war torn countryside.
After its blast came the overtone whistling
Of the Huns, their chilling songs ringing
All across the vast landscape.
There was no stopping now,
Battle was on.

Time seemed to slow to a halt,
Even as chanting soldiers continued
To scream and hurl biting insults
Upon the Huns with increasing crescendo.
Sighlut looked toward the Franks
To his back, shields and spears
Lifted high as shouts of confidence
Masked their inner fears,
And sweat trickled down his brow.
Some distance to his left he saw the *aquilifer*,
Whose iron grip held fast the eagle's likeness,
The very bird behind which
The might of Rome had long rallied.
A row of shields bearing the Chi-Rho
Lined up behind the proud bird,
And dust swirled up from feet
Stamping as they went into formation.
The *legio comitatensis* unsheathed swords
Shining in the sunlight like torches
Blazing in a field of dry grass.

Even from afar, all eyes could see
Attila parading about his troops,
Thrilled as a lion circling about
Its well-earned kill, and in the air

He raised Kolbulut's keen edge
Shining brightly in the sun. But then
Attila did what none had expected.
He waited. None knew why,
And it was only after the fight
That word of his purpose came upon
Roman ears, that the dreaded War-Sky,
Battle god of the Huns, looked
Without favor upon this battle.
Those signs left in the entrails
Of the sacrifice offered but grave portents
For Attila, saying that disaster
Would fall upon his host.
The only comfort that was given him
Was the tidings of the soothsayers,
That a commander of the enemy
Would breathe his last this day.

So relieved, he spoke his officers,
Kings and chieftains called to his side.
"Be it Aetius or Theodoric,
I shall be pleased to see them slain,
One or the other. In this
I shall place my contentment
And so bide my time, waiting
Until the ninth hour of the day
Before drawing battle with them.
It shall be in the darkness of night
That battered hordes beneath me
Will find their hope for escape."

But as the blazing afternoon sun
Hung overhead beaming bright,

SIEGE OF EUROPE

At last battle was made,
And all the land trembled below
As Aetius led his legions forward.
Sighlut hastened his Frankish kinsmen
Ever upward to the crest of the ridge,
Each step shortening the gap
Between them and their destination.
Like a cloud of thunder,
A myriad of arrows let loose
By Hunnic bows darkened the sky.
Even from afar they shot well-aimed,
And only shields raised in defense
Could stave off their whizzing barrage.
As Germans and Romans continued,
More volleys were sent their way,
Each one taking more lives
Than the volley preceding.
Coughing up dirt kicked upward
By stray darts, Sighlut watched
As arrows drove clean through
The necks of Franks all around.
As Sighlut and those all about
Stumbled over the piles of dead,
Amoricans hurried from behind
To fill in the gaps left by the dead.

But to all amazement, Sighlut could see
Allied Visigoths ascend the ridge,
Their horsemen coming first and
Infantry close behind, but it was clear
That they had out-hastened those
Caught underneath Attila's command.
The ridge had been taken,

BOOK EIGHT

So much was clear as Attila saw
Others hasten to Theodoric's side,
A line of Chi-Rhos holding fast the crest,
Fortune betraying the Scourge of God.
But he stretched out his hand.
Command was still his, and the power
To his name was without measure.
His own horses went up against them,
And Romans came crashing down
On Huns and Gepids arrayed there.
Unleashing javelins, they entered the fray,
And fell and swift their onslaught was,
For horses uncounted were skewered
Upon the fine ends of Roman shafts.

Sighlut's contingent reached the ridge,
And all across the plains below
He could see arrayed the vast
Immensity of Attila's horde,
An endless sea of soldiers
Drowning out all greenery in its path.
But as he looked on, he and those
All about him were met head on
By Attila's finest footmen,
Crashing upon wooden shields
As water rushing down on stones.
No longer could they be restrained,
And all the Catalaunian Plains trembled
As Attila's host fought to hew its way
Ever on through Germanic armies-
Franks, Alans, and Burgundians alike.

The first to come were soon impaled

SIEGE OF EUROPE

Upon Germanic spears, yet still
They went on running through the shafts
Toward their bearers, either beheading them
With clean strokes or instead gurgling
Forth their own spewing blood.
Suicidal those charges may have been,
But soon they seemed to work,
Opening up more gaps in the spear wall
And allowing other Huns to pour in,
Breaking through the front lines
And with their swords cutting down
Roman allies by the hundreds.
Caught by carnage on all sides,
Sangiban's hopes were dimmed
And his losses were grave.
All around the stench of death lingered.
The screaming of the dying came as a deluge
As blood and gore drenched the fields
And flowed down the ridge
Like a river red with oozing blood.
But as despair seized battered Sangiban,
Theodoric hearkened Visigoths about himself,
And down the ridge his horsemen went.

Bursting into song, battle-fury overtook them
As they came against the Ostrogoths
And against their king Valamir.
Fierce and terrible was the onslaught,
And dreadful was the dire moment
Opposed horses met each other.
Fewer in number the Visigoths were,
Yet through the Ostrogoths they drove
Like a spear through wounded game.

BOOK EIGHT

From Theodoric's right hastened his son,
Battle-eager Thorismund, young and proud,
He drew his sword and slew Valamir's attendants.
Lost in the thick of newfound glory,
Theodoric was lost from all friendly eyes.
He met a spear hurled his way,
Set loose by fearsome Andag,
And from his horse he fell to the earth,
Trampled unknowingly by his own riders
Who followed after the prince's bravado,
The cracking of a hundred bones
Drowned out by triumphant proclamations.
The fighting grew more furious;
Chaos rose to a crescendo as trumpets
Brayed and horses cried, goaded on
By their baleful masters to war.
The Huns here were thrown into disarray
And hastened to the defense of their king,
Surrounded by a ring of wagons
Set up to hinder those who would pursue him.

And as the sun began to sink down,
Sighlut boldly led his Franks onward
Until at last they neared this wagon fort.
But then they were caught, surrounded
As all the hosts of Attila's empire
Bore their wrath against them,
Goths and Gepids and Thuringians
And Heruli and Huns swarmed about.
But with a clamorous shout
The Franks fought to push them back.
Even Laudaricus, blood-kin of Attila,
Rushed in to see Sighlut fall

SIEGE OF EUROPE

But was himself ended in the fracas.
But then fearsome Franks were met
By a foe few among them knew,
Swart Elf mercenaries, summoned forth
From the far reaches of Karoputaru
Joined in turn by a hulking brute
Tall as two Elves stacked one on the other.
Franks trembled in terror
As the shadow of this brutish spectacle
Summoned forth from the farthest reaches
Of the Swart Elves' domain
Came in fury against their lot.

Sighlut watched on as Etunaz,
Champion among the lumbering Thurs,
Joined Elves against the Franks.
With a colossal axe in hand,
He hewed his way through Frankish shields,
Sending splintered shields and hewn limbs
Splattering all about him.
Surrounded by Elves and by trollish brute,
Sighlut was without escape,
And all around his comrades were slain.
Theodard fell pierced with arrows,
Dagobert mauled by a ferocious hound,
And Franks were piled up in great heaps
As Etunaz trampled over them,
Singing a hateful song as he went.

Last among them was Theodamar.
His weapons shattered, he seized then
The sword of a slain Hun and fought
To cleave his way to Sighlut's side.

BOOK EIGHT

Countless times was his face stained
With the blood of the slain
As a sea of foes engulfed him,
Spurned on by Etunaz's mocking laughter.
With a leap he drove his blade onward,
But was instead caught by Etunaz' grip.
The brute seized Theodamar by the limbs
And pulled him part, tossing aside
The limbless body into a heap of corpses.

Even as Theodamar flew through the air,
No time was left for Sighlut to grieve,
As his own survival still hung in the balance.
But still wrath consumed his spirits
Against the Huns, Elves, and those others
Who so came against the Franks.
So enraged he was that he cast aside
For a moment mighty Gram
To slay his foes with his bare hands
Intimately, more personally than a kill
Offered by any sword could.
Into the thick of the fray he crashed
Cracking open the skull of an injured Hun
As into bone his fists flew.
Fists flying, Sighlut fought more
Like a devil than any man
Amidst this sea of foes.
Skulls were cracked, limbs broken
And spines shattered by brutish might
Ere he readied honed Gram.
His weapon drawn once more,
He proceeded then to spill open
The bowels of many encroaching foes,

SIEGE OF EUROPE

And all around him the field was buried
Underneath a flowing coat of gore.
His blade cracked through the vertebrae
Of yet another rival when he rose
To see once more the tide of battle.

But Etunaz still went laughing about,
Singing slaughter as he went.
A mighty axe he swung through
A contingent of Sarmatian riders,
Among the last of a once proud people
Whose lands had been overrun
By the likes of Attila's kin.
Mutilated horses and loose limbs
Were tossed about like child's play,
And Sighlut's rage abided.
Watching the slaughter of the beast
And Attila's countless allies
Caused him to tremble where he stood.
He could no longer fight.
His only hope was to wait it out
And hope the carnage could calm.

A horn sounded!
Endless through were Attila's armies,
The Huns and their allies uncounted
Seemed now to be pulling back,
Gathered around Attila's wagon fort.
And all around Attila's camp,
The air rang with fire and slaughter.
Thousands more on both sides were slain
In the fighting before his palisades.
A hundred nations hurled to war

BOOK EIGHT

Came against each other
As the afternoon began to fade,
Overwhelmed by a tide of blood.
As Sighlut waded through the chaos,
He felt grapple at his ankles
The trembling hands of all those
Who dying pleaded for some aid,
Begging to be put down and so end
The torments that ravaged their souls.
Sweeter they deemed it would be
To die there than to so endure
The hells war unleashed on them all.

A Hun reached out to Sighlut,
Arms stretched as he gave that plea
Many others delivered before him.
Half of his leg was gone, and an arrow-shaft
Rose like a sail from between his shoulders.
Sighlut gave the man his wish, driving Gram
Through the collarbone down into his gut,
And so delivered unto that wretched Hun
The sweet release which death long offered.
And Sighlut remained by the body,
Hands trembling as he wept.

Though a hundred tribes and nations
Fought tooth and nail for the plains,
No king ruled among them all,
Not even dread Attila himself
Or Aetius, scion of proud Rome
Whose days had come and gone.
Here only one master reigned supreme.
In war, Death is lord over all.

BOOK NINE
FIRE AND SLAUGHTER

Sightless night fell upon them,
And no light remained now
Save for that which flickered on,
Kindled by the pyre in Attila's camp.
Billowing smoke snuffed out
The faint glimmer of twinkling stars.
Like Sighlut, Thorismund beheld the pyre,
For in the fury of his onslaught,
He without knowledge led his closest riders
And himself into Attila's encampment,
Surrounded on all sides by Huns
And by raised fortifications.
Illuminated by the glow of the fire,
The Scourge of God basked in blazing light.
Casting up Kolbulut into the air,
He let out a terrible shout
And all his forces trembled there
As he spoke. Visigoths pulled back their horses,
And even the Romans dared not make a move,
For a dread terror sank on their hearts
As they saw Attila before the roaring flames.

BOOK NINE

With a cry he spoke for all to hear.
"You know not the things I have seen,
The terrors that dwell beyond our mortal plane!
I have seen with my own two eyes
The War-Sky himself, wrapped in glory
Upon the back of his pallid steed,
And even now he conspires, raining doom
And woe upon Rome's last remnants.
Though for a time you triumph in battle,
No lasting victory can ever be won
Against the true Lord of War."

The cries of the Huns sank upon
Those Visigoths caught in their camp.
Trapped in the thick of the melee,
Thorismund hastened his riders on
To speed through the wreck,
Stumbling over mounds of the dead
And hastening past whizzing arrows
As they fought their way out,
Going by the very path that first
Led them into the palm of the Huns,
Fighting with the fury of famished lions
Surrounded by flocks of bleating sheep.
But as their escape drew near,
Their exodus was blocked by a new-come force.
Clothed in red, an ancient helm
Sat upon a face like a dread mask.
With one arm he bore a shield
And with the other he held a spear,
And with each swing a surge of roaring flame
Would follow in its ghastly wake.
At his coming horses quivered

FIRE AND SLAUGHTER

And valiant Visigoths lost heart.

With a twisted laugh he beckoned to them.
"My hour has come," he declared
With a harsh, screeching cry.
"Die now, hapless barbarians!
Wither as Death's cold grip
Seizes you and claims your souls."

Visigoths fled before his frightful visage,
Dismounting their horses and scrambling
Over the raised walls of the wagon fort.
Thorismund too would have joined them,
But the specter's attention was robbed,
And his fell gaze turned toward the North,
As if distracted by some other presence.
Then at once he vanished, resolved
Thenceforth to meet this new arrival.
Both he and Thorismund heard a distant tap,
Like the beating of far-off drums
Well away from the hosts of Aetius and Attila.
Sighlut likewise heard its pounding,
And so did steel-eyed Aetius, separated
From Roman riders in the thick of the fighting
Had now come upon the Franks.

"Do you hear that?" Aetius spoke,
"Perhaps the Huns' second force has come,
Or that unknown terror assailing them.
Are the rumors true then?
Are we doomed, caught now
By fresh foes set against wearied arms?"
"History shall see," Sighlut answered,

Having calmed his fears for the moment,
"Whether these fears are realized.
But we must learn these things for ourselves.
Let us go, you and I, and hasten
Into the shadow of looming trees
To see for ourselves what force now comes.
Attila's own host has been pushed back,
If ever there will be a chance to go,
Now is it. Let us not delay."

"We are of one accord," said Aetius.
"Should a new threat come, we shall retreat,
Pull back to caution our allies
And warn them of foes to come.
Yet perhaps this rumored assailant
Will yet prove itself an ally to our cause.
Let us pray for the best. God willing,
We will yet survive this onslaught."

From the gore of the battlefield they rode,
Spurring riderless horses they had recovered.
Having fled the chaos of the impending rout,
Into the gloom of imposing trees
Their path led them on,
Shielded from unwanted eyes
As Roman and Frank passed off,
Hastening to face the unknown.
They weaved through a labyrinth of firs
As quickly as their horses could carry them.
It was nearly pitch black,
And horses already unsettled by war
Were spooked now by unknown forms
Darting along overhanging tree limbs,

FIRE AND SLAUGHTER

Navigating with hardly any effort
Their arboreal course, swiftly speeding
And rustling leaves in the dead of night.
After their course Sighlut and Aetius went,
Weaving ever onward through the forest
And riding on as night slowly faded,
Dawn creeping just around the corner.

Then they were met by pattering feet,
Which carried one who sought them out,
At once Sighlut recognized him.
Rega the Swart Elf it was,
Mentor and foster-father.
"What a time you have come," he said.
"Dear Sighlut, it appears that
Our mutual friends are behind this-
Dewo be with them both.
They've made quite the mess, worse
Than after my first taste of Kunasan beer."

Even now they heard Huns calling,
Not shouts as they first thought,
But rather screams and panicked wails
Which heralded their hastened approach.
The first among them came into view,
Followed by several hundred others
Fleeing the mess that ravaged their host,
Abandoning their allies to their fate.
Among them came other folks,
Warriors of the Scirii and Rugii,
Most on foot with but a few horseback,
Bodies quivering and brows sweating.
Before them went hulking Etunaz,

Who had led the contingent to this place.
He waved his axe and taunted his foes.
Fearful though his allies were,
None could tolerate enemy soldiers.
"Run while you can, little men."

Yet Sighlut answered him saying,
"Already have you slain
One who was my friend and kinsman,
By Theodamar, son of Chlothar.
His death will be avenged,
And from you we shall not flee."

"That is a pity," Etunaz laughed,
"I would have enjoyed the sport."
Then he hastened towards them,
Rustling leaves overhead as he strode,
Poised to swing down sharpened axe.
Gram shook in Sighlut's hands
And he trembled before the brute,
Yet unnoticed came Theodamar's vengeance.
A triple-horned Triceratops in full ire
Crashed upon the Thurs, impaling
Hulking frame upon the ends
Of keen keratinous lances.
Staggering Etunaz fell back
Only to again be met by lethal assault
Arrayed against his mangled mass.
At once the Huns panicked,
And lumbering in came another bulk,
A fearsome Dacentrurus,* its tail

---

* In Wešikeriaya: Oropukonu

FIRE AND SLAUGHTER

Adorned with twin columns of honed stakes.
Its fearsome lashes sent ill-fated Huns
Flying through the air from their saddles.
From above leapt honking Guanlong,
Driving Huns from their horses
While others rushed to finish them off.
Terror filled their minds with such madness
That many Huns still alive threw aside
Abandoned armaments and scurried away,
Fleeing into the dark of the forest,
Driven off by the prodding given them
By herds of dome-headed Pachycephalosaurus,*
Though left alone once they had passed
Away from the bounds of battle.

Leaving Rega to his own devices,
Sighlut and Aetius hastened through the fray
Until at last forests gave way to open plain
And those first faint bands of dawn
Came upon the eastern horizon.
There on a hillock they beheld
An orchestra of crested Parasaurolophus
Draped in regal tapestries,
And Ezana led them in their songs.
They rose beaked snouts into the air
As they rose up on their hind limbs.
One after the other, each let out its call,
Booming honks echoing over the battlefield.
Up their notes went and down they fell
Until Azaba, the last among them, rose
And ended the anthem with his own note,

---

* In Wešikeriaya: Aikaza

Low and drawn out, its ringing tone
Hovered over the battlefield until
Once more the chorus was silent,
Its anthem replaced by the clamor of battle.
The baleful onset of the Host of Dragons
Had completely overthrown whatever order
Once held by the Huns now assailed.
Battalions of riders were split apart,
Driven into thin wedges as huge beasts
Thundered in and rent their formations,
Joined in turn by Swart Elf allies
Who with piercing darts and shimmering spears
Picked apart Huns scattered by the fracas.
Patagotitans went stomping onward
Through the fray, most among them Aïasa,
Known for his temper and his rage.
Wherever they went horses would not go,
Swerving away only to be snatched up
By the serrated teeth of cunning hunters.
Overhead flew the winged Hatzegopteryx,[*]
Its span cast a shadow upon all fighting below,
Joined by a flock of its own kind,
Screeching as airborne doom dove down
Against the shattered hordes.

To Ernak and Dengizich it was clear
That to resist these creatures was fruitless.
So terrible was their onset that all
Trembled standing before them, shaking
In their hands as they let their arrows fly.
Huns uncounted retreated to the forest,

---

[*] In Wešikeriaya: Dunosulu

FIRE AND SLAUGHTER

Where they were left unharried
By those who drove them away.
Others elected instead to gather round
In a single ring, collected together
At the heart of the battlefield,
Shielding their princes from assault.
Onward Sighlut and Aetius hastened,
Met by Romans who had earlier retreated,
And together they drove through the chaos,
Riding beneath sweeping tails and
Weaving through legs tall as tress,
Unhindered by the Host of Dragons.
Yet Ernak's royal retinue went against them,
Horseback Huns clad in scaled armor
Imported from the heights of splendid Ctesiphon.
Before them went hulking Arbaz,
Yet the Thurs was barreled to the ground
As a dagger-jawed Tyrannosaurus faced him down,
Jiggles sinking serrated teeth into his neck.
On the great beast's back rode Honoria,
Who Aetius once knew long ago
When she still called Ravenna home.
But now she seemed not like Roman royalty,
Nor some lonely exile out in the wild,
Clothed instead in splendid plated armor
Forged by skilled Swart Elf hands,
And she wore a myrtle crown.

At once Sighlut stuttered, afraid once more
By the forces that had been summoned.
Warm streams summoned by shock
Ran down his trembling legs.
But Aetius called to Honoria, saying

BOOK NINE

"Friend, What fate brings you to us!
By what road have you come this way
With such a dreadful host to your back?"

"It is a long story," Honoria answered,
"One better left for another day.
More work is left to be done."

Just behind her drove Evoric,
Bearing regal armor just as she was,
And he rode in upon Sophia's back.
Cleaving through Ernak's retinue,
Horned Triceratops barreled in
With thunderous wrath, horses skewered
And riders soundly trampled underfoot.
Evoric rode then to Honoria's side,
The architects of this destruction
Seated here before Sighlut and Aetius,
And speaking to them he said,
"The strength of the Huns is shattered.
Those who have not fled gather now
With Dengizich's own retinue,
Ringed around their princely leaders.
We shall not kill them, but another power
Lingers here with which I must contest.
I can sense its coming, some dread power
Which far predates that of my own.
I have been brought to bear against it before.
Follow me if you so desire,
But I must drive it from the plain."

Evoric spurred Sophia onward,
Charging on towards the rallied stragglers

Gathered around to protect their princes.
His companions stood back
As Evoric leapt from Sophia's back.
Five thousand Huns stood before him,
Forming up a wall of spears
And shields covered with ibex hides,
Arms trembling as Evoric approached,
And even now he could see
Many would flee now if so allowed.
Yet lucky for them, their lives
Were not what Evoric sought now.
Before the schiltron now stood.
The terror Evoric anticipated,
That same Thorismund had seen the night before.
To his sides stood the twin Thurs
Falisaz and Galmaz, always ready
To follow the Lord of War into battle
As he rode forward upon a ghastly horse.
From the specter's unseen mouth
Came a laughter at which friends and foes
Backed slowly away. Staunch Aetius
Would have sworn he heard this voice before,
Planting dread rumors into his ears,
Though little more could he say
Save that at its dread utterance
His heart was overborne with worry.
And yet staunch Evoric stood firm.

"You have met me before," the figure spoke,
His face twisted with vile amusement.
"Deep in the darkness of the Under-City
I made a game of testing your power.
Through the annals of the historians,

I have gone by names uncounted,
Though to the Huns I am the War-Sky,
Called upon in this dark hour
By my favored Attila."
"Some patron you must be," Evoric said,
"If your favored you have permitted
To be so soundly defeated this day."

"You do not know to whom you speak,"
The War-Sky answered back saying,
"But your ignorance I will pardon,
For how could I expect otherwise?
You know not my ambitions, wretch.
Behold now the terror of my power,
All you nations of the earth, and despair!
Flee now while still you can,
And perhaps you may yet escape
The fires of war and the damnation
That shall follow afterwards."

"You are a fool," Evoric answered,
"No matter what title you bear."

"Do not bandy ignorance with me,"
The War-Sky slavered, gurgling
On the hideous cries of his throat.
"A legion of monsters stands against me.
If flee you do not, then cruel slaughter
Shall be the only path ahead of you.
Further battle is inevitable."

"These are not monsters," Evoric said,
"And neither are the Huns behind you.

FIRE AND SLAUGHTER

They are free to go if so they wish,
To return to their doting families
And live on their lives as they did
Ere calamity came upon Europe."
Murmurs broke out among the Huns
Eager to accept such generous terms.
One lowered his sword with acceptance.
Ruga he was, conscripted years ago
And long eager to see home again,
To be with his wife and twin daughters,
To hold them against his breast
And sit in silent contentment.
And so the War-Sky singled him out,
Ordering him to take up arms
And fight against Evoric's marshaled beasts.

"I cannot speak for us all," Ruga said,
"But as for me, I only wish to go home,
And these people only want
To preserve theirs and safeguard them.
Who am I to snatch away from them
That which is dearest to me?"

And so Evoric spoke again saying,
"All you Huns have family back home:
Parents, siblings, slaves who perhaps
Have even become like friends to you,
And I know you love them dearly,
For have you not gone to war
Under the hopes that your people
Would be made greater indeed
Than ever before they have been?"

BOOK NINE

"And yet this war," Ruga added,
"Has brought but death on both ends.
What greatness has been won for the Huns?"

His comrades nodded with consent,
And more among them lowered their arms.
Enraged, the War-Sky slew Ruga
Right where he stood, punching
The shaft of his spear clean through
The man's body, his friends around
Slowly backing away, fearful that
The fires of his rage would consume them
As so they engulfed Ruga's charred flesh.

"Harken to me, you spirit of war,"
Evoric proclaimed, the War-Sky recoiling
As a blinding light shone forth,
"For I will not treat with one
So blindly devoted to slaughter
Merely for slaughter's own sake,
A blind slave gripped by the sport
He has falsely professed to master.
We have come from shadows forgotten
To defy you and all for which
You so stand. No place is there
In this world for one like you.
Already your servants defy you,
Knowing full well the clarity
With which these words ring. Begone!"

The War-Sky gave a great cry, overcome
With the fear that now assailed him.
No more battle was there to be found,

FIRE AND SLAUGHTER

And Evoric's audacity was enough
To challenge the wraith's own resolve.
Turning he spurred on his pallid horse
And fled thenceforth from all eyes.
After him went Falisaz and Galmaz,
Unafraid to trample any allied troops
Still standing in their path.
Those that remained saw the fruits
Left to their long endeavor,
The anger of their dreadful god
Turned aside with meager words
And the sacrifice of a single soldier
Who dared declare the folly of this war.
And so they threw down their weapons
And sued for mercy. Even their princes,
Renowned Ernak and Dengizich
Followed after their example.
With a word of assurance, Evoric
Let them off, free now to fly
Wherever they may, unassailed
By the Host of Dragons as they went.

Thus the battle came to an end,
Though no songs were sung of it,
Neither by Romans nor by Huns,
Nor any of those countless Germans
Whose kin bled and perished there.
This was no day of glory,
For heavy sorrow consumed all.
And though the campaign ended,
Attila's war was far from over,
And in its wake would the world
Be forever changed. Rome's last hurrah

BOOK NINE

Had come and gone, though little
Had been won that day save limp bodies
Piled up in tattered heaps.
It was well into the morning now,
And men were hard at laboring,
Sifting through the mounds of dead
Piled up where the fighting was thickest,
And it was in these heaps
Where Theodoric was uncovered,
Laid upon a fine cloth and brought
From among the mangled bodies,
Flanked by torches as Visigoths
Bore him back to his tent.
Thorismund's eyes were wet with tears.
Limbs trembling, he gave little heed
To anything other than this loss
He had suffered so soon.
Stumbling over hewn corpses,
His eyes often turned to the wagons,
Watching in contempt as Huns
Prepared to march back whence they came.
Horns sounded the retreat
And Attila rode alongside them,
Holding aloft Varus' lost standard
As he went, back held erect,
Dignified and confident even in defeat.
Yet Roman spectators knew better,
For the savagery that had occurred
Proved to the world a lesson.

"Attila has been defeated," said Aetius,
Speaking to embittered Thorismund,
"Now we know he can be bested.

FIRE AND SLAUGHTER

He shall not be regarded as Alexander,
Who drove undefeated all the way to India.
Now is the time to nurse wounds
And to tend to our fallen comrades.
A time may come when we can
Set our eyes upon Pannonia,
But such a day is long off.
Tend to your people as
I shall tend to mine, as king
You now set your vigil eastward."

Aetius stood alone in the field
Overwhelmed by the stink of blood
Mingled with the pungent reek
Of vomit and of splattered feces.
An unbearable stench, yet there
He remained, looking on
At all the damage wrought,
And there he met with Honoria,
Who recounted to him
The long road she had taken
Since last she left Ravenna.
Clad in her splendid panoply,
She appeared to him more as a lost hero
From the poems of Homer
Than as rejected sister to the emperor.
And so he asked of her, "Shall I
Report to Valentinian of your survival?"

"I leave that to you," she answered.
"I doubt I will again go to Italy,
But no longer do I fear his anger.
My road now leads me away,

BOOK NINE

For once the Dragon is dealt with,
I will go into the East,
Consult with Marcian in Constantinople,
Establish a presence on the Danube
And then deal my deathly blow
Against the dreaded Scourge of God.
Then, once and for all, shall I
Remove the head from the snake."

Aetius nodded his consent and said,
"I will not keep you then.
Go and speak with your allies.
I must tend to the aftermath.
But this I will say, for what it's worth.
If my station was Valentinian's
And I were emperor of the West,
You would be welcomed back
With arms wide opened.
No matter what the world may say,
You have shown your mettle
And redeemed former deeds."

A single tear ran down her face,
And she thanked him there.
Then off she went to find Evoric,
Who stood alongside Ezana.
All around gathered the Host of Dragons,
And with a wave of his hand
Ezana beckoned to the beasts.
"You have served the task ordained for you.
Let us go now, denizens of Karoputaru.
Let us be off and leave Rome
To do the business of Romans."

FIRE AND SLAUGHTER

At once the host bowed,
And swiftly countless hundreds
Of those colossal beasts drew off
And Ezana spoke once more
To Honoria and to Evoric.
"I shall yet aid you from afar
After I have lead them away,
Back into their ancient lands
Where beasts might sleep and play."

With Ezana leading the way
The Host of Dragons at once drew off,
Vanishing in the thick of the forest
As they began their homeward trek,
Thundering through the landscape
With a boisterous cacophonous anthem,
Their presence lingering on in song
Long after they were lost from sight.
"So much death," Evoric spoke
As Honoria stepped to his side.
"How many dead here left behind
A wife? Children? What tangled
Thread of lies led them on this long
Road to blood-soaked Catalaunian Plains?"

"Such is not your doing," she answered.
"God only knows just how worse
This slaughter would have been
If fear instilled by your machinations
Did not drive the second host away.
You would have made a terrible Roman,
Though I suppose even Aemilianus was brought
Down to tears, weeping for the destruction

He brought to bear against Carthage.
Do you regret what we have done?"

"I do not regret our actions," he answered.,
"What I take remorse in is
That most humbling reality
That nothing else could be done
To avert this fearsome fight.
Peace has been won for a moment
By these hard labors of war.
We have severed a diseased limb,
But still the plague lingers on,
Festering and biding its time."

"Indeed that is so," Honoria said.
"I have a plan, and Aetius himself
Has agreed to what details
I have divulged to him. In him
We have an ally, even if brother
Valentinian has long rejected me.
But Attila's campaign on Italy
Is surely upon us now.
Fanefiru must be dealt with first,
Then perhaps my plans may be realized."

Evoric nodded and answered her,
"I have held back Sophia and Jiggles,
So they will remain by our side.
Perhaps I could recall a few others,
Just a small sampling of our host.
I am certain that Attila shall hold
The lives of his hordes in higher regard,
Faced now with the revelation

That they can be soundly beaten."

Honoria smiled wryly and spoke again,
"Indeed there still is hope for Rome,
And I am grateful for your friendship
And for the help you have offered.
Neither will I take for granted."

Elsewhere among a sea of corpses,
Sighlut searched for Theodamar's body.
All around him were the slain,
Franks, Huns, and Elves alike
All mangled and twisted before him.
Rega met him there where he sat,
Drinking from his bottle of wine.
"No small victory is this," Rega said.
"Fortune indeed has favored you."

"Perhaps for me," Sighlut answered,
"But not for the sorry fool
Whose limbs were torn for sport, nor
The countless others slain thus.
My mouth is dry and ashy,
But an endless supply of wine
Shall not sate my parched throat.
Long had I hoped this fight
Would be a contest of glory
As my ancestors won ages ago,
But none of that is there.
There is only emptiness,
Emptiness and anger.
I feel smaller than I did before.
I had hoped that our names

Would go through the annals,
Remembered for ages to come.
The old songs of the bards
Are just that- simply songs,
Nothing more than hopeful lies.
That much I know now."

"Yet your struggle is not over,"
Rega spoke, arms stretched out.
"If not for the glories of your fathers,
For what then shall you fight?"

"There is nothing left," said Sighlut,
"But vengeance alone. Yes,
Let me avenge all those who fell,
Theodamar and the rest.
If not glory, then revenge
Shall become my coveted prize."

"Attila is still a threat," said Rega,
"For still he wields a mighty weapon
Which may yet win him the war.
The Dragon, surely I hope
That you've not so soon forgotten
My fallen brother Fanefiru.
May Zaršu-Mot claim his soul
As another thrall for his halls!"

"As surely as I live," Sighlut answered,
"I will come upon the Fire-Waurms
As he slumbers in his den
And I will run him through.
The Dragon shall die."

BOOK TEN
CHAOSKAMPF

Those who survived the grim battle
Went at once on their separate ways,
Kings and chieftains each going back
To secure their homes and thus prepare
For further bouts of bloodshed.
In this way Aetius returned to Ravenna,
And there met with the emperor himself,
Valentinian, king of the West, angered
At the news that still his sister lived.
With glaring eyes he gazed out,
Leaning against the parapets and peered
Over the swampy expanse around Ravenna.

"It cannot be!" he declared. "That siren
Nearly brought the empire to its knees.
But I know her ways, wretch that she is.
She will throw herself down in prostration
Before the feet of another man who may
Grant her the chance to supplant me.
I reckon already she was such ambitions
With the barbarian you call Evoric.

BOOK TEN

May she throw her life away, hurled
Headlong into the Dragon's gaping maw.
Only by her death may she yet gain
Some semblance of honor in my eyes."

Yet even as he said such things,
Off his sister went into gloomy Gold Tor,
Marching with Evoric at her side.
They hastened after vengeful Sighlut,
Who went ahead of them without notice,
Eager to end the Erepši and to
Run him through on Gram's keen edge.
Through an arched passaged tucked
Deep within remote Gallic mountainsides,
Their treacherous road led them on.

They left their mighty beasts behind,
Horned Sophia and dagger-jawed Jiggles,
That they might safeguard the entrance
While masters ventured down below.
But even as they came upon that door
Which led into Fanefiru's infernal domain,
A note in parchment was left for them,
Written in Swart Elf script- Rega's writing.
"Leave, Evoric and Ildico," it said
"This is your only warning."*
Ominous though the note was, still
They went on, worried now that Rega
Conspired dark deeds deep in his heart,
As if he harbored some other motive
For setting Sighlut against Fanefiru.

---

* Wešikeriaya: *Eporaku ite Ilediko pagaes. Tauko seko toto eme.*

CHAOSKAMPF

Thus cautioned against Rega's ambitions,
They hurried in silence down into the tunnel,
Following cracked stairs as they made their way
Into the abode of the dreaded Erepši.
As on they went into the deepening gloom,
No sound was heard but the tapping of feet
And water dripping down from crevices.
Adamantine sconces stationed on the walls
Emitted blue lights of ethereal magics,
Guiding onward their slow procession,
Even as they trudged through murky streams
Where slippery Diplocaulus* swam about,
Salamanders with skulls like arrowheads.
They darted away from new-come travelers
When one or the other stepped too near,
Though Honoria did tap one of them,
Gently planting her finger on its back,
Spastically twisting its body as it fled.

At last the passage drew again to land,
And before them stood Gold Tor itself,
The vast treasure hoard dear to Anadavara
Surrounded by a ring of shallow water.
One after another, they could hear
Stay coins fall off from the back,
Clinking down along the cliffside
Opposite the hoard from them.
On the other side of the mound was a pit,
A vast abyss huge beyond measure,
Spanned by a mile-wide bridge
Which itself led to a doorway,

---

* In Wešikeriaya: Peteyopuga

An exit by which one might go
And again see the light of day.
Coughing, Honoria waved aside
The smoke that clouded her eyes
And peered off into the darkness,
Hoping with well-trained eyes
To make out Fanefiru's monstrous form.
Evoric, too, sought out in vain
To eye the Dragon in the dark.

"Who knows where Fanefiru lies,"
Evoric remarked, looking ever on.
"Vast are the tunnels underneath,
And in any among those thousands
Could our foe now slither through.
Let us hope, your highness, he is soon found."

"But hearken now," Honoria said,
Scuttling onto the mound of gold,
Coins giving way as she trod over them.
All across this heap of wealth,
She could see left there an imprint
The shape and size of a Dragon no doubt,
Hot blood oozing over a thousand tiny coins.
She tossed one such token to Evoric,
Who took a whiff of the metallic aroma.
It was the blood of the Dragon,
For now it seemed Sighlut had dealt
Some blow to the beast while he slept.
Having buried himself beneath the riches,
Sighlut ran Gram upward as lumbering
Fanefiru slithered over him, driving Gram
Clean through Fanefiru's armored breast,

Carving through scales like shields
Until at last his blade dug itself in
And out spilled blood as a rushing fountain.
The blood-trail led them on from Gold Tor,
From the mound of wealth long abandoned,
And took them to the open chasm,
Where across shadowy abyss stretched there
The mile-long bridge, silence still broken
Only by the dripping over of a loose coin
Tumbling down to the Heart of the World.
Following along precarious cliffside,
At last their path abandoned the edge as
Scattered drops of blood trailed westward,
Where the mound of gold was usurped
By a labyrinth of looming pillars.

There stood a huge, empty hall
Black as the walls flanking its edges.
Nothing lingered there in the dark
Save for those hewn towers of stone,
Figures of beleaguered titans holding up
The roof of the mountains carved into
The forms of supportive columns.
And this same cavernous hall engulfed
Gold Tor on one side and the other,
Leaving the mound of cursed riches
An island in a sea of colossal pillars,
Held in place by imposing gloom
And the lost memories of distant days.

Sighlut must have taken this path,
Seeking cover from Fanefiru's flaming blasts.
Indeed his chances would be better there

BOOK TEN

Than out in the open, exposed
To infernal breath and draconic ire.
The blow he dealt to the Erepši,
Grievous a pain though it may have been,
It was not fatal, and still the beast,
The object of his vengeful hunt
Was an adversary most dreadful.
In the distance flickered a pale light
And an echoing cry bellowed after it,
This shout was faint, though clear enough
To see the Dragon stirred in the deep.
Booming footsteps thundered in the void,
Sending loose stones tumbling down pillars,
Shaking the earth beneath its coming
And trembling crumbling rock overhead.

So Honoria and Evoric ran, taking flight
And seating themselves upon the bridge.
From there they might better assess
The circumstances they were now caught in.
So in the middle of the span they stood
And in the middle of the span they waited,
Watching the light wax and wane.
With every flicker the light grew nearer,
The pounding of feet more thunderous,
And stones continued tumbling downward.

Soon could they see a shadowy figure
Leaping amidst the Dragon's flames
And taking cover behind stone colossi.
Behind him followed Fanefiru's huge, red mass
Frothing with rage as he galloped along,
Flaming wings splashing against pillars

CHAOSKAMPF

And sinuous neck weaving through statues
As in vain he sought to snatch up Sighlut.
A trail of ash and smoke followed in his wake,
Blanketing the ground in a fine grey coat.
Shrouding smoke flooded from his nostrils,
And flames leapt ever upward, lighting up
The vast underground halls, unbearably hot
As he continued his bombastic assault.
Fanefiru halted as he neared the bridge,
Huge forefingers creeping over the cliffside.
Vast his flaming wings were spread aloft,
Wrapping themselves around nearby pillars.
His neck he held high with boastful dignity
As a deep groan churned in his throat,
Blood oozing slowly from where in his chest
Gram's keen edge clove between hardened scales.

At last Fanefiru spoke, his voice deep and dreadful.
"It comes as no surprise to me that Evoric,
He of all people, would be involved in this
Foul deed, the murder of an old serpent.
Yet here you have come now in vain,
For your deaths matter little to my cause.
Bold you are, stranger who has run me through,
And brash like Attila and the old battle-gods.
Come face me then, head-on if you will!
I am the dread Erepši, sovereign of flame!
Cower as my wings eclipse the sun's light
And despair as doom engulfs you!"

Dragon-fires within began to churn,
Surging forth from their master's maw
And unleashing hellish wrath upon those

BOOK TEN

Who would dare stand against him.
Yet as the infernal blast drew itself near,
Evoric mustered the power he could
And conjured there for them a ray of light
That turned aside the Dragon's breath
And cloaked Sighlut in a shield of radiance.
And onward stalwart Sighlut darted,
Enduring the hellish heat of Fanefiru's assault,
Continuing on as Evoric's light claimed itself
The victor over awful Dragon's breath.
Two foes hurled themselves against each other
And Fanefiru took a snap at Sighlut,
Who swerved to the side and slashed at
The Dragon's dagger-filled snout
With a swing of well-forged Gram.
A second wound Sighlut dealt,
And then a third quickly afterward.
Then he leapt onto Fanefiru's head
And brought down his full wrath.
Crying out with a mighty shout,
He slashed again at the Dragon's head,
And each time Gram met Fanefiru's flesh
Deeper and deeper the blade's keen edge
Cut into its victim's immense skull.
It was not long ere thick bone gave way,
Revealing ripe brain matter in its wake.
Still Sighlut kept slashing, until at last
Fanefiru threw Sighlut off, and there
The Dragon screamed in dying agony.

"Now you are slain," Sighlut declared,
"And thus your alliance with Attila
Brought low ere it could be fulfilled.

CHAOSKAMPF

Sleep now where you lie, worm,
And let the punishment beyond be cruel!"

But Fanefiru spoke again, mustering
What little strength was left to him.
"Well done, warrior, stay your arms
And let me breathe out my last.
I would speak with you, vanquisher,
For I have but one request to give.
Honor it, and you will be rewarded
Not by me, but by the consequences
Of this good deed thereof.
A ring sits wrapped around my finger,
Anadavarenu- that cursed band
That first gave me this dread form.
My brother Rega, perhaps you know
His name and of his parentage.
Evoric knows them well, as did
He once know me ere I turned
Into the monster now before you.
Rega is not who he says he is. Indeed
I can perceive he wants this ring now,
For he alone knew the truth,
The truth concerning my allegiance
Yet he did not turn you aside."

"What do you mean?" asked Honoria.
"Were you not Attila's ally, poised
To enter Italy once he did the same?"

"Such was the story," Fanefiru answered,
"And such was as I told Attila,
And yet my father sought to buy off

BOOK TEN

The Scourge of God with this very gold.
Why would I have intervened thus
Unless I wished to thwart this deal?
The ring I kept to myself- yes-
And thus bore this curse on my own.
Rega would undo my deeds,
More a friend to Attila than you.
I told Attila I would join him,
But in truth I would remain here,
Alone in isolation, bearing still
The burden of my gamble
Now thus thwarted by you.
Rega knew all this, it's true,
So now you know his true allegiance.
However you chose to go from here,
Please heed my last request.
Rega must never have Anadavarenu."

Gagging forth spurts of hot blood,
Fanefiru writhed in agonizing pain
Until at last he crashed into the dust,
Little more than a lifeless shell oozing red.
There upon the ground Fanefiru lay,
His jaws agape and eyes rolled back.
The Dragon had been slain.

The wreck of the immense serpent stank,
Reeking with the stench of blood and smoke,
And frothy saliva bubbling oozed forth,
Creeping out from an unhinged jaw.
All stood there gripped by silent awe,
Amazed at the feat that had been done.
A Dragon was slain- no small task

CHAOSKAMPF

Even for the mightiest of heroes.
Down Sighlut walked along Fanefiru's length,
Until at last he neared limp hands.
Upon his finger still sat Anadavarenu,
And Sighlut heaved aside huge digits
As he removed enchanted band from bearer,
And as the ring was stripped from its host
It shrank down to fit on human fingers.

Throughout mountain halls clapping echoed
As Rega's voice hailed Sighlut from afar.
"A mighty feat you have done, my boy!
Of this glorious victory folk shall sing
All throughout the long ages of the earth,
And others may yet twist and adapt it
For their own less worthy epics.
You have won the honor you sought."

"Indeed," Sighlut answered.
He held Anadavarenu into the air,
Eyeing it closely as he began to speak.
"And yet what a strange feat it is
That so much power by one curse
Could be interred in this simple band?"

"And that is why," Honoria said,
"That this ring must now be dealt with.
Imagine the damage that would be wrought
If such a power turned to Attila's side,
Or the terror its curse could inflict
Even if used by our own mortal hands.
It is clear Anadavarenu must be lost,
Either buried or perhaps soundly shattered,

So no wicked hands may seize it."
Rega nodded at the words she spoke
But said nothing, looking on
At the band as Sighlut held it up.
Its beauty held Rega's heart,
A crimson gem adorned its side,
And all along the sides of the band
Was engraved an encircling Dragon,
Its gaping maw opened wide
As if prepared to engulf hapless prey.

But as he watched from afar,
Evoric cut short his adoration.
"I shall be blunt with you now,
For I can see no other means
By which to deal with this matter.
You heard what Fanefiru said, I reckon.
Your brother told the truth, did he not?
Never had he any true desire
To join Attila against Italy."

"I cannot speak for him," Rega said.
"He is dead, after all, and it would be
Presumptuous of me to assume
The ambitions held in his mind.
I have not held discourse with him
For the better part of a year."

"Enough of your lies," answered Evoric
With a boldness Honoria had not before seen,
He who was so usually mild of temperament.
"All this time you have done nothing
But skulk around in the shadows

While Sighlut achieved your ends.
Fanefiru sought to waste the power
Held fast by the band Anadavarenu
And keep it neutral in this war;
You sought its power for yourself."

"What right have you," said Rega,
"To condemn me as you do?
In all my years I have only sought
To do what was right by my people,
A matter Fanefiru never understood,
Nor did so-called *Ildico* here."

Sighlut frowned, unsure what to make
Of what Rega said in his defense.
"What mean you regarding Ildico?
How has she failed her people?"

Rega smiled and revealed what he knew,
"They did not see fit to tell you then?
Could you not see during the battle
That Aetius was a friend of hers?
'Ildico' was never her name at all,
Despite those lies she may have said.
Indeed the only truth she said
Was that Ravenna reared her up.
In truth she is Justa Grata Honoria,
Indeed she is the same Honoria
Who threw herself at Attila's knees
And thus brought him in his wrath
To bear his war against Europe."

At once Sighlut broiled with rage

And cried in anger against her.
"It is because of your lies that
Attila has brought the world to war.
Theodamar's death and the deaths
Of so many others lie on your shoulders.
Does all this mean nothing to you?"

At once Honoria sought to plead,
To defend herself against Sighlut's anger.
"What do you think the answer is?
Have I not all this time sought myself
To amend the damage I have wrought
With the work of my own machinations?"

"Do not speak to me of redemption!"
Sighlut grabbed her then by the throat,
Poised to strangle her then and there.
"It is you who has brought all this pain
Upon the nations of the world.
Because of you is Theodamar slain.
In the age of battle-specters
And armies of colossal monsters,
It is you who unleashed these woes."

But Evoric intervened, shouting "Enough!"
And at his voice Sighlut's grip was loosened
Though the Frank had not ordained it.
"When our tempered emotions have cooled
We may then discuss these matters.
Rega is toying with our heated tempers,
Diverting the attention from himself."

"As for myself," Rega answered back,

CHAOSKAMPF

"I shall claim the ring Anadavarenu
As wergild for bloody murder twofold,
Both for my late father and my brother.
No more just payment could there be.
Try all you may, there is none now
I shall allow to hinder me."

At once he stretched out his hand,
Snatching the ring from Sighlut's grasp,
And in one swift motion leapt onto Evoric,
Grabbing the Goth and holding up
An unsheathed knife against his neck.
Stepping back, the Elf placed his heels
Up against the edge of the bridge.
If anyone charged his way, or if
Evoric sought to free himself
All that was left for Rega to do
Would be to hurl himself and Evoric
Over the edge, donning the ring
And flying away on Dragon-wings
While his captive sank into oblivion.

Upon the crags and cliffs overhead
And down, down from within the deep,
Hideous Unnamed Things crept from crevasses,
Crawling along the rocks with unformed limbs.
With pale skin and horned mandibles,
Watching with compound eyes they jeered,
Poised to scavenge off the remnants
Of mythic class between Human, Elf, and Dragon.
Hooting cries echoed throughout Gold Tor,
And Honoria quickly covered her ears,
In vain trying to drown out the awful sound.

BOOK TEN

"Now we have company," Evoric groaned.
"None among us should ever want
To see what indeed would happen
Should our clamor awake their lords.
Rega surely has heard the tales before,
That no mortal has seen with their eyes
The dread Masters of the Unnamed
And come out again to tell the tale."

"The barbarian speaks true," Rega answered.
"And that right there's a reputation
Even Dragons or Attila's god can't claim.
On my way you will let me go
Or all you here shall surely die,
If not by my hand then by theirs.
Then shall your phantoms be counted
Among the myriads held fast
By dread Zaršu-Mot.
Even now I hold Anadavarenu;
The power here is my own."

"And yet," Sighlut proudly declared,
"The ring is not yet on your finger.
Thus I still can act against you."

And all that happened in that moment
Happened in the blink of an eye.
No time was there to ponder
Or otherwise make sense of the chaos.
Enraged Sighlut lunged after Rega,
Crashing against Evoric's body
As he launched his assault on his mentor.
The three all entwined together,

CHAOSKAMPF

At once they petered over the edge,
Tipping over as their descent began.
But Honoria too leapt after them,
Clutching fast onto Evoric's heel
And catching him as the others fell.
Sighlut and Rega continued on,
Tumbling down into the shadowy abyss
While Evoric dangled safely there,
Watching ever onward as faint figures
Of Man and of Elf clashed with each other.
It was not long ere they were lost from sight,
Consumed by the blackness far below.
Hooting and shrieking, hideous Unnamed
Went scrambling down after then,
Eager to witness as best they could
The end of their ill-fated confrontation
Down at the bottom of the world.

What reports from in the deep abyss
Were brought to the world of sun and breeze
Beyond chilling rumors of dread immemorial?
Down into the dark Rega and Sighlut fell,
Each one striving with his bitter rival
For control of the ring Anadavarenu.
Down they fell into a deep domain
Were dark things dwell, where never
Light has reached, nor shall it ever.
All around their pain-struck ears
Rang the cries of the Unnamed.
Like a swarm of biting insects
They came forth from ancestral crevices
As mortal foes fell further downward,
And the further down they descended,

BOOK TEN

The hotter surrounding stiff air grew
As hardened slabs of solid earth
Gave way to a realm of molten rock,
And yet the ghastly chill presence
Left by the those Unnamed Fiends
Seemed to stave off a scorching death.
How many blows were then exchanged,
No living mortal can now report,
But indeed it can clearly be said
That Man and Elf spent all their strength
In hot contest for Anadavarenu.

But at last the fateful moment came
When Sighlut overcame his foe.
With a clenched fist he struck Rega,
Sending him screaming to his doom,
Engulfed by an endless wall of magma.
The ring had now been loosened,
Falling through the air as Sighlut was.
Reaching out he sought to seize it
So that he might himself take upon
A Dragon's form and fly to safety,
Escaping whatever hells awaited him
Down in the Heart of the World.
So he struggled as man and band
Continued their plummet to its bitter end.

The demon stirred! Awoken within
The bowels of the deep earth, forces
Nearly as old as the world itself rose,
Awoken from their ageless slumber.
Their awful features indecipherable,
Grotesque forms emerged from the shadows,

CHAOSKAMPF

Bearing ravenous limbs upon their victim,
A mere gnat engulfed by cruel titans.
Deep within this endless dark dating
Back to the beginnings of the world,
Silence seized Sighlut as they closed in,
Poised to take him and swallow him whole.

Mustering forth the strength in her arms,
Honoria hoisted Evoric from over the edge.
As soon as he sat upon solid ground,
Firmly she wrapped herself around his body,
Crying softly and offering a tighter hug
Than any she had given in all her days,
And tears streaked down Evoric's face
As he returned the embrace given him.
His rapid pulse slowly calmed down
As the two huddled alone in the dark.
At last he spoke, "Twice that makes it now,
That you've saved me from certain doom."

"Don't do that again!" Honoria declared.
"I do not think my heart could bear it."

"Nor do I, highness," Evoric answered.
"I mean, if it were the other way round,
But I- I will just stop my babbling.
Lucky are we simply to still draw breath!"

She laughed and then their eyes met,
And it was there in that fateful moment
Honoria understood the stirrings in her heart.
Long had she been in Evoric's company,
And many paths had they trod together

BOOK TEN

Through wild wilderness and perilous war.
In all her years as royalty in Ravenna
She had not the understanding friendship
He so easily offered her way,
And she knew he trusted her as well,
Taking pleasure in her company
And counting strongly on her friendship.
She had in her arms now the love
She sought even before her past scandals,
A love that accepted her even when
All the world was right to condemn her,
And she had it not within her healing heart
To be in a world void of Evoric's presence.
Overbearing these sentiments seemed to her,
And her hopeful prayer now was simply
That Evoric felt likewise toward her.
But still she held fast those sentiments,
For the time to speak had not yet come.
Still holding one against the other,
They loosened their grips and looked on,
Heads turned to an immeasurable abyss.
Long already Sighlut and Rega had fallen,
How much farther they would go,
No mortal knew, for few indeed
Had ever gone so deep into the earth.

"Let us hope," Evoric grimly spoke,
"That this at last will be the final time
Anadavarenu appears in human history.
As pained as I am to say it,
I hope neither of them survive the fall
By seizing the ring and using its power
To bear their bodies safely away.

CHAOSKAMPF

The survival of the ring would only mean
Yet more troubles to befall the world.
It is better for all that Anadavarenu
Lingers where none can reach it."
Honoria nodded her assent and answered,
"I know that Sighlut in his anger
Was prepared to kill me then and there,
And yet I don't begrudge him that.
I struggle to imagine all that he lost
In this long war against Attila,
In the cities sacked or on Catalaunian Plains.
So many on both ends died there that day.
I know it may not truly be my fault,
But still that does not excuse me
From ignoring my duty to make things right,
To suffer alongside the world in its pain
And to take joy in its gladness."

"Then perhaps," Evoric answered saying,
"That may be our purpose in all this,
To bear whatever healing our arms
Have the strength to give this dying world.
It will survive, this I know, for God
Has not decreed its undoing just yet.
But for so many in this calamity,
Apocalypse must surely seem inevitable."

"Then let us be off," Honoria spoke again,
"And throw aside this dreadful place.
Our road leads us now to Constantinople,
Where Emperor Marcian might welcome us
And hear out the plans I have
To at last relieve Europe of this plight."

BOOK ELEVEN
VICAR OF CHRIST

I sing now of the terror wrought
And doom launched upon the West.
Where once was light and splendor
Now ruled naught but bleak carnage.
Italy, seat of one of the greatest empires
The world has ever beheld,
Wept as from underneath her breast
Her children were snatched without remorse.
No aid came from those northern kingdoms
Who left her in the hands of fate,
Lost, unable to turn aside this doom
And return the world to how it was.
What dread news the North Wind
Brought down on that terrible day
When from the peaks of the Alps
Came down a rider on rufous horse,
Attila charging forth in seething fury
And leading his onslaught into woodlands
And through those soggy marshes,
His confidence fueled by a host
Boasted to number half a million.

VICAR OF CHRIST

Surely he must have exaggerated,
For how could one mortal man alone,
Even the Scourge of God himself,
Muster forth so many troops for war?
From the walls of Aquileia,
Flavius Aetius awaited his coming,
And as the sun sank down in the West
He saw above the scattered Hunnic yurts
Dread winged shapes loom in the twilight,
Like those huge Hatzegopteryx Evoric called
Against Attila nearly a year before.
He knew of the Huns' expedition
Deep into the distant Land of Dragons,
Though he had heard it was a failure.
Yet even now it wielded some success
As winged forms hovered over the city.
Their wailing cries rose and fell,
And already Roman spears faltered.
Those creatures swooped within bowshot
Before soaring safely back out again,
Repeating this waste of Roman darts
As Huns pushed forth their siege engines.

A trumpet rang, and Aetius sought
To push back those upon the gates,
Galloping through the line of fire
And driving Huns back in a tumult of cries.
Yet once more the enemy came forth,
Marching behind Varus' lost eagle
As they did against the host in Gaul.
A hail of arrows came raining down
Upon Aetius' doom-struck sortie,
Sending horses and riders to the dirt

And kicking up a storm of dust and gore
As on the deadly barrage continued.
Dismounted riders frantically sought
To find riderless horses and thus escape,
But were instead caught in the shadow
Cast upon them by sweeping Hatzegopteryx.
Winged beasts entered the fray,
Skewering panicked Romans on honed beaks,
Cruel jaws long and sharp as pikes.
With jabbing blows they felled the horsemen,
If not by dozens, then perhaps hundreds,
And Aetius struggled as best he could
To hasten so very few survivors away.

Some among the hellish flock
Landed and strode about on all fours,
Impaling Romans left and right,
And bodies slithered down hulking necks
To be burned by boiling acids
Churning in their turbulent guts.
Hideous wails rent the skies asunder
As all about them Romans were sent
Screaming down into the grave.
No escape was there from the horror
Nor solace for the wearied soul
As monsters from time immemorial
Brought their judgement down on those
Who still fought for a dying empire.

In this way bleak carnage continued.
Gracefully speeding through the air,
A Hatzegopteryx struck a rider at the neck
Before its own trachea was pierced, hit

VICAR OF CHRIST

By a well-aimed blow from dismounted Aetius.
Dropping to the grass it gasped,
Writhing and gurgling in agony until
Aetius released the beast from its misery,
Watching on in solemn lament
As the light faded from its glassy eyes.

A clamor rose from Aquileia's streets
As flames leapt through like a breeze.
Screams and wails rent the air asunder
As the calls of the flock beat down
Relentlessly upon the horrid slaughter,
And Aetius watched as Huns like beetles
Scrambled over Aquileia's battered walls.
As he watched, so too did Attila,
Seated now upon his ebony throne
And smiling as the carnage ensued.

Then came rushing up to Aetius' side
Horseback Callistus, one of the last
Of those officers who had survived
The mess of this ill-fated sortie,
And he gave Aetius his demand.
"Fly now while still you have strength,
Taking those few that you can
While we and the rest linger on behind,
Holding fast to doomed Aquileia
For as long as our strength will allow.
Italy needs you alive, Aetius.
God knows that Emperor Valentinian
Will not offer Italy the leadership
She needs in this age of slaughter."

BOOK ELEVEN

At once Aetius sprang onto his black horse
And rode in haste far from the city,
Accompanied by a small host of riders
And followed in turn by soldiers
And civilians several hundred strong.
In shame and terror he from afar
Watched as Aquileia met its awful fate.
Wings of shadow born aloft by winds of gore
Took to the air as Attila's wrath
Consumed Aquileia, stripping the city
Of all its plunder and of its riches,
A pillar of smoke rising from the wreck.
Aetius' ears and his heart ached
With each wail ringing out on the plains,
Horrified that there was no power to him
To relieve those folk of their cruel end
As a city of stone was reduced to ash.
And on this mound the Huns raised up
The lone image of Varus' lost eagle.

Attila laughed as all this was done,
Certain then that it would be he
Who brought down this mighty empire,
Ushering in for humanity a new age.
As Aetius rode away from the ruin,
Surely he must have known in that moment
The Western Roman Empire now ran
The last leg of her ending race.
She would fall, and with her collapse
None knew what the future held for Europe.

The Hatzegopteryx turned their gaze
Upon those who fled from the carnage.

VICAR OF CHRIST

Swooping in with their hellish fury
Or trotting upon membranous forelimbs,
They wheeled in to pick off their prey
Who were driven now into a full rout.
Soldiers threw down their weapons
And civilians wailed as those cruel beaks
Like honed pikes ran them through.
Some among the Huns drew near,
Hoping to pick of those squadrons
That had just panicked and scattered.
Already their arrows came whizzing in,
And dust rose as more bodies fell,
Kicking up a dense fog shrouding
What faint vision there was in twilight.

But there was one who in haste rode
Ahead of the Huns, throwing his hands up
He spoke then with a soft whisper.
A beam of light fast permeating
The dense firmament of twilight,
And the horses of the Huns frothing recoiled,
Backing away from this blinding blast.
The winged terrors withdrew their assault,
Swooping away from the rout
And flocking around the rider.
At last the moment came when Aetius
Recognized him from Honoria's company.
"I will take these beasts with me," Ezana said,
"And lead them back into their land
As is now my charge for all creatures
Harvested by the Huns from Karoputaru.
Either harass the Huns or now retreat
Back to the heights of high-born Rome.

BOOK ELEVEN

Honoria has done her part; Marcian
Saw fit to go along with her ambitions.
Soon we shall go across the Danube.
The Harrowing of the East is nigh.
Keep this horse, for I shall need
A faster way to reach those beasts
Scattered across the wilds of Europe."

With that Ezana leapt from the horse
To climb aboard one of the winged fiends,
Running his fingers gently through
The soft fuzzy coat on its body.
Spurred on by Ezana's whispers,
The Hatzegopteryx ran at a moderate pace
Before crouching down and vaulting upward,
Pushed aloft by the might of its wings,
Soaring high above the lands of Italy,
Followed in turn by the rest of its kind.
As they left so too did Aetius,
Hastening on as fast as he could
Until at last he reached the Eternal City,
But a hollow shell of her former self.

Within the walls of high-born Rome,
Seated still upon her seven hills
Though now she lingered in decay,
Leo himself, the Bishop of Rome,
Went walking down her haggard streets
Passing out whatever bread he could
For the huddled masses of the poor.
With outstretch arms they accepted
The offers given from Leo's hands,
Eager to consume what little they could.

VICAR OF CHRIST

With gentle eyes he looked upon
Each to whom he gave this food,
Saying a little prayer as he passed them by.
From a distance watched Valentinian,
Who fled Ravenna to the old capital.
No longer had he the luxury
Of spending his days in idle comfort
In the baths or cheering at chariot races.
Now he saw the true face of Italy,
Engraved in the half-starved expressions
Of those who had not the fortune
Of being born in royalty's throng.

"Why do you bother?" the emperor said.
"These fools are all dead anyway,
Or so they will be soon enough.
The hand of doom comes for us all.
None are exempt, even behind these walls."

"Would you have them give in now?"
Leo answered him, waving his hand.
"These people have endured much more
Than you have in your years, my lord,
For barely have you left the splendor
Of your palace and already you falter.
Your sister, too, has endured much,
Much more than ever you shall.
It has been nearly two years now
Since you drove her from Ravenna,
And ever since that painful day
She has strived unceasingly,
Tending to the clamors of the world.
Gaul would have been lost without her,

BOOK ELEVEN

And even more shall yet be spared
On account of her intervention.
She has learned what you do not:
That her trials do not define her,
And that when faced with doom,
Still she has the choice to keep on,
To hold on to what hope still lingers.
Did Job simply curse God and die?"

"Yet even Job," Valentinian answered,
"Even he never enticed dread Attila
By opening by his legs in harlotry."

But Leo paid no heed and answered him,
"You would do well to take after
Honoria's example. We all would.
But as for now, there is little more
Left for us other than to wait.
Attila shall soon show himself.
Yet for all of his cruelty, I do
Believe that we have yet to behold
The full measure of his character.
Before the Hun's bow is at last broken,
We may yet see some honor on his part."

But as the Vicar of Christ finished,
Rome's gates were thrown open
As Aetius' company rode straight in,
Followed in turn by tattered civilians
And hundreds of rallied soldiers
Clutched together in an uncounted mob.
A mass within the city flocked about
The famed general as he rode in,

VICAR OF CHRIST

Wearied and worn from his journey.
"Aetius! Aetius!" they welcomed him,
But he gave no answer to them,
His mind fixed instead first and foremost
On finding Valentinian and reporting
All that happened under his watch.
So he did, to emperor and to pope
He recounted Aquileia's obliteration
And how he stopped from time to time
To harass the Huns as they marched on,
Picking off stray trains of supply
And hunting down lost scouting troops.

Though he had not the power
To openly contest with Attila,
Another force in Italy stirred,
One that could fell any army.
A plague had struck the Hunnic horde,
Stripping them of much-needed food
And trimming down some soldiers as well.
It had not decimated the army
As any Roman might have desired,
But still it was a thorn in their side,
Giving a constant prick even as
The Scourge of God ravaged Italy.

But when he heard of Ezana's assurance
That Honoria's host would be on the march,
Valentinian was at a loss for words.
A portion of his heart wanted to rejoice,
To take in the hope that perhaps
Her presence might turn Attila back.
But hateful bitterness got the better of him,

And truly he said in his own thoughts
It would be better if she died there.
Then the world would be rid of her,
And she would have her redemption
Dying for the empire that she doomed.

"But if Attila is to retreat," Leo said,
"He must first know of this attack
Now pressed against him on the Danube.
Envoys must be sent to break the news,
For was that not the purpose of their campaign?
Where now is Attila encamped?"

To this Aetius answered Rome's bishop,
"At the ford of the river Mincius, there
He has stopped for a while, allowing
His troops to rest for but some time,
Sapped of their morale by the plague."

"I will not go," Valentinian declared,
"Not unless unruly mobs seize me
And thereby grant me no other choice."

"Then I will go," Leo there declared.
"I speak on behalf of the people of Rome,
For am I not the bishop of Rome?
Aetius must wait behind, seeing to
Rome's defense should this envoy fail.
The consul Avienus and Trigetius
The praetorian prefect, them I will take
By my side should they be so willing."

At this Valentinian laughed,

Certain that such a ploy by the pope
Could only lead to certain ruin.
"None among you shall ever bear
The right to call me mad for my
Rejection of my sister while she
Goes about the feats that she has.
You do not seriously think you can converse
With the dreaded Scourge of God himself,
The barbarian of all barbarians,
And come back to see again
The faint light of high-born Rome?
Best of luck to you, hapless fools!"

"Well unless you see a better course,"
Aetius answered, anger stirring within
The chambers of his hot-blooded heart,
"This is the way it must be done.
I do believe that it is high time
You serve your role as an emperor
For the first time in all your life,
Doing more than simply spurning
The best option you presently have,
Or condemning the deeds of your sister
While you procure your every lust,
And weep for your own imagined slights."

At Aetius' words he slumped backward,
The emperor angry with his defiance.
He withdrew his spiteful mockery,
But glared on at the defiant general,
Anger festering deep in his heart.
"Then may God be with us all."

BOOK ELEVEN

From what little security remained there
Behind the walls of high-born Rome,
Leo and his entourage left just as soon
As dawn arose the next morning.
With him went Avienus and Trigetius,
The both of them fine men, loyal
And of one mind with the Vicar of Christ.
Armed troops bearing forth the Chi-Rho
Marched alongside, offering some protection
From any ambushes that might be hurled
Upon this envoy, stirred by Attila's anger.
Beneath beaming sun and twinkling moon
Their hopeless trek continued until at last
They neared the banks of river Mincius.
The cloudless sky was thick concealed
By a hazy fog of dust kicked upward
That only grew the thicker as Leo neared,
Swirling ever up as the envoy approached
The palisade surrounding Attila's camp.
The earth itself seemed to tremble,
Stirred by thousands of stamping feet,
And a myriad Huns going about their duties.

Even now panic seized the hearts
Of those gathered around Leo.
As the earth shivered beneath the Huns,
It became clear to all that those few
Stationed upon the walls of Rome
Could do little to stave off their advance,
Trouncing through Rome's Western Empire.
Yet the gates of this ramshackle fort
Were laid open for the Romans,
Allowing the envoys to pass on through

And see that Aetius reported truly;
A plague had struck the war-stead.
Shafts the pestilence came in form above,
Rattling through the dark of night
And in the light of Italian days.
Bullocks and horses and hounds were slain,
And so too were a number of warriors.
The pyres of the dead were burning,
And all the camp reeked with the stench
Of smoke and blood and pus.
At last the Romans neared Attila's yurt,
A temporary dwelling forged from
A latticework of imported timber
Bent into shape by steam-treating
That offered pliancy without fragility,
And all upon this wooden skeleton
Were laid the hides of goats and ibexes.

Attila sat there before his round tent,
Planted upon his richly inlaid throne
And flanked on both sides by his riders
And by a pair of hulking Thurs
Hired off as mercenaries from the crags
Of far remote Dawwo-Hanhilaz,
Southernmost reach of Karoputaru,
Where even Swart Elves dare not tread.
Yet some among the Huns made it there
And hired those of the Thurs
Gripped by wanderlust and greed.
So here stood Harnaz and Luką,
Ready to defend their newfound leader
And squash those who opposed him
With grim axes bared for battle.

BOOK ELEVEN

At this sight the Romans quivered
In the presence of such massive brutes,
Leo too, though he remained resolute,
Hoping to God that by his bravery
They may yet survive the day.
Sweat began to beat down his brow,
And he made the sign of the cross
Several times upon his chest,
Praying fervently under his breath,
"May God see us through this day."

"What a meager host this is," Attila taunted,
"That comes to exchange blows with me.
Far from crumbling walls have you come,
Bishop of Rome. I'd hoped Valentinian
Would surprise me, come with bravery
And say something intelligent, but instead
I meet a man of the church. Who are these others,
Tell me there names and of your purpose,
Why have you left faltering Rome?"

"I bring Avienus and Trigetius," Leo said
"And with them come brothers-in-arms,
Fellow Romans eager to save their city.
Yet we have not gone this way to fight,
Rather to negotiate and give our terms."

Attila saw the Romans arrayed there,
Grey with fear at the looming Thurs
And the Scourge of God's own grim visage.
He laughed, for it seemed to him
This arranged parley would favor him.
"Have you come to in vain bargain

VICAR OF CHRIST

For your own pathetic lives?
Fine then, tell me your pleas.
I will hear them out as I may."

But Leo answered him stern and grim,
"We do not bargain for our own lives,
But rather shall you yourself bargain
For the safety of your empire."

At his audacity Attila again laughed,
"Oh ho! Now I like this clergyman here.
You've more stones to you than
That weasel who lords over Italy,
Pitiful Valentinian, the entitled brat.
I would not mind sharing a feast
With the likes of you, man of piety.
That said, I fail to understand
The weight of your issued threats,
For I am not able to be turned aside
By the meager might of your ilk.
Aquileia has been annihilated
And countless towns scattered thus.
It will be but a short time now
Ere I dance upon Rome's dead.
As with Alaric and his Visigoths before,
Rome cannot turn my power aside."

"And yet," Leo answered with zeal,
"Even Alaric fell so soon
Upon plundering Rome's seven hills.
So too will seizing the Eternal City
Spell certain doom for your horde.
Already have your uncounted riders

Been long wearied by this here march,
And the blight following your trail
Has done little to bolster morale.
The fight for Rome shall be bitter,
Having been occupied for countless ages,
And every last defender must be slain
Ere you can claim the famed city
As a prize among your plunder,
Though the rewards you would gain
Will not be worth the effort exerted
To seize her from our own hands."

But at his words Attila answered him,
"You think I have gone all this way
Merely in search of more lands,
More resources to bolster armies!
How mistaken is your whole lot,
For my desires are not so provincial.
If your lives you deem more worthy
Indeed than utter annihilation,
Pay heed to what I am about to say.
This is but a mere sample of my host,
A force so vast vales tremble in its wake,
And my marshaled beasts so numerous
Rivers are drained by their thirst."

But to this Avienus rose up saying,
"Have you so soon forgotten all that
Which has happened in your wars.
Allow me to remind you, for clearly
Your frail memory has already failed you.
That last time you crossed into our lands,
Thousands of your own dead alone

VICAR OF CHRIST

Were buried in the rolling fields of Gaul,
Their lives claimed by swords in our hands
And by the bared fangs of creatures
Far greater than your own horses.
Still you trounce around Italy acting
As if all the world should shake in fear
The moment you rear your ugly,
Worm-eaten abomination of a face.
So now shall I ask you this:
Shall you surrender and withdraw
Ere we inflict another grave defeat,
Or shall you plunge your own people
Into extinction in vainglorious pursuit?
For as you march upon Rome,
So too shall your very own empire
Be snatched from beneath your grasp."

At this Attila rose from his inlaid throne,
Angered by the words hurled at him.
"Now everything is clear to me.
Marcian it seems, has finally arisen,
Sending someone across the Danube?
That alone could explain the confidence
With which you so richly defy my name
When famed Aetius oh so lately
Fled from me, tail tucked between his legs
Like hapless pups punished for impudence.
But even this emboldened confidence
Is sorely misplaced, for mere bravado
Shall not deliver your fractured empire.
My host will, his entire legion whole,
Swallow without a shred of remorse.
Of him no trace will remain after this doom."

But at his seething anger Trigetius spoke,
"Then you should know who rides forth.
Give him the news, holy father,
For it is time Attila learned the fate
Waiting for this glorious empire of his."

But Leo had no need to tell him,
For already Attila knew in his heart
Of whom the Romans were speaking.
"Evoric," he groaned, the Thurs shaking
As the very mention of his name alone,
For many of their kind were lost
To the Host of Dragons summoned
To the blood-red Catalaunian Plains.
"Do not bandy your lies with me!
I can perceive now this accursed Goth
Once again sends his demons my way.
What thanks he has given me
For electing not to hunt him down
When he escaped from my company.
I suppose then the lady Ildico
Has gone off with the cur, too."

His face grew twisted with rage,
And no longer did Attila haughtily laugh,
For it was clear to him even now
Little time was left to him in Italy.
Rome could never hold against him,
But likewise could he surely not afford
To allow this second host to trounce around,
Passing through his lands unopposed.

"Hearken to me," Leo spoke,

"For but two options are left to you.
Withdraw from Italy and so secure
Whatever peace you might obtain,
Or continue on this march to Rome
And thus have your vast empire snatched
Directly from underneath your feet.
You may return to Pannonia unharmed
Should you accept this final offer."

"These terms I will accept," Attila answered.
"Consider yourselves fortunate indeed
You have the outlaws now doing
All of the dirty work for your lot.
Remember that, for the next time
I cross the Alps it will not be so."

"Do not presume ahead of time,"
Leo then declared, firm as always,
Undaunted by Attila's darkest threats.
"You know not what tomorrow may bring,
Much less your very next campaign.
Depart, and take all utterances
Of your awful war-god with you!"

Giving a great cry, Attila quickly
Sprang upon his rufous steed as
The other riders galloped close behind
And Thurs clumsily ambled afterward,
Themselves grunting and panting heavily.
The Huns sounded bombastic horns
And from among the Hunnic yurts
Rose a great and clamorous yell
As dust smothered the parched air

BOOK ELEVEN

And Huns began their long march home.

And thus was Attila's second incursion
Against the Western Empire pushed aside.
Now quickly hastened the Scourge of God
To avert the collapse of his own kingdom.
He could eventually return to Italy
If need decreed thus of his lot.
But to reclaim an empire lost from him
Would be a far more arduous task,
A daunting labor even Attila deemed
Could not be done in his lifetime.
So in haste he departed from Italy,
His anger turned aside yet again.
Never again would he see Italy,
Nor would he claim Rome's seven hills.

BOOK TWELVE
LOVE AND WAR

Indeed Marcian came to Rome's aid.
He heard out wandering Honoria and Evoric,
Who had gone cross Europe's wides expanse
Until at last they neared the shores of the sea.
The heroes side-by-side gazed out in wonder
As blazing sun threw down its beaming rays
And smote the face of imposing walls.
When they neared the city heights
They were met with the ringing of trumpets,
For Evoric had sent ahead of their coming
His winged servants, scavenging Istiodactylus,
To proclaim to Marcian the hour of their arrival.

Behind them marched in full glory a host,
Surely not the entire Host of Dragons
Which so lately faced the Huns in war,
But a smaller sampling from among their kind.
Among their number were Evoric's dearest,
Triple-lanced Sophia and fearsome Jiggles,
The mighty Tyrannosaurus loved by Honoria,
And all around them went the honking
Of Ezana's nine Muses, those Guanlong.

BOOK TWELVE

Behind them went a massive Patagotitan,
Lumbering Aïasa with his rod-like neck,
Bearing a fearsome battle-tower on his back
While by his side ambled wondrous forms,
Creatures weird and wild, great and small,
Scuttling beneath his immense shadow.

If any city could ever hope to hold out
Against Attila's fury, it was Constantinople,
Though struck by the fury of a fractured earth
But a few years earlier, its very walls injured,
It was not destroyed- far from it!
In but sixty days the walls were repaired,
And even now they stood in pristine condition
Though once they lost fifty-seven towers.
Thus was the defense offered by Theodosian Walls,
Providing Constantinople its famed triple-defense,
Notwithstanding further walls and battlements
Tucked deeper within Constantine's city.

On the outer ends stretched a great moat
Ten meters deep and twice that distance wide,
Lined on its inner flank by a rising battlement.
Beyond the moat loomed the first wall proper,
Lined with many dozens of lofty towers,
Nearly as tall as the moat itself was deep,
And separated from the moat by rising terrace.
Yet from behind this outer wall grew a second,
Taller even than the first, holding fast
Against whatever threats might assail the city.
From the Golden Horn of the Bosporus
Down to the shores of the Marmara Sea
These daunting fortifications stretched on,

LOVE AND WAR

Not to be taken lightly by any adversary,
Even the dreaded Scourge of God himself.
He once sought to seize for himself this place,
Coming upon it while the walls still were cracked,
Battered by the earthquake that came so lately,
But even then those cracks were sealed in haste,
The walls repaired well before his hordes arrived.

As Honoria and Evoric drew themselves up,
The triumphal arch of the Golden Gate
Was thrust wide open for them, an honor
Bestowed upon a select few indeed.
Huge towers flanked the marble arch,
And as they went through three arched gates
They marveled at the vast array
Of statues laid out before their eyes,
Figures of great crosses and of Theodosius,
The second emperor of that name
Conveyed in a chariot by mighty elephants.
Passing on through Constantinople's heights,
Honoria and Evoric were led on
By splendid mail-clad troops with plumed helms
Past the hippodrome and beyond
The majestic Hagia Sophia itself
Until at last they came upon the slope
That stretched on down to sea shores,
Going through the looming Bronze Gate
Into the Augastaion, where they were met
With feasting and with jubilation,
A welcome Honoria would certainly
Not have received back at Ravenna.

Wise was Aetius to have reported

BOOK TWELVE

Word of Honoria's deeds in war,
For surely she was here appreciated
Far more than by her spiteful kin.
Without hesitation, Marcian requested
That fattened livestock be butchered
And promptly prepared for consumption,
And all the emperor's cooks sought
To prepare a meal worthy of royalty,
Slaughtering their prey and burning the thighs,
And all invited came to this banquet,
Dignitaries from the earth's wide reaches,
All the way from mercantile Aksum
And the heights of splendid Ctesiphon.
Only the finest wine was brought forth
To be enjoyed by all who drank of it,
Reveling in the presence of heroes
And hearing well the tales of their feats,
Eagerly listening on to their exploits
While their guests recounted them all.

Marcian too listened intently, taking in
Each last aspect of their account,
From their trek through the Land of Dragons
To their strife on the Catalaunian Plains
And the clash with dread Fanefiru himself,
And as he listened on to their story,
He could see with his own eyes
Just how far these two had gone together
And how much they had endured.
While Honoria said nothing of her sentiments,
He could see those blossom too,
Be it in the glistening flicker in her eyes
As her gaze turned to Evoric, mentioning

Heroic deed or humorous saying of his.
Other things there were as well,
And all of them quite subtle, but
Nonetheless clear to his perceptions,
For Marcian saw much in his long years.

When at last their long tale was ended
All burst into triumphant applause
And Marcian beckoned his herald.
"Come! For our honored guests
Mix more wine in bowls overflowing,
Pour rounds for all the banqueters,
That we may offer all our prayers
To our gracious Lord who thus has led
These heroes into our blessed fold.
Then shall I hereby grant whatever
Request our guests might have for me."

So they did, and those last rounds
Of sweet wine were then poured out.
When at last the drinking was done,
Marcian took his guests aside, in private
Strolling down the shoreline's length
As they convened, and all was silent
Save for the peaceful murmur of waves
Encroaching upon sandy shores
And workers finishing their daily chores,
The calls of gulls fading in the distance.

"It is truly remarkable," Marcian said,
"Just how far you have gone and indeed
How much you two have accomplished
In the span of but a single year.

Your brother does not bestow on you
The credit or respect or you richly deserve."

"That may be so," answered Honoria,
"But I strive now not for his approval,
Or even to stave off his fuming anger.
My struggle now is only to ensure
That there is some place for posterity
To call home after the war has settled
And Attila at last laid down to rest."

"And for that I commend you," Marcian said.
"You understand the duty you bear
And you bear it so willingly.
A finer emperor you would have made
Than your simple-minded brother,
Valentinian, who seems to spend his days
Either fuming in anger against you
Or watching chariots and making love,
No conquerer of armies or nations,
But rather of luscious bedsheets,
A man of idle pleasure, better fit
To rule in the days of yore, back
When Rome's might was unchallenged.
But no longer is that our world,
And I think such times will not return.
But come now, enough of my talk.
You have ambitions, so you say,
A plan by which we may at last
Thwart Attila and bring him down."

"Indeed I do," Honoria said to him,
"But for my machinations to succeed

LOVE AND WAR

I shall need your aid and approval,
For I shall march across the Danube
With a mighty host to my back.
Not as Honoria will I go, for such a name
Would soon betray by purposes,
But rather as Ildico, scorned daughter
To some Gothic chief cruelly slain
By the raised rod of the Huns.
By that name already have I gone
Across the wide expanse of Europe,
And it is solely by that name
That the barbarians know my face.
Romans and rallied Goths liberated
From the yoke of the Huns I will lead,
Winning victories against the Huns
Once Attila has turned his sights
And invaded Italy, as he soon will.
Only then, when his empire is exposed,
Shall we strike with our full fury,
Forcing the Scourge of God to turn back
And try to stave off our advance.
But he shall fail, for at our side
The creatures here with us shall come,
Their reputation goes before them
And as they near Huns shall quiver."

At her proposal Marcian nodded
And answered back with his approval.
"Such audacity you bear before you!
This plan is bold, yet I like it. May it
Not be said that I withheld my duty
While my neighbors in the West
Succumbed beneath his heavy yoke.

It will take some time, it is true,
But I will marshal Romans for you,
Gathering whatever might I can.
There is another here called Aetius,
Confusing though that may be,
I will grant him direct command
Over those soldiers I will have rallied,
But his actions and tactics in large part
Shall be determined by your will."

"For that I thank you," Honoria answered.
"I count myself as indebted to you."

"As do I," Marcian answered her.
"Now let us be off, for much is there
That must yet be done, to determine
What numbers we shall need,
For Constantinople cannot be undefended."

"We do not need a numberless horde,"
Honoria answered, relieving his load,
"For I am not set on destroying the Huns
And wiping them clean from the earth,
But striking where they are undefended
And thus forcing Attila to again withdraw.
Perhaps in his newfound desperation
I may at last find my opening
And see him finished once and for all."

"Once in his domain," Evoric spoke,
At last joining the fateful discussion,
"There may yet be nothing left
To hinder Attila from coming at us,

LOVE AND WAR

Unleashing the full mass of his empire
To crush us without any remorse.
We will buy time for the Western Empire
To recover from the clamors ahead,
Though none may be left for us."

"I hope this is right," Honoria spoke,
Her heart leadened by grim matters.
"Let it be said that I would rather die
Doing my part to usher in the coming age
Than sit by in idleness while war
Consumes all that live around me.
But the day has been a long one,
And nothing now sounds sweeter
Than to lie down in restful sleep.
I will take off then, and speak more
With both of you another day."

So Honoria hastened away, taking off
To reach the lodgings she had been granted.
In silence Evoric and Marcian remained,
Watching waves crash on the shore.
Evoric too thought that he would take off,
Catching up on the lack of sleep
He had suffered the long night before.
But as he went to depart, Marcian
Cut him short one last time, hoping
To share a final few words with him.
"I see a wonderful thing blossoming.
Heed what I say: do not waste it."

"I do not understand," Evoric said,
Unsure of what the emperor spoke.

BOOK TWELVE

"Sixty years I have spent on this earth,"
Marcian answered back with full assurance.
"Thus have I picked up upon a thing
Or two in all this time. Is it not obvious
What buds between you and Honoria?
In the subtleties of your movements I see it,
The way in which your pitch is altered
When one speaks about the other,
How she looks at you and you at her."

"Your vision is clear," Evoric answered,
"And my heart shines with a light
As radiant as the rays of Venus
Ere other celestial forms overwhelm her.
But these are days of war and slaughter.
Long has her road already been;
I shall not lay on her another burden."

Then Marcian spoke, "I will not tell you
How best you ought to live your life.
But listen to me and do not squander this.
Do not stand opposed to your heart
When God has directed it thus,
Lest the words you should have spoken
Be forever locked within your heart
And regret your sole companion."

Evoric kept these things in mind, and
Long they remained in Constantinople,
Waiting for that fateful occasion
When Attila would campaign again.
Then they would hurl their blow
And strike the Huns when vulnerable.

LOVE AND WAR

As time dragged on, the hour growing near,
Ezana came to the city and pledged
To hasten to Italy and to Rome declare
That Honoria had crossed the Danube.
And all this time Evoric pondered
The things Marcian said to him,
And Honoria too pondered her feelings
Stirred within for dear Evoric.
Nearly nine months passed from their arrival
Until at last they departed Constantinople,
Putting behind them the regal city
And hurling headlong once again
Into warfare out on the wild expanse.

Oh the many victories they had won
Once they crossed the Danube's banks!
Were I to sit down and take the time
To record every last one of them,
Such a record would surely merit
A volume just as long as this one.
One by one they came to Hunnic forts,
Freeing Goths caught in their villages
And rallying them against Attila's might.
Ever so slowly their army grew,
A ragtag force of Romans and barbarians
Until indeed none dared oppose them.
Rarely had they need to fight,
For more often their foes surrendered,
Succumbed to fear at the presence
Of motley crew and dread animals.
A hundred trembled forts succumbed thus,
Throwing weapons aside and in this way
Allowed invaders to roam their land freely.

BOOK TWELVE

But a few months had come and gone
When little resistance remained here
In Attila's fractured Pannonian Empire.

So battered by incessant campaigning,
Ernak and Dengizich's rage was tempered.
Attila's sons eager for hot battle,
They marshaled together a mighty host
And went off in pursuit of their foes,
Who led them ever on a wild chase
Through all the far reaches of the earth,
Toying with them as still they conquered.
Of the countless feats they achieved,
Even as they led their pursuers on
This bothersome retreat farther north,
Many more were bested besides the Huns.

Far to the north their road took them
As Honoria sought to cleanse the wilds
Of all foul forces who sought ill
Upon the innocents of the world,
Though only briefly shall I sing of them.
Into marshy Toradaaku far in the north,
Home to the warrior-women of old
And where lingered there dreadful spirits
Endlessly assailing beleaguered villages.
But through their webs and dens
Honoria led her host on through,
Driving them back and facing on Atayayiq,
Dread father of the swampy rivers,
And banishing the wraith from that place.
And so she made peace with Amazons,
Who kept from that moment on

LOVE AND WAR

A watchful eye set against the Huns,
Aiding ramshackle host from the dark.

It was among these haunted marshes
That Evoric came upon Honoria.
Hard-pressed by Marcian's words,
He thought he might at last divulge
The stirrings that plucked at his heart.
Gallant though in war he was,
At last his nerves were robbed of him,
And all he could muster was a simple
"Good day, your highness" before walking alone
Through forests filled with ancient memory.

From this place they went north
Toward the far fringes of Hyperborea,
Where from the earth rose like mountains
The forgotten bones of Arana herself,
Mother to all the monsters that walked the earth
Before Dewo stood on her monstrous hips
And with his club shattered her skull.
Her blood carved deep trenches in the earth
As he called forth the mighty North Wind
To bear her bones away to secret lands.
When great Arana fell, she fell into
The fits of a maniac, and her shrieks
Shook the stars from the heavens.
Even now the echoes of her wails
Carry through the breezes of this land.
The other gods and their monsters
Were trampled beneath Dewo's boots.
He drew them in and smashed their weapons,
Casting them in nets and sat in a heap.

But at this site of that ancient battle,
Whence forth the old gods were scattered,
There Honoria met again the Hyperboreans,
Huge folk them all, and Ketjin to his guests
Threw upon them stores of sweet mead
And gave their guests some of their beasts.
Great shaggy creatures they were,
Led by the great twins Pur-kuposki and Sesipti,
The mightiest among their breed,
And with them a contingent of their riders;
Hyperborea's finest sons and daughters
Joined Honoria's unending advance.

Among the crags of Arana's bones
Far removed from the world of Rome,
At last they met their Hunnic foes.
Through narrow mountainous passes
Honoria's force was divided up,
Romans holding fast one channel
And Goths clinging onto another.
Against the Goths were sent the Thurs,
Who dealt grievous blows to their lines.
But against lumbering brutish axemen
Came the Amazons in their chariots
Carried forth by huge Scythian deer
With antlers entwined like great bushes.
Against huge Ðorbaz went Sarukê,
Illustrious queen of the golden wreath,
Who upon her godlike stag she rode
And drove her lance through Ðorbaz,
Punching her shaft through scaled nipple
As with her sword she clove his face,
Nearly shaving his beard as with a razor.

LOVE AND WAR

As he fell the Thurs faltered,
And Goths rushed upon their rout.
While the Romans were poised against
The retinues of Ernak and Dengizich,
The hardy hosts of Hyperborea
Came atop their lumbering beasts of wool,
Elephants with huge tusks led by the great
Pur-kuposki and Sesipti, and with them
The huge rhinoceros Nixojwa, who tossed aside
Battalions of Huns into the ravines.
So too rampaged Aïasa, champion Patagotitan,
For on his back was placed a tower
Held fast by Amazons and by Swart Elves
Hurling catapult shots against the Huns
And upon the rocks above their heads.
Beneath the shadow of his long neck
All Huns faltered, and even now
Their princes hoped they might flee.

But the clamor awoke others here,
Foes that long slumbered in the crags,
And from their ancestral dens
Emerged once more primeval lindworms,
The most hated of Arana's spawn.
Writhing like a mass of twisted snakes
They surged from deep crevasses
And threw themselves upon all,
Romans, Huns, and Goths alike.
Many losses were dealt by their fangs
And by the chill breath of their lungs,
But many of them too were slain,
And it was said that dagger-jawed Jiggles
Trounced upon the craggy slopes

BOOK TWELVE

Proudly holding one in his jaws
As he threw it upon its horrified kin.

Scythed Amazonian chariots raced in
And tore through their mangled bodies
Trampled underneath Hyperborean steeds
And by ongoing Roman legions,
Who hewed away at primordial serpents
Long forgotten by the rest of the world.
The Huns fell back, guarding their princes
While they hoped to skewer the lindworms
And so seek out a chance to escape
And venture back to Attila's halls.
As the Huns prepared their departure
From the ridges of ancient Arana's bones,
All of Honoria's host rejoiced at
The momentous victory they won that day.

But such a victory came at a price,
For coming down from white peaks
Rushed upon them a snowy inundation.
Triggered by the clamors of the battle,
An avalanche tore through both hosts,
Killing few but separating all,
Battalions driven apart by mounds of ice.
Like the others, Honoria and Evoric
Scampered in search for secure cover.
From tempestuous avalanche they took flight,
Running underneath the gloomy skies
Until at last they found a hollow cave
Carved into lonely hillside, a shelter
That could afford wandering Goth
And Roman princess-turned-warlord.

LOVE AND WAR

But they did not enter in unharmed,
For of the arrows sent their way
Launched from bows of goat-horn make,
A single dart from a dozen found its mark,
Speeding through the air toward Evoric
Until it glanced upward from his buckle
And there drove into his gut.
When she saw the blood flowing out
Honoria grew pale with fear, shouting
Evoric's name as he fell to the ground,
Rolling in slushy snow red with blood.
But some relief did come to them,
For the threads that bound the arrowhead
To goat-horn shaft were outside the wound.

The arrow dug in but a short distance.
And yet it nonetheless did its job,
Rendering Evoric out of commission.
Solemnly Honoria helped him up,
Together going into the hollow.
As Dido and Aeneas ages before,
Predating the dawn of high-born Rome,
In there they clutched each other
For warmth, of course, but perhaps more.
Evoric still clutched the oozing wound,
Applying pressure to slow the blood.
Honoria bent down to offer aid,
And at last Evoric was overborne
By the words Marcian spoke long before.
This was his final chance, he thought,
To reveal his turmoil and at last voice
Those sentiments he shared with her.
Do or die, this was his chance.

BOOK TWELVE

Thus to her he spoke clear and boldly,
"The emperor saw this as well, so now
I think there's no more point in subtlety.
Long have we been near each other,
And far indeed has our journey gone.
I worry, though, what should occur
Once Attila sees who you truly are.
He will try to take you, I fear, drag you off
And punish you for imagined slights,
Or otherwise add you to his harem.
I cannot say which fate is worse.
It was me who pulled you into all this,
And still I'd hate to harm you
On account of my strife with Attila."

Honoria looked at him and answered back,
"Long has your war been my own, too.
Fear not! I shall be well for a while longer.
I still can fend for myself, as well you've seen
On this long road we've taken together."

So she answered him and sat there
Thinking over his voiced concerns
Until at last she too was overborne
By those same sentiments she first felt
When in the Dragon's den she clutched
Evoric by the heel and saved him thus.
So again she called to him saying
"Ah! What dreams have long stirred
The fires blazing in my tempered soul!
What nightly visions have disturbed my sleep!
Can I say them now? How will you answer
At once to my confessed secrets?"

LOVE AND WAR

So Evoric answered her again,
Looking up in her eyes as he spoke,
"Many months ago Marcian said to me
That your secrets were the same as mine.
At least it was as how he perceived.
Long have I pondered the merit to his words,
Though I was afraid to voice them out.
No longer, for our army is bruised
And Attila's coming is surely close.
These thoughts I must voice now,
Lest I never again face the opportunity.
Long have we been companions, yes,
And I have counted you a dear friend.
But as we strove and awed together,
Closer have you been drawn to my heart.
Aha! Enough of this flowery speech.
I speak plainly now, for I do not want
To live in a world without Honoria."

Honoria stopped, motionless there
Until again she put her thoughts to voice.
"How long have I craved this,
Not simply from you, but anyone.
Long have I been mistrusted by the world,
And though I've gained honor renewed,
I'm renowned as a fearsome warlord.
I am fearful that even now I may yet
Become like the Scourge of God.
So I pray that this may not be!
Little more do I desire now
But to finish this fight and thus retire,
Retreating away from all the clamor
And living in peace with another.

I knew I wanted this the moment
You nearly fell into those vast depths
Beneath Gold Tor with Sighlut and Rega.
What you have just said I told myself
In that very moment, that I wanted
Not to live in a world without Evoric.
Thus do I declare my love for you."

So with warm embrace they met each other,
Holding fast with arms wrapped around,
Clutching tightly, and then Evoric said
"I do not know what the future holds,
But this very much I swear to you:
By our strength and by God's grace
We can work this out. We will!
Regardless of what happens next,
Regardless of what the world says,
Welcoming Marcian or hateful Valentinian,
I so swear you will have my love."

So Honoria nodded her assent,
And together they waited out the storm
Until at last the tumbling snowfalls ceased.
Hand in hand they went from the cave,
Each one's eyes fixated on the other's.
But as they laughing left the hollow,
They saw arrayed before them the ambush.
Scores of archers stood at the ready,
Poised to fire at a moment's notice,
And before this line of archers
Stood the dreaded Scourge of God himself.
Attila, lord of the Hun, laughed grimly.
Having joined his sons in secret,

LOVE AND WAR

At last he caught his quarry in this trap.
"And here we have Evoric and Ildico,"
Attila said, marveling at his catch.
"Long have you been a thorn in my flesh,
A constant pricking pain thwarting
Even my most ambitious campaigns.
But now at last the prey is caught.
I have but to give the word, and
Upon you a hail of arrows shall fly.
Give me but one reason why yet
I should spare you and let you off."

Clutching at his wound, Evoric rose
And so answered Attila saying,
"Because my order will avenge me
As they are so wont to do. If indeed
You thought the Host of Dragons
Was a terror too much to bear,
Imagine the damage that shall be wrought
If again such power is thrust upon you
By my combined might of all my kin
And those others fallen into their fold!"

"Then what a web we have woven!"
Attila answered with outstretched arms,
"For your survival is yet my benefit,
And yet I still cannot tolerate
The presence of your mighty force,
Battered yes, but nonetheless dangerous."

"We may yet withdraw," Evoric said,
"If fair terms can be agreed on
And you remain beyond our borders."

"I know what prize I want," said Attila,
Eyes fixed upon Honoria's frame
Even as she knelt by Evoric's side,
Checking to see if any more
Hot blood threatened to spill out
From a wound not properly bandaged.
Attila saw in how she tended Evoric
And in how her eyes met his
That she was in love, infatuated
By the Goth who caused him much pain.
Though now a second campaign
Had been thwarted by these two,
Perhaps Attila could have his due pay,
Depriving young lovers of each other.
"This woman with you, this Ildico,
Her body is well-formed, one like this
I have long sought, yet Valentinian
Time and again would deny me her.
Give me her, let me bear her away
To the heights of walled Jalaŋgül,
For within those palisades I may add Ildico
To my brides, and from her womb
May yet be born more sons to my name."

"She is not mine to give," Evoric spoke,
"Nor is she any man's property.
She is herself, not some wench or slave
I can simply sell off for pretty profit."

"You'd best reconsider," Attila answered,
"For this price is the only price
I will accept. You may go off
And speak with her for a moment

LOVE AND WAR

If you so need, but heed my words
And do not deny me my prize.
Send her to me, or you will die."

So the two hastened back into the cave,
And grave Honoria was first to speak.
"I know you will protest, but I will go.
I have to, no matter how much I hate it.
I cannot have you die on my watch.
So as it was in Gold Tor, so too
Has history repeated itself thus.
Our love must wait if we're to survive.
You cannot stop me, and for that
I hope you will one day forgive me."

"Honoria," Evoric contested.
"You need not be hauled off
To slave away in Attila's lands.
I will muster what strength is left
To my name and quench this madness.
If I must die, then so be it. Gladly
Would I lay down my life for yours."

"I know you would," Honoria choked.
"But please, do something better.
If you will not do it for your own sake,
Then do it for mine. Live."

Evoric nodded, his face wet with tears
Streaking down his face. "You will not
Dwell with him until the end of your days,
This much I promise. When I am healed
And my old wounds at last sealed over,

I will come and avenge you. None may hinder
Us as through Jalaŋgül our host cleaves."

"Don't," Honoria said, stern and resolute.
"Do not come to my aid. Gather up
Our allies scattered by the storm
And disband our host wherever you will.
This all started with an army,
But armies cannot stop this war.
See to your wounds and outlive them,
For I will end this once and for all.
Attila will not survive the night
He takes me to join him in his bed.
At long last he will have Honoria,
But Honoria will be his undoing.
His ploy has all but doomed himself."

She wept and hugged him there,
And Evoric answered her saying
"No matter what happens, remember
There will be a place for you in my heart.
May God be with you even now
As you plunge into the jaws of death."

They remained for a moment there,
Weeping and hold fast to each other,
But then at last the moment came
When Attila called them out and
So demanded their final answer.
"I will go," Honoria said to him.
"You have for yourself another bride
So long as you let them off,
Evoric and all the rest with him."

LOVE AND WAR

"As truly as I live," Attila answered,
"I am a man true to his every word.
They shall withdraw from my lands,
And for a while I shall remain
Tucked in the walls of my own domain,
For you've put me in quite a pinch.
Come, and very soon you shall see
How generous a husband I can be!"

At once Attila led Honoria away,
A train of bowmen following behind.
Evoric was left alone by the cave
As he held back his tattered flesh,
Free to return to his allied host
And lead them away from here.
Where his road would now venture
He could not foresee, but always
Would his thoughts be fixed here
And on Honoria held in Pannonia,
Trapped in the stronghold of Attila,
Held fast by the Scourge of God.
But as they left, Evoric waited,
Watching as his vision grew dim.
Hidden toxins began to do their work,
And all the strength was sapped
From his blood and his bones.
In came a figure wreathed in dread
Who with an outstretched hand
Made at once for the fated Goth.
His eyes were shut with sleep.
The shining snow gave way to a void.

BOOK THIRTEEN
LORD OF THE HUN

Away from far northern peaks
The Huns went with their captive
Until at last they saw Pannonia's plains
Laid bare before their eyes, where
In all directions stretched a grassy expanse.
Little here was there to be seen,
Even in the heart of Attila's empire,
Only passing flocks of horned sheep
Goaded on by their horseback herders
And overtone whistles echoing on,
Carried over the land by a soft breeze.
In those notes could traveling ears hear
The harsh winds of the steppe,
Streams rushing from mountainous sources,
And hoofed herds roam across the hills.
An alien song- yes- but hauntingly wondrous.

Tucked deep within the Carpathian Basin
In a place that will soon be forever lost,
Forgotten by the annals of the historians,
Honoria drew upon the wooden palisade

LORD OF THE HUN

That held Jalaŋgül within its shell,
Stronghold built by and for Attila himself.
A lone island caught by a sea of grass,
No place seemed more held in isolation
To Honoria's eyes as she beheld it,
And ominous grey clouds rolling in
Did little to stave off her growing dread.
Through a maze of yurts she was led,
And all around her loomed riders
That seemed like centaurs of old,
Such was the bond between the Huns
And the horses that bore them away.

All around her was the packed chaos
Of those caught in the bustling to-and-fro,
Women weaving baskets with intricate detail,
Common folk gripped in idle chatter.
Further in were the prisoners of war
Hunched over, spewing vomit profusely
As Gothic captives grappled each other,
Wrestling for whatever scraps they could.
Captors stood back and jeered
As they writhed and rolled in the muck.
Nearby sat another prisoner huddled up,
Nursing wounds with hand upon his stomach,
Feeling at the hot blood so lately spilled
From the gash he had suffered,
Groaning and cursing under his breath.

But even as the prisoners suffered,
Honoria could see they were not alone
In the long miseries that they endured,
For in the eyes of the Hunnic folk,

She saw no joy, no laughter or revelry
Even as warbands gathered for jubilation.
Here she saw a world of nomads,
Yet the further she went on in,
Passing through the bustle of Jalaŋgül,
Portable yurts were usurped by log huts
Built up by timber imported from far away
As a people of the plains were so coerced
To remain walled within a single city
And labor while their king egged them on,
Spurring their bitterness to deeds of war.

But surely they must have gained from this,
From all the feats won by illustrious kings.
All around Honoria she could see
Just how rich in abundance Jalaŋgül was
Despite an absence of fine marble streets
Or towered walls of stone looming high above.
Among mounted warriors and gaunt laborers,
Great stores of wealth were laid out,
Silks and pearls imported from India,
Silver platters, goblets, gold-studded bridles,
Dates and other fruits from foreign lands.
Spinners in wagons wove fine fabrics
In mimicry of designs taken from Ctesiphon.
All this she saw and so much more,
Heaps of shimmering gold, yearly tributes
Once handed over by quaking Roman hands
Now withheld from Attila's grasp.
It was no Gold Tor perhaps, enchanted
And multiplied by Anadavarenu's might,
But splendid indeed it must have been
To possess such stores of wealth even here

LORD OF THE HUN

In this backwaters town of barbarians.

All this the Huns acquired by war and trade,
All this and other prizes just as plentiful,
But in Jalaŋgül there was no joy.
No children ran around in idle play,
Sneaking off behind their parents' backs.
There were no lovers sharing kisses
Or elders going on about days of yore,
For they wept for their sons slain
And for their daughters widowed by war.
Like them all Honoria lived in misery,
Waiting for the night she would be joined
By matrimony to Attila's side, waiting
For the chance to run him through
And thus relieve all the world of him.
As wedding preparations were underway,
She saw little indeed of Attila,
Remote and distant, his other wives
Had not the time to bed with him.
None knew why he had gone so remote,
But in ignorance rumors abound.
Some said he prayed to the War-Sky,
Knowing his final hours drew near.
Others said that he drew up tactics
In preparation for his next campaign,
One to end Rome once and for all.
Whatever the case, if was clear
That all was not well in Jalaŋgül.

But even in Jalaŋgül gripped by sorrow,
Isolated from the rest of the wide world,
Honoria counted here a familiar face.

She knew him and his frame at once,
Zerco, dwarf of Mauretania, taken
Years earlier by migrating Vandals.
Two decades ago he was bought,
And as a jester he travelled to courts
All upon the face of the Roman world,
Switching back and forth between
Hands of owners both Hunnic and Roman.
Aetius held him once, Bleda too,
Attila's brother slain eight years before
And with whom Zerco went on campaign
Donned in armor built for his shape.
Small in stature, his lisping voice
And hunched shoulders won him
The Huns' mockery and Attila's contempt.
Zerco was once free of the Huns,
Given back to Aspar the general of Rome.
But to the gloom of Jalaŋgül he returned,
Convinced by Edeko to come back
For the sake of his wife, a handmaiden
To Bleda's queen of years long past.

So here in mockery he lingered,
Brows raised as once he beheld
Honoria's form pass him by,
For he had been in Ravenna's court
And seen her with his own eyes.
At first he struggled to speak
But in private caught her by the tunic
And at last mustered his wit saying,
"Dear lady, Ildico they say you are.
Do you remember my face? Most do,
Even if but to laugh at its ugliness.

LORD OF THE HUN

I am sure you must be Honoria,
Sister to Valentinian himself, long
Sought after by Attila's lustful ploys."

Honoria drew close and answered him,
"Yes, truly I know your face, Zerco,
Though long years passed since last
Our mortal eyes beheld each other.
Yet even now you cannot speak to me,
At least not exposed out in public,
Lest you expose my disguise and thus
Bring me and all I love to ruin,
Trapped forever in wretched Jalaŋgül."

"It's more pleasant in the summer,"
Zerco answered. "Not by much, but more."
Then Zerco handed her a small glass vial
And some strange drink rippled inside.
"Take this then, if I correctly perceive
The ambitions you shall undergo.
After the wedding you will be borne off
Into Attila's private yurt a mile beyond
The palisades of wretched Jalaŋgül.
Beneath this roof of ibex hides
You will have your night of passion
And he will pour out drinks for you both,
So he does with every wife he claims
Upon the hour of their consummation.
Long have I wanted to end him,
Though for fear of dear Teŋir.
Long has my wife been good to me
When all those around deride and scorn.
I knew I would be discovered

BOOK THIRTEEN

The moment I dealt the killing blow,
And for my crime would Teŋir
Bear the punishments so decreed."

Honoria took the vial and assured him,
"As surely as I draw breath, I will.
Attila shall die by the drops of this concoction,
And should my quest prevail and I survive,
So too shall you be delivered, you and Teŋir,
And off you may go wherever you like,
To Constantinople perhaps, for now I deem
That no safer place could be found
Than behind Theodosius' triple-walls."

As she said this Zerco thanked her,
And he handed her the venom's antidote
As a precaution should some blunder be made,
And off he went to warn his beloved bride
Of all these fell deeds soon at hand
And thus prepare for their great escape.
Then at last the fateful day arrived
When Honoria would be wedded off,
Still under the name of Ildico the Goth,
To Attila himself, the dread Scourge of God.

When the handmaidens had washed her
And anointed her with flowing oil,
They brought to her clothes of wool
In place of regal tunics, and on her head
They threw down her wedding veil,
Shrouding her face from mortal eyes.
No longer did she bear the proud attire
Of Roman royalty or Swart Elf conquerer,

LORD OF THE HUN

Draped now in the garb of Huns.
Not a Hun by blood, but by marriage
She would be counted until her final breath.

Then the handmaidens brought her forth
And through the throng of guests she walked,
Kings and chiefs from across Attila's empire,
Warlords who earlier led their tribes
To fight upon bloody Catalaunian Plains.
There was Orestes, Roman by blood,
Though long a secretary in Hunnic court
And clothed in Hunnic garb like she.
Attila's wives were gathered in full throng
And before them were blooming daughters,
Attila's sons as well, Ernak and Dengizich,
Ellac too, who last laid eyes on Honoria
When through the Land of Dragons she trod,
Taming mighty Tyrannosaurus with her voice
And forming battle-plans against his father.
Ellac saw her too and he nearly wept,
His heart leadened to see her bound
In matrimony to his warmongering father.
But again he beheld her calm demeanor
And in her eyes he learned her schemes,
For in that moment he understood
This night would be his father's last.

"Come now, my lady," Attila beckoned,
Arms outstretched as he embraced her.
"Of all brides out in the wide world,
Of those already admitted to my fold,
None are so fair as you appear tonight.
Your face and your well-toned figure

Are of the sort kings would fight for,
Sending a thousand ships to Troy,
Or as I too have twice campaigned
To be joined with Valentinian's sister,
Though twice has my heart been denied.
But for a consolation prize received,
No finer gift could ever be given,
For your beauty surpasses all,
Your audacity too, you who have
Proven yourself a mighty warrior
And a conquerer to be rightly feared,
Calling forth from the bowels of the earth
Untamed beasts from time immemorial.
So come now and be joined with me,
A Goth to a Hun, but vanquishers both
Worthy of remembrance in the annals."

Thus Attila spoke and Honoria nodded,
Holding back the tears that nearly fell,
Cloaking her sorrow and her bitterness.
Even as she was bound to Attila
Her heart and mind went off to Evoric,
Hoping earnestly he survived the wound
And did not bleed out on cold cave floor.
All this she endured on his behalf,
For him and for all of the West.
Though her sorrow gripped her now,
She knew it would soon pass away,
If for but a little longer she could endure.

"And you I do accept," Honoria answered him,
"Though for long years we have been rivals,
You have proven the merit of your strength,

LORD OF THE HUN

Your cunning too, who as a single king
Has all the world tremble before him.
If so bondage to you is to be my lot,
Then by my life and by my forefathers
Do I now accept the roll of the dice."

In this way two were joined as one,
Attila at last wedded to Honoria
Though still it was in blind ignorance.
And all the Huns sat down in feasting,
Gorging upon fattened roast loins,
Crowded around on soft sheepskins
Lying down upon the grassy fields
All around Attila's lofty log hut.
Then they brought forth a herd of goats
Bleating and butting heads together,
Sacrificing them all to the War-Sky,
Afterwards eating up their innards
And burning their thigh bones on embers.

Attila gave forth his prayers saying,
"You rise, king of heaven and of battle,
In perfection above the sky's horizon,
And you fill the lands with your perfection.
You reign high above all, and your rays
Of war embrace the lands you have shaped.
Against the land to which your spear tip points
Comes destruction and death,
Thick like the blanket on lovers' beds.
But the land which sits behind you
And your protecting arm of might,
In that land is all darkness dispelled,
Consumed in the festival of your light.

BOOK THIRTEEN

You dwell deep in my heart,
And none may know you as I.
Bless, then, this perfect union,
For all work is put down when you rest
And taken up again when you stir,
Long of the open steppe and of war,
The king of heaven and earth's calamities,
Old yet young, living forever and ever."

One by one the goats were led up
To have hot bowels spill from their guts.
Attila slaughtered them all himself,
Driving his sword through their hides
And slicing them from the neck.
Soothsayers rose from their seats
And offered promises of glory
For those bound together tonight,
And Attila held aloft keen Kolbulut,
Still red with splattered goat-gore,
Proclaiming out loud the divine favor
That long had been bestowed on him,
The blessings of the battle-god
That spurred his nation on to war
And thus secured for nomadic Huns
A place forever in history's mind.
Huns pulled meat from off the spits
And took turns passing flesh around,
Banqueting for many hours on end
Until twilight darkened all the earth.

When at last the festivities ended
And Huns went back into round yurts
Or huddled under hastily built huts

LORD OF THE HUN

Laid out by timber imported from abroad,
Attila took his newlywed bride
And led her forth from Jalaŋgül's walls.
A short distance they trounced the plain
Until at last they neared a private yurt
Lined with tapestries rich and marvelous,
Imported from the far reaches of the world.
Some were woven as far off as India,
Others in Persia or down in Egypt,
All of them fine and all of them vibrant.

Thus into this tent of color they went,
And he went underneath thick bedsheets,
Pulling his bride down on top of him
And beckoning spoke to Honoria.
"The time has nearly come, my bride,
For us to consummate our union.
Offer a prayer for the union we have made,
For it is in joy we have joined each other
And it is proper to thank the War-Sky
Even now for his bountiful benevolence.
Pour out some wine, too, into
These engraved chalices from far Scythia,
So that with the ecstasy of wine
We may be joined with one another."

Honoria received the ornate cups
Handed her from Attila's grasp,
And down she walked to a table
On which were laid fine bottles of wine
Imported from distant Spain.
Flowing out from glass bottle
The wine rushed into cups below,

And once Honoria filled the glasses
She took from within her robes
The vial Zerco gave to her,
Turning back her gaze to ensure
Attila's eye could not catch a glimpse
Of the addition made to his drink.
Dripping poison came running down,
Rippling the pool of red wine.
Honoria sniffed it once or twice
And then at last took up the cups
And delivered her lethal gift.

Attila brought the chalice to his lips
And wiped his peppered beard stained
Red with wine like ambrosia flowing down.
"Fit for kings this fine drink is!"
He declared, beaming eyes wide open,
"And indeed no finer way to usher in
The consummation of this our union
Could we have guzzled down tonight.
Now lie down, your bosom to my chest,
And let us have our night of passion!"

The king forced himself upon her,
Met in turn by a tense Honoria uneager
To open herself up to him so soon.
She would rather he choke right there,
Spewing retching vomit on her face,
Than let him plant his budding seed.
Oh how she winced even now,
Waiting for the moment when at last
The toxins would take hold, ending
The Scourge of God where he lay.

LORD OF THE HUN

And yet much to her newfound relief,
Never was she to consummate
This loveless marriage even now,
For Attila drew his body back from her,
Holding fast his trembling stomach.
With haste he leapt up from the bed
And out came his wedding feast
Like a deluge onto the earthen floor.
He staggered back, drunkenly slipping
Head and heels over vile regurgitation.

"Witch!" he cried, wiping away putrid refuse.
"By what powers have you ensorcelled me?
Is this some curse of Evoric as I presume,
That at your very touch my health is stripped?"

"This is no evil magic," Honoria answered,
Holding aloft her emptied vial; little more
Than residual drops were left inside.
"This all is my own doing, not Evoric's,
And long have you deserved the fate
That now stands ready to engulf you.
Tonight you said to me another you sought,
Honoria she was, sister to the emperor
Of the fractured Western Roman Empire.
Now you know the truth, for I am she,
Exiled by a spiteful brother and by war
To long traverse battle-wearied wilds
Avenging honor and redeeming wrongs.
After two campaigns turned aside
You have the bride you long sought
As pretext for your bloody wars,
But she has become your undoing.

At long last Honoria has prevailed."

Attila hurled again upon the floor
And wiped away blood dripping down
From his nose bleeding raw and red.
"And so you have avenged yourself
But tell me this: are you satisfied
At this pitiable sight before you,
At this pathetic shell of a man
Coughing out his own life force?"

"I do not laugh with joy," Honoria said,
"But no longer will I rest without sleep,
Knowing at last your terror has ended.
No longer shall justice cry in vain."

"So you say," Attila staggered back,
Nearly slipping again on the mess,
Gazing with sunken eyes upon she
Who put him down this wretched way.
"So you think your cause has won,
But my death has not stopped war.
The fight will simply take for itself
Some other gruesome shape.
You have driven off a symptom,
But not the dread disease itself.
Return to these steppes in a decade
And you would see the land in turmoil.
The lowly will hold exalted positions
And those who were pious
Shall go on their own way.
To save one empire, you have so
Condemned another to the same decay."

"Would you not have done the same to mine?"
Honoria answered him in turn.
"Would not the empire of Rome
Be made to crumble under your watch?"

"So you say," Attila smiled.
"Perhaps we are more alike than I thought.
But Rome's might has already passed.
In my absence, her demise shall only
Be slower than you thought it was.
Now everything makes sense to me.
Listen close and hear me out,
One final story from my lips
Until this poison's done its work
And at last I join my fathers."

Honoria listened in, and Attila
Continued to speak to her saying,
"Some time back, when I gathered
All the nations of my empire
By the shores of winding Danube,
I beheld an omen in the skies.
An eagle tore itself clean through
A flock of lesser birds scattered
As the predator rent them apart.
But once his kill was claimed,
The eagle went off to the unknown.
I knew then and there that this,
This was an omen of my god,
And so I asked of Evoric,
Still in my custody at the time,
To decipher this sign for me,
And this was what he said:

'Many shall flock to war-
Kings, chieftains, champions of legend-
None shall be exempt!
Only one, however, will outlast them all.
But this one too will then depart,
Lost to obscurity,
Forever a memory among the rest,
Though this one's presence
Will have been felt by all.'
I thought he spoke of me,
Oh how mistaken I was!
Even then he spoke of you.
Omens foretold your coming
And the deeds you would do.
The War-Sky thought not of me,
Nor ever has he favored me,
This much I can see now.
Long has the Lord of War
Craved for himself unending battle.
How could I expect less?
He sent down his stone from which
Keen-edged Kolbulut was forged
Not because he favored me,
But he knew I would offer him
The fighting he so desired.
Thus have I broken my people,
This much you've seen.
There is no jubilation now,
Save for my own celebrations.
There are no parties or revelries,
No songs sung of ancient days.
My people are utterly broken,
Gripped by eternal lament

For all those they've lost for me
And for the will of the War-Sky.
I too lost that day our hosts met
Upon blood-soaked Catalaunian Plains.
Laudaricus who went up against
Franks led by unmatched Sighlut,
A kinsman close to my own line,
Never again shall we embrace,
And all of this for what purpose?
What reward came from his death
But a few more stores of wealth
And funerals dragged on too long?
Europe shall be made destitute,
Though its kings shall be numerous."

And then Honoria felt for him
A sensation she never expected
To bear for the Scourge of God- pity-
Pity for all those even he had lost
And for the misery of his people
Which so lately engulfed her spirits.
So she knelt down to his side
And offered him a gentle embrace,
Ignoring the vomit on his chest
As she revealed the antidote
Given by Zerco for the poison.
"Take this, then, and buy for yourself
Another chance to redeem your people
And bring them from the brink of collapse."

But Attila pushed the vial away.
Wiping aside tears and refuse,
He looked at her and answered,

BOOK THIRTEEN

"All of my life I have been told
That to slaughter was my destiny,
That I would become a mighty king
And so usher in a replacement
For dated and corrupted Rome.
And thus in pursuit of glory
I have doomed Huns everywhere.
This empire will not outlast me.
That demon has doomed my people,
So please let me defy him
As he bred me to usher war,
I may at least have my own say
In denying him the battle I may bring."

Honoria spoke to him,
"Come on, you fool. Take the drink
And win hope for your kingdom.
Be a redeemed leader who shall save
His people and lead them to peace."

"Your confidence in me is assuring,"
Attila smiled, "but I've one last life
To lay low- my very own. But you,
Perhaps you can be that redeemed leader,
A queen of comfort and respite from strife."

In silence they sat next to each other,
Bitter enemies of war now as friends
Mournful of the troubles they suffered.
And so Attila continued retching, and
Hot blood poured from his nostrils.
His shivering body grew cold and pale.
He revealed a token he long kept to himself,

LORD OF THE HUN

A fine ring with a blood-red stone.
"Long ago you sent this to me,
Hoping I might save you from
A marriage unwanted. Instead
I claimed you as my own, against
Your volition. I think it's fitting
You have it back. It is yours."

Honoria's eyes glistened with water
As she accepted the gift, nodding
Softly and mouthing her thanks.
Then at last Attila said to Honoria,
"Though the world hates us both,
In my eyes you've shown your worth.
You are a good woman, Honoria,
Far better than the man I've been.
Go with Evoric, give him my blessing,
And may you at last find your peace.
No one deserves it more than you.
If my god will not pardon me,
Then perhaps yours can find it
In his heart to spare this wretch."

Then Attila breathed his last,
And off his spirit was whisked
To whatever fate awaited beyond.
And all the empire wept for him.
And on the following day,
Long after rosy-fingered Dawn had risen,
Attila's attendants broke through
And saw Honoria clutched on their king's corpse
Weeping bitterly through her wedding-veil.
Ellac followed in after them,

And as he saw Honoria huddled there
He understood all that had transpired,
Though he said nothing to his brothers,
Content still to keep the truth a secret.

No wound did Attila bear, no sign
Of any machination against him.
The emptied bottles were proof enough.
This many of fifty years was past
The time when his physique was prime.
He drank too much, so they assumed,
And his body could no longer bear
The consequences of his debauchery.
Still the attendants morned for him,
Though custom would not permit wailing
To honor such a mighty warrior.
They tore the hair from their heads
And marred their faces, mutilating
Them by knives and leaving deep wounds.
Such was the way to honor men, they said,
Even though their man-of-all-men
Spent his final moments weeping.

Upon the fields they placed his body,
Tucked underneath a silken tent
For all his admirers to there behold
His pallid corpse one final time.
Around him the finest horsemen rode
As games were held in his honor.
All his deeds were then recounted
And a dirge sung for his fate.
They sang of his glories won,
Ignorant of how in the end

LORD OF THE HUN

He learned to detest these so,
And they sung of his death,
Which they deemed came not by foe
Nor by treachery of former friends,
But in peaceful celebration.
In this brief moment his vast empire
Could say it held some peace,
However short-lived it was meant to be.

A strava was held at Attila's tomb,
Celebrated with revelry at last
As grief was mingled with joy.
Then in the cover of dusky night
Off they bore his body away,
Tucked inside three coffins.
The first was bound with rich gold
And the second with silver,
For he had won the honors of empires,
And the third was bound with iron
Because he had subdued the nations.
Alongside his body were there placed
Gems of immense worth, the arms
Of enemies won in bitter contest,
And princely relics from all across
The nations and tribes he lorded over.

Even Varus' eagle was laid on his chest,
Forever buried with its latest bearer.
But as his body was laid to rest,
To hide the corpse and his prizes
From the eyes of mortal curiosity,
Those who were appointed the honor
Of sending him off to the life beyond

BOOK THIRTEEN

Were rewarded with a sudden death.
Thus was the location of his tomb
Lost to all the minds of the earth.
None know where his body remains.
None shall ever know. Attila is lost,
Forever alone as he was peerless in life.

Soon word spread of Attila's death,
For even in well-walled Constantinople,
Marcian suffered sleepless nights
Awaiting news of Honoria's campaign.
But on the night Attila died
His frightful dreams were interrupted
As spear-bearing spirit came before him.
Though Marcian knew not his name,
It was none other than the War-Sky,
Dread battle-god of the Huns
Now rejected by his prized servant.
And at Marcian's feet the War-Sky
Laid down a phantasmal image,
The likeness of a broken goat-horn bow
Held but days before in Attila's hands.
And in the shattered bow he knew
The Scourge of God at last was dead.

But then the War-Sky addressed him
And with scornful laughter said,
"By Honoria's hand Attila is slain,
So Rome has won this single fight.
Yet Evoric has been lost to war.
Even now I hold him in lofty Panhušu,
From which I am known to many
As dread Zaršu-Mot, Lord of Phantoms.

LORD OF THE HUN

I am feared by the mightiest of Swart Elves.
The Erinuša are my handmaidens,
And about my throne sit manticores
Eager to feast upon beleaguered souls.
In the deep Mist-Crags sits my citadel,
Down, down in the gloomy Netherworld.
Neither you nor Honoria will see him again
While still the Hunnic empire lives.
So have I revealed to Honoria
Far off in wretched Jalaŋgül.
And yet war shall not be ended,
For even now your western brothers
Run the final leg of their race.
Doom shall not come from horseback Huns,
But from a foe older still,
Rome's bitterest enemy of all,
Though forgotten by all in this age.
Attila's empire will soon be broken
And high-born Rome will smolder.
Though your battle has now been won,
This victory shall last but a moment.
You cannot forever avoid the call of war.
In bitterness shall both empires die."

BOOK FOURTEEN
FATE AND PHANTOMS

As quickly as the Hunnic empire rose
From the shadows of obscurity,
In this way did its power falter
When at last the king was dead.
Honoria was true to her every word,
And once the opportunity presented itself,
Zerco met with dear Teŋiŕ
And at once fled miserable Jalaŋgül
To spend the years left for them
Safe and secure in Constantinople.
But Honoria remained behind,
Watching as the empire of the Huns
Piece by piece began to crumble.
Long she waited for word of Evoric,
Hoping the War-Sky had taunted her
With little more than wicked lies,
Though never were her ears graced
With the news of his survival
Or of his present whereabouts.

Ellac took upon himself the charge

To preserve this dying empire
And by his side he kept Honoria,
Still known to the Huns as Ildico,
Who rode upon a snow-white steed.
Ellac sought from her wise counsel
To help him navigate dire straits.
But all the help she could provide
Did little to stave off this collapse.
Attila's other sons contested with him,
For Ellac claimed that he was
Most fit to lead their people on.

Ernak and Dengizich challenged him,
Others too, a myriad of sons
Born from Attila's insatiable lust,
And together they suggested
Portioning out their father's empire
Among scores of regal heirs.
But as countless heirs squabbled,
Word spread of their periled state,
Coming upon the ears of Ardaric
King of the Gepids who earlier fought
On Attila's behalf at Catalaunian Plains.
At last he saw for mighty Gepids
The chance to cast aside the yoke
Long pressed upon them by the Huns.
So they took up arms in fierce revolt,
A hundred nations following after them
To join the Huns in hot battle
Along the banks of the river Nedao.

Upon the plain the rebels marshaled,
And as a solid mass allied Goths stood

BOOK FOURTEEN

Holding up their towering pikes
Like Alexander's Macedonian phalanx,
Which in ancient days won many fights
And with allied horsemen went forth
Conquering all from Thrace to India.
Shafts gently tottered back and forth,
Swaying in their bearers' firm grips
As around them gathered countless
Other tribes and nations so compelled
To aid Goths and Gepids in their fight
To at last rid Europe of the Huns.
To their aid came the Alans
Clad in heavy mail armor,
And along them went the Heruli
Light-armed and mobile, skirmishers
To reinforce the Alani bulk.

Before them went the Rugii
Hurling themselves upon the Hunnic line,
And their armor rang so fiercely that
Even the very sound frightened foes
As from profusely oozing wounds
They dragged clean out spearheads
Planted there by Hunnic shafts.
Shields were driven against each other
And as torrents from their battalions
Came rushing blood that stained the earth
Until at last the Rugii were beaten back,
Nursing fresh wounds and slipping
Over the bowels of fallen friends
As they fell back from the line of battle.

And as the Rugii flew back

With tails tucked between their legs
All the rebels staggered and faltered,
Fearful they too would be bested
And thus subject again to the Huns.
So Ardaric rode before them
And crying out with a great shout
He beckoned to all the host saying,
"Come now, this host of nations,
Do not now lose your resolve
And be thus beaten by the Huns,
For before me is an army of free men
Standing against a horde of slaves
Bound in fear to the memory
Of a tyrant whose day is gone.
These are no gods arrayed against us,
Thus still can they be beaten back
By the strength of our arms."

Thus the king of Gepids proclaimed,
Urging them across the plain,
Thousands stampeding over the field
Through the dust and to the battle-line
Once more upon the Hunnic ranks,
Eager to at last cast aside
The burden left by their former masters.
Heruli let loose their javelins
And all around the Hunnic flanks
Rode Gepids seated on foaming steeds.
All around Ellac swarmed about
A thick mass of striving Huns
Fighting with hide shields, spears and swords,
Thrusting and hacking at the waves
Hurled upon them as against stone.

BOOK FOURTEEN

Upon his own horse Ellac rode,
Weaving through the thick of the fray,
Leaping over the gore and retching
That littered the field of battle.

So Ellac hastened through
The wreck of his falling empire.
He unstrapped a polished bow
And readied his honed arrowhead.
He flexed his arm and then released.
The bow sprang and arrow twanged,
Piercing the neck of a Gothic pikeman,
A fountain spurting from his lower neck.
Arrow after arrow he sent flying,
Each of them hitting their mark
And sending foes to an early death.
But all around him his forces faltered,
And from afar Honoria beheld
The shattering of Hunnic might.
Gripped by desperation, Ellac strived
To rally together battered troops,
Parading through crumbled hordes
As all around him the mangled dead
Were piled up in great heaps.

Upon a lofty pillar of stone
Overlooking the woeful carnage,
Ellac beheld a dreadful figure
Seated there, laughing haughtily,
The dread War-Sky Attila once revered.
Upon his back was draped a crimson robe
And underneath sat scales of armor.
He wore a horned helm on his head

And beneath its shadow all foes faltered.
He stood there with spear in hand,
Rejoicing at the slaughter about him.
At once Ellac called out to this foe,
A former patron now betrayed,
"Oh great god of my fallen father,
Shall you come down from your perch,
Or is the play down below
Too rough for the likes of you?"

"What need have I," he answered,
Laughing with an awful voice,
"To slaughter beggars when they
Do such a fine job of it themselves?
Now comes the prince of all paupers.
Shall I break you too as I have
So many kings greater than you?"

At once Gepids sprang upon Ellac,
Who brought upon them unsheathed blade
And fought against their dozens,
Spilling out a sea of hot bowels
That slithered out all about him
As Gepids flailed and faltered in droves.
Then he rose, consumed with rage,
And leapt upon the god of his fathers,
Who thrusted time and again
The shaft of his flame-followed spear
Until at last Ellac was toppled over,
Bested not by shimmering spearhead
But by the butt of the shaft.
The wind knocked from his breath,
He writhed upon the ground as over him

BOOK FOURTEEN

His vanquisher taunted, "Hearken,
The king of an empire once mighty
Now quivers struggling for survival.
Let me thus relieve you now
And put an end to your misery."

From the cover of distant trees,
Seated upon her white horse,
Honoria watched as the final blow
Was brought down upon Ellac.
Clean through his sternum the spear drove,
Planting him firmly to the earth,
And all around him the land was drenched
By roaring blood flowing ever outward.
Onward Ardaric pressed his strength
Until at last the Huns broke into a rout.
Thus the might of their empire was broken.
Though still Hunnic tribes would linger on
In history for a brief while longer,
Their name as a deadly power was gone.
Thirty thousand fell in all that day
And many more survived this still,
Though from the battlefield they bore
The faltering memories of bygone days.

Satisfied with the day's slaughter,
The War-Sky turned then to Honoria
And called out with a harsh cry.
"Harken now, woman of Ravenna.
I know the one whom you seek,
For I am he, the Lord of Phantoms,
Dread Zaršu-Mot in my lofty ivory citadel.
Once have I told you this, now give chase!

Perhaps I may yet show mercy."

From the scene Honoria fled not,
For Honoria remembered that, like Evoric,
She had the gift to call upon the creatures
Of Karoputaru's ancient wilds.
Perhaps she already bore other gifts
Which he had previously displayed.
So she sang a song before the scattered dead,
And then she gave chase to the War-Sky,
Who led her far and wide across the earth.
As she followed after him, one by one
She was joined by the beasts of Karoputaru,
The Host of Dragons once more rallied
To her cause. And so they gave chase
To the dread War-Sky on his pallid horse.
From the banks of the Nedao he rode
Upon a ghastly steed pale as wintry death
And she upon a white horse of war
Bred among the Pannonian hills,
Bounding over hills and through woodlands
For countless weeks out in the wild.
What road she took no mortal can recall,
For from the land of the living she left
In haste for the hellish glooms
Of worlds fouler than that of Rome
Or of the ancient Swart Elves,
And in secret the Host of Dragons followed.

Honoria recalled when in days long gone,
When through the Under-City she walked,
She passed the door to Aegaeon's prison
And the realm of the Mist-Crags.

BOOK FOURTEEN

To that door she returned, having gone
Once more among Toratanatu's heights and
Passing through gates of marble and obsidian.
Among treacherous crags she stood,
Her feet resting on pitch-black soil
Spotted with ethereal asphodels
And spirits flickering like fireflies.
Among underground mountains
Crept serpentine limbs larger than rivers
Like tentacles on the ocean floor.
A deep voice shook the Nether-World
And Aegaeon called out to Honoria.

"I know you have come, trespasser.
I can smell your breath, and I hear
The patter of your feet. I can feel
The fluttering of your frail little heart.
Come now, do not be so bashful!
I wish to treat with thee, for I
Am he who topples mountains
And levels armies. Older than the world
Am I. My eyes have seen it perish
And be born anew time and again.
I instill terror in the hearts of gods,
For why else should they condemn me
As door-warden for the most hated among them?"

"Of your might I have heard,"
Honoria said, "oh Aegaeon the Vigorous,
The King of Cataclysms. I do not think
My praises shall guarantee my survival,
But still I pray you may let me pass."

FATE AND PHANTOMS

The unseen voice answered her
"Then come and tell me why
You come to trod this ancient land.
Do not lie to me, for no surer way
Could you guarantee your own death
Than to speak with a lying tongue."

"I come to confront your jailor,
None other than Zaršu-Mot himself.
Honoria I am, and long through war
Has my road led me. Now he holds
As a prisoner dear Evoric, of an order
Which perhaps you god-kind know.
Of all who still draw breath,
He is among the last left to me
In this cruel world. I shall go
And bargain with the god of phantoms
Or I shall claim the living by force."

Aegaeon laughed and answered back,
"Indeed I have heard of your exploits,
For even far beneath the earth are those
Whose roads have entwined with yours.,
And even some which you think have died
Still count among the living. Indeed,
Among the ancient Unnamed Things
Which even gods dare not cross stirs that
Hated ring of Elves which shall yet shape
The web and flow of human history
Before your time ends. But come!
Gaze into these chasms and for yourself
See what I have professed."

BOOK FOURTEEN

Honoria peered down into the gloom
To eye what Aegaeon spoke of.
In an endless dark flickered a light
That came and went like huffing breaths
Far, far below. Worlds away it seemed,
And yet already she knew the truth.

"The ring of Anadavara yet lives,"
Aegaeon chuckled, "And so has
Its bearer, though his rival has fallen.
I know well the hand you had in these affairs.
But come now! Don't be alarmed!
You have wisely appealed to the hatred
Which has long festered in my heart
Against my jailor in his ivory citadel.
Go then with my blessing, that I
May once more laugh at his anguish."

Serpentine limbs slithered far down
Into the endless gloom beneath the crags.
So relieved, Honoria continued on her road
Through winding cliffs which by the spell-craft
Of vigorous Aegaeon opened up
And revealed to Honoria glowing fields
Of uncounted shimmering asphodels.
Beyond ghostly meadows stretched a marsh
Fed by two rivers, one reddened by algae
And the second yellow like foul pus.

All around thronged ancient phantoms,
The specters of those long dead,
If not their true spirits then simply
Their likenesses planted here to taunt her.

FATE AND PHANTOMS

Ancient rivals were kept together,
Deprived of their journey beyond
Into the halls of the afterworld-
Brilliant Achilles and horse-breaker Hector,
Alexander and Darius, Scipio Africanus
And Hannibal with his spectral elephants.
Among this procession of the dead
Went forth Honoria's imperial predecessors,
From Augustus to Hadrian to Constantine,
All of them robbed of the right
To stand before their final judgement,
Held fast by dread Zaršu-Mot
For countless ages in foggy halls.
And into the mist Honoria went.

Through the growing fog she swam
As if through a vast sea she went,
And high above her soaked head
Faint starlight broke through the surface.
Down all around her sank the bodies
Of those countless slain in the war:
Romans, Huns, Goths and Gepids,
A thousand tribes lost to history,
Each one going down into the deep,
Into the darkness that engulfed them all.
Down with them fell mighty warships,
Shards of hulls and battered oars,
And darting through this labyrinth
Of hewn bodies and snapped ships
Came sharks eager to fatten themselves
Off the spoils of heartless carnage,
Twisting and pulling chunks of flesh
Before they too went into the deep.

BOOK FOURTEEN

Upward Honoria paddled herself,
Desperate to catch a breath of air,
And as she continued, ever upward
Dangled near the surface a Patagotitan;
The whale-sized long-neck drifted down
As all the bodies that came before
This majestic beast of Karoputaru.
Rotted sharks and other foul fishes
Swarmed about the giant's legs
And tore flesh off colossal limbs
Without risk of harm or injury.

At last she broke through the surface,
Her escape from the gloom below
Welcomed by the squaws of gulls
Perched upon the Patagotitan's back,
Swarming the beast in great congregations
And taking off little nibbles from
A creature that would have weighed in life
Ten thousand times as much as they.
Just nearby passed a spectral vessel,
A Roman ship with lateen sails
Sailing through the rivers of the deep.
Onto its deck Honoria scrambled,
And as she climbed up onboard,
She saw there surrounded by a throng
Of discounted Huns armed with spears
Famed Aetius; long months had passed
Since last her eyes met his.

"Do not come!" Aetius shouted,
Holding in his hands a bottle of wine.
He took a sip of it and spoke again,

FATE AND PHANTOMS

"You cannot save Rome. We never could!
We have tried to stave off death,
Though in so doing we deal it out.
Now I pass on into the life beyond.
I'll save a few bottles for you,
For one day you'll be there too."

"Don't go!" she yelled, nearly weeping.
"I can yet save you if you'll let me."

"Do not bother," Aetius answered her.
"You thought you could save the Huns
By throwing down their cruel leader,
Giving Jalaŋgül some measure of hope,
But all you've done is doom them too,
Caught on all sides by embittered foes.
Not only them, but us. You've destroyed us all."

"This isn't you, Aetius," Honoria answered,
But he gave her no heed, raising up
The bottle to his lips, never removing
Them from its brim. On he kept drinking
Until he fell passed out upon the floor,
Huns booing and jeering as he fell back,
Gnashing their teeth as he hit wooden boards.

So she hurried then to the general,
Pushing bystanders aside as she hastened,
And as she knelt by Aetius' side,
A club banged against the side of her skull,
Sending Honoria falling to the ground
Just as the one she sought to deliver.
Just overhead she saw Valentinian,

Hateful brother holding club in hand
And smiling as he knelt next to her.
He did not raise his club to kill his sister,
Instead contend to laugh and thus speak.
"Don't you see? Everywhere you go
There is naught but death and woe.
Just as you've brought down Rome,
So too have you destroyed Pannonia,
And what has come from all this
But more bodies added to the heap?
Everywhere you go, every friend you make,
All are undone by your guiles."

"Shut up!" Honoria cried out with rage.
"Do not stand over me taunting thus,
You who doomed me to this existence.
You would have murdered me
Had I so chosen to remain in Ravenna
And share in Mother's final moments.
You did all of this to me,
Although I cannot deny my part.
I'm just as much to blame as you,
Despite the hurts you've dealt me."

"All this and more," Valentinian said.
"I met your Evoric, running back
From your ill-fated expedition.
I asked him to speak with me
So we could help heal this world.
The stupid fool listened to me
And came into my palace.
You want to know what I did?
I took this sword beside my waist

FATE AND PHANTOMS

And drove it up through his chin
Until like a Phrygian cap
It rose from the top of his head.
Poor wretch stained my carpet,
But I'm the emperor. That I can fix.
As he was dying I knelt down
And I said this to him:
That his affections for you were misplaced.
He was only a means to an end,
And you had him wrapped around
Your fingers, ready to be cast aside
The moment you found another man
Who might threaten my seat.
And as he breathed his last he knew-
I could see it in his eyes-
That he died for a harlot,
Less than a harlot, actually.
I'd make love to a harlot.
But you, you are irredeemable."

Honoria rose to her feet
And stood wroth before her brother.
"Enough of your lies, you
Who once I called a brother!
I could kill you here and now.
Maybe then some justice would be down,
If not for me, then for Evoric."

"Try it then," Valentinian taunted.
"Perhaps you'd finally prove your worth.
Come at me and show to all the world
You're more than a scheming seductress."

BOOK FOURTEEN

Her mouth frothing and foaming,
Honoria rushed upon her brother
And with a single stroke drove her sword
Clean through Valentinian's gut.
But as she ran him through,
She saw no affect laid on him,
As if through a phantom her sword was driven.
With a club he struck her again,
And as Honoria rolled to the ground
He grabbed her by the nape, dragging her
Across the ship until he opened a door
And thus led her below the deck.
But as through the door they went,
The world around them seemed to change.
He dragged Honoria not through a ship,
But into her palace in Ravenna,
And there she saw herself
Clutching blankets to her breast
As Valentinian stood over her
On this the night it all began.
Off to the side stood their mother,
Placidia scowling with contempt
At the schemes of her daughter.
Honoria remember that night
More vividly than any other.

"So it was with Eugenius," her brother said,
"And so it was with vile Attila. So again
Has it been with that little rat Evoric.
As a dog returns to its vomit,
So my sister perpetuates wickedness.
She cannot deny her true nature."

FATE AND PHANTOMS

"And so you threw me aside," said Honoria,
"Kicking *augusta*- your sister- to the floor,
And in her place rose a warrior filled
With a fire that cannot yet be quenched."

"As I have long desired," Valentinian answered.
Then all around them gave away
And no longer were they in Ravenna,
But upon a lonely mountain peak
Where down below marched a mighty force,
The Host of Dragons marshaled for war.
From the crags looming overhead
These vast vales of the Netherworld
Emerged the alien forms of those Unnamed
Who rule the depths beneath the earth,
Spying the army as onward it marched
And waiting to strike the surface world
And corrupt all lands with their filth.
No longer did Valentinian pull her on,
For now his form had been transformed,
Taking on the likeness of the War-Sky
Who slavering knelt and spoke to her.

"Surely you must remember that day
We first met deep in the Under-City.
Do you remember what Evoric said,
What he suggested that I was,
That perhaps I was of his order
Though I abandoned my given charge?"

Honoria nodded but she said nothing,
Looking on as thousands marched below,
A myriad monsters ready for battle.

BOOK FOURTEEN

So again the War-Sky spoke.
"I was once like Evoric, it is true,
And once there was another age
That so needed the Host of Dragons.
I summoned them and led them forth
Against a host of rebellious Swart Elves
Joined in arms with other nations
Bent on bringing down the empires
That lorded over their present age.
I gathered the beasts to my side
And allied myself with the pharaoh,
Besting our foes far off in Retjenu.
Victory was ours, though at great cost,
And onwards I continued my charge,
Calling forth the Host of Dragons
Whenever some threat reared its ugly head,
Just like Evoric, and just like you.
By and by, the time came
When the call to war consumed me,
I could think of nothing else
Beyond urging hordes on to battle.
Attila was only a means to an end.
You, however, you bear potential,
Overborne by anger and loneliness."

"But I am not alone," Honoria rose,
Her voice stern and clear.
"Though none stand at my side,
I will never be on my own."

"To whom do you refer?" he answered.
"To Evoric? To your God? Childish hope
Can not bear you from this cycle of woe.

FATE AND PHANTOMS

You are utterly broken. Never will the day come
When you can live in peace.
When wounds run this deep,
What peace could you ever have?
What hope is there for you?"

"Enough!" Honoria said loud and defiant.
"I will listen no more to your lies!
Begone, for I will grant you
Any control over my will."
"That we shall see," the War-Sky answered.
"In due time you shall break."

"There is a force greater still,"
Honoria said, "than your cruel hate.
My love surpasses your evils,
And I will face the god of phantoms
Who rules over this dread realm-
I will face you-
If so my charge demands."

"Come then," the War-Sky beckoned.
"You are nearer to me than you think.
Prove your mettle, show to me
Your spirits haven't been broken
By the long toils of war."

At once he vanished, and all the visions
Around Honoria began to fade away.
Rising then from these dread visions,
She found herself in the heart of this land,
Standing before the gates of Panhušu,
The citadel of Zaršu-Mot himself,

BOOK FOURTEEN

Most feared of all the gods of the Elves,
Yet loved by the Huns as the War-Sky.
She stood upon the bridge before those gates
To declare her power and her cause
Against he who dwelled inside.
The Host of Dragons stood behind her,
All the mighty beasts of Karoputaru
Which she ordained to follow after
Her trail through the wild in secret
Prepared at once to bring their fight
To the fell denizens of Panhušu.

And Honoria spoke to them saying,
"The wizardry and spells of Evoric's order
I have at last uncovered, that same power
Which by providence flows through
My own tempered veins. Long has Evoric
Been of aid to your causes and mine.
Let us go then and free him,
His memories sapped by long waiting
In the halls of the gloomy dead."

And though the visions had departed,
The phantoms of the dead still lingered.
Ancient heroes of the Swart Elves
And Babylonian kings stood side-by-side,
Roman emperors and others too
Known to Honoria in earlier days.
Hannibal of Carthage came to her side,
Smiling as she approached and spoke.
"At last among the living comes
One who might see us off
To face our well-deserved judgments.

FATE AND PHANTOMS

Such has been the fate of many
A conquering king to be held here,
Stolen upon the hour of our deaths
To bide ages uncounted in these halls."

But Aetius knew the truth of her journey.
"She has not come to deliver us,
Though deliverance she may yet provide.
Evoric was claimed by Zaršu-Mot,
Wounded by Attila's venomous darts,
And now she comes to save
The one love left to her in the world
Of those who breathe living breaths.

Honoria nodded and answered back,
"Still may you come with me and so
Win your freedom from
The dastardly Lord of Phantoms.
Then perhaps you might gain
A chance to see the life beyond."

But there was another among them
She had counted still as living,
The proud form of Valentinian,
Her brother now a slave among the dead,
Imprisoned like the ancient kings
Seized by Zaršu-Mot's agents
To labor away in his ivory citadel
And postpone passage to the life beyond.
Rome's emperor was dead.

BOOK FIFTEEN
RAZING HELL

"This cannot be!" she declared,
Trembling in her brother's presence.
"Are you not still emperor of Rome,
Seated upon her seven ancient hills
As since last my eyes saw yours?"

But Valentinian would not answer.
Crossing his arms, he turned away
From his sister and cast his gaze
Instead upon the other shades.

"Brother, will you not hear me?"
Honoria pleaded. "Must you
Wear your hatred even in death?
Please speak to me for once!
This world has enough hurts.
Can we at least relieve ours?"

"Alas," Aetius spoke up
As his own specter approached.
"I do not think he will again

RAZING HELL

Speak with you face-to-face,
And no good was ever conceived
From his enmity towards you.
Hearken now and hear how we died,
How a mighty emperor was unmade.
Once word of Attila's death spread,
All thought that peace had come
And the Romans were at last secure.
Long had my bitterness festered,
Jealous Valentinian was of my achievements
And angered by my confidence.
Now he grew suspicious, influenced
By whispers from Heraclius,
That eunuch of renowned influence.
Lies he heard also from another,
From that senator Petronius Maximus,
Who said I sought to supplant him.
I had married off my boy Gaudentius
To his daughter- your niece- Placidia.
Valentinian thought I meant to supplant him
And instill my seed as the emperor.
So he sat on his richly inlaid throne
Going over machinations in his head,
Thinking how best he should dispose me.
At last the fortuitous moment came
As I came upon his throne with
My thoughts bent on financial matters.

"At once he leapt from his seat,
Fingers pointed at me before him.
'How long must I tolerate this babbling?
What inane nonsense pours from your lips!
Do you think I should take to heart

The drunken counsel slipping out
From he who dealt Rome such strife?
All of Rome's troubles lie on you!
And now you plot your twisted schemes
To seize the throne and thus supplant me!'

"So I sought to defend my honor.
'My lord, have you been hard at drinking,
Wasting your nights away with women
In the taverns, those not yours to bed?
All these long years have I strived
To preserve Rome from threats uncounted,
From dangers without and within.
Why now would I so thoughtlessly betray
All for which I've long labored?'

"But he would not hear me out,
So blinded by his maddening rage,
And with Heraclius he rushed upon me,
Standing alone and unarmed.
In my gut they plunged their swords
So that out from my marred flesh
Blood went seeping into all the cracks
Lining rows the tiles of marvelous mosaics.
And in those pristine halls he marveled,
Glorying over the splendor of his kill.
'Well it is that I have done this.
At last the scheming mongrel is dead
And a good deed done for Rome!'

"But as Valentinian finished speaking,
From the crowd looking on,
A counsellor rose and said,

RAZING HELL

'Whether well or not, I do not know,
But know that you have cut off
Your right hand with your left.'

"Thus in his folly did he destroy
He whom he supposed his usurper,
Though in truth he slew his protector,
And now Rome's emperor stood exposed.
From across the seas Vandals watched,
Seated within the heights of Carthage,
That ancient city which ages past
Waged two long wars with Rome
And two times were beaten back
After years of bitter turmoil.
Then at last the Romans came
And razed Carthage to the ground,
Full on genocide.
But in Africa they rebuilt Carthage
And made it a Roman colony.
Long under Rome did she prosper
Until recent history, when from the West
Came marauding Vandals expanding their domain.
They seized Carthage, making her
The seat of their newfound power.
So in Carthage their king Gaiseric sat,
Waiting for Rome to soon expose
Her weakness festering within.

"And that time would soon come,
For even now Petronius Maximus-
That same man who egged him on-
He conspired against the very same man
He so lately encouraged to me.

BOOK FIFTEEN

Now for vengeance Petronius acted,
Knowing that his dear wife Lucina
Had been forced upon by Valentinian's hands,
Raped by the man who for years
Condemned you as a harlot.
Oh! If only he could have seen his error
Before it was too late to repay his sins!

"Petronius met with the veteran Scythians
Optila and Thraustila, who in days past
Had gone to war beneath my standards,
And with them he hatched conspiracy.
One day Valentinian dismounted his horse,
Setting himself up in the Field of Mars
Where he unslung my bow and there
Prepared to fire away at targets.
Upon his temple Optila struck him,
And as their emperor turned around
The same Scythian bashed in his face
While Thraustila leapt upon Heraclius,
Slicing open his gut with a keen blade.
From the remnants of his battered mess
They seized the royal diadem and robe,
Placing them upon Petronius.
He held the support of the Senate,
And with a few well-placed brides he
Secured for himself imperial succession.
In this way were we undone, and all know not
What fate awaits high-borne Rome."

At this news Honoria wept,
Arms wrapped around the general
Who long she hated in her heart.

None of that mattered now, for
What healing could enmity provide?
"I do not know what judgement waits
For you before the gates of heaven,
But so I swear that you and all the others,
Even Valentinian who scorns me so,
Shall be freed of this prison when
I deliver Evoric from the ghost-lord's grasp."

And Aetius answered, "Even if
Our damnation cannot be turned aside,
Still I can count myself glad to at last
See the healing of your heart. Forgive me.
Truly you'd have been a better emperor
Than he who will not speak with you."

"She may have been," spoke regal Augustus,
Who had hearkened to their side
With a legion of shades to his back.
"But *if's* do not matter now."

"Indeed," said Aetius.
"And though Petronius claims
For himself the mantle of the throne,
Now I proclaim you, dear Honoria,
The successor to our empire."

"Now prove yourself once more!"
Augustus declared. "A kingdom
You shall yet rule, though not upon
Those seven hills. Lead the way."

So Honoria prepared the charge,

And countless of Zaršu-Mot's thralls
Thronged about her side- Celts
And Myrmidons, mighty Elves,
Men from across the far seas
Who carved colossal heads of basalt,
And lords of far eastern dynasties
Were but a few of those who mustered
Beneath the standard of Honoria.
Macedonian phalanxes stood behind
And Hunnic riders went before her,
And all about proceeded that mighty host
Of monsters from the Land of Dragons.
Many thousands rallied to her side,
And all the deep places quaked
As her mighty host moved forth
To make war agains the god of phantoms.
And Honoria cried out, "I am
A woman who loves her city and
A man imprisoned beneath the earth.
I've found my way across the world,
Crowned by those who came before
To continue on an age-old fight
Against the forces of evil and hate.
Come what may, I am *Augusta*."

Honoria rose before the black gates
Of ominous Panhušu and uttered
Words and power, and they
Were at once shattered before her.
The cries of unnumbered phantoms rose
As the gates crumbled down,
And Honoria went at once
To contest Zaršu-Mot and

RAZING HELL

Win Evoric back from his clutch.
Riding upon dagger-jawed Jiggles
She crossed the bridge, followed
In turn by the shades of ancient kings
And the living forms of mighty beasts.

From pits beneath came his many thralls,
Gripped both by wonder and dismay
At the power that had been displayed.
Long had they lingered in the shadow
Cast upon them by their dread lord,
And in all the ages spent down here
Not once had they seen one come
So willingly into his ivory halls.
Some at once withdrew from her splendor,
Draped once more in the regal armor
And her crown of myrtle leaves
She donned when to war she rode,
Dressed like the Swart Elves of ancient legends
Who with gods and monsters contested.
Others fell in fury upon her host.
But of the Host of Dragons,
Those with lances on their heads went first,
Triceratops, Diabloceratops, and all their kin
Armed with skulls like phalanxes,
Marching alongside human lances.
Spears keratinous and Macedonian both
Were at once adorned with the bowels
Of skewered thralls littered here and there.
Others were trampled or driven apart
By contingents of swift cavalry,
So that the fanged beasts close behind
Could pick apart scattered ranks

BOOK FIFTEEN

And so clean up this messy affair.
The citadel trembled as daemons howled,
Fearful of Honoria's dread approach.
Their slaves at once took heart and fled,
Not knowing where their road would lead,
But simply glad to at last be rid
Of the god of phantoms and his ills.
So great was the horror of her approach
That the War-Sky stirred in his throne
Even as she came to speak with him.

He wore a mask of the dead upon his face,
And crested plumes rose from his helm.
Flanked by towers of ivory and by manticores
Gnawing at the bones of ancient monsters,
He sat alone upon his fearful throne
And to the mortal before him he declared,
"How is it that one among the living
Should find herself in my phantasmal halls?
You have withstood my awful visions
Which years ago broke the king of Huns
And made a convert out of Attila.
Tell me then what request you might have,
That I may grant it and send you off
To live again among those who live
Rather than among mere likenesses
Of those whose time is past.
Why should I suffer your presence
When already my host fears you?"

Honoria gave him her request.
"You know well my desires,
For it was you who seized Evoric

RAZING HELL

As he stood prepared to die,
Or if not you then your servants.
Return him to me, and let us both
Hasten away to our own lands.
He does not belong here
Any more than I do. Neither
Do the uncounted dead rallied
Beside my standard, and they too
Shall at once be delivered
To await their final judgment."

"Your companion was a fine prize,"
He answered. "Here he was healed,
And from his lips I learned much
Concerning these present days of death.
But you shall not have him. Already he
Remembers little of his days with you.
So happens to all who abide in this realm.
He is mine, and never again shall he
Walk beneath the luminous rays of the sun."

"If not by bargaining I may claim him,"
Honoria brandished her keen blade,
"Then by force he will be recovered.
I will not suffer his endless anguish
Here in the abode of your specters."

"Have you come," Zaršu-Mot taunted
"To count yourself as Diomedes
Who ages past fought against gods
And lived to tell the tale? Come then
And try your luck if you so please.
Give me the battle I seek from you!

BOOK FIFTEEN

Only with the price of spilled blood
Can the freedom of the living be bought."

Honoria readied her sword,
And the War-Sky laughed as it was drawn.
But she did not aim it anymore
Towards him or his countless thralls.
She turned it instead toward herself,
Pointed upward to her head.

"What madness be this?" the War-Sky cried.
"Come now, you fool, and give me battle.
Blood must be spilt in exchange
For hapless Evoric's release."

"And Evoric shall be released,"
Honoria answered, "for blood
Shall be spilled. My own."

"Do not toy with loopholes!"
The Lord of Phantoms cried.
"You are to fight me."

"I can't fight you if I'm dead, can I?"
Honoria smiled wryly. "Nor can I
Offer you battle in days to come."

"Yet you are a woman of war,"
Zaršu-Mot frowned, "commanding
Armies of Romans and Goths
And ghosts and beasts. Why claim
Through sacrifice what's rightly yours
Through the art of conquest?"

RAZING HELL

"I've seen enough conquest,"
Honoria answered in defiance.
"The world's got enough killing.
I should know, as I've contributed.
To this hideous mess. Why then
Should I take when I can give?
My blood in exchange for Evoric
And for these specters is as fine a price
As one could ever bargain for."

The War-Sky yielded and there declared,
"This insect's cunning has quite the sting!
I will allow these slights for now,
For perhaps you may yet prove useful
In future god-strifes. Begone then!
And take a myriad souls with you.
I cannot trust you to fight when you're dead!
But in days to come, perhaps,
I can make a battle-thrall of you."

He finished speaking, and with his handmaidens
He withdrew at once into his inner chambers,
Wanting no more to deal with her ilk.
From hidden doorways emerged Evoric,
And he dusted off the remnants of battle.
As he went to see of the Host of Dragons,
Honoria once more met with those kings
And conquerers who joined her host.
Some offered her friendly words.

Aetius gave her a warning, "Should now
You travel off to claim your title,
I would be wary, for forces stir even now

That would seek to supplant you.
As Aegaeon told you, from beneath
The Heart of the World stirs one
Who still would have you punished.
But go; you'll make a fine emperor."
And Honoria wept with Aetius.

She called out one last time
To Valentinian. "Brother!
Will you at last forgive my crimes
As I have forgiven yours?"

This time he looked at her,
But still he would not speak.
"Then go," Honoria said.
"Go in peace to your judgement,
To whatever that may be."

"Now let us be off!" declared Augustus.
"Honoria must join her beloved Evoric
And return at last to ancient Italy.
We go now to face our judgment
And accept whatever it may be.
Many are the sins among us,
But this woman here may yet
Prove herself a nobler leader.
History shall see if I speak true."

Then the shades of those kings smiled,
Relieved to at last be freed of this place
And slowly their forms boarded triremes
Ghastly both of hue and of form,
Captained by mighty seafarers Ulysses,

RAZING HELL

By Hanno and by Xu Fu.
Away from Panhušu the ghost-ships
Were blown like dandelions in a breeze.
Away the folk of old went to meet their maker
And embrace the charge laid on them all.
But as their specters were blown away,
The last that remained was Valentinian's,
He who had died the most recent.
But as his image too passed from sight,
Honoria saw him raise his hand to her,
And he smiled. Then he too was gone
With the rest, never again
To be seen by the living.
The Host of Dragons withdrew,
Content with the victory that was won.
None remained behind save for Jiggles
And for horned Sophia, who hearkened
To their dear companions and there remained.
Evoric watched the shades from afar,
Amazed to see them rallied and so
Depart from this mortal life. Then
His eyes turned back to Honoria,
Who long he hoped to meet again,
Imprisoned as he was in these halls.

"You followed me all the way down
Into the Netherworld?" he remarked.
"A bit creepy," he joked, "but nonetheless
I appreciate the commitment."

Honoria laughed and rushed upon him,
Eagerly wrapping arms around his shoulders.
"Oh how I've missed you," she declared.

BOOK FIFTEEN

"I thought- he told me you were dead!
But here you are hale and whole,
And no happier for that could I be.
But I'm tired, Evoric. I am so tired.
How can we ever hope to fight evil
Without becoming as the enemy?"

Evoric nodded and answered her,
"I am at a loss. I do not know.
But you've done your task, Honoria.
You need not struggle any more.
Perhaps it's time that you at last
Rest and pass on to obscurity,
Living on as you may in peace,
Forgotten by this bitter world."

"The War-Sky was like you," she said,
"So he told me so just before
I called together beasts and kings,
Compelled by duty to summon forth
The Host of Dragons as we had.
To stop Attila we became him,
Forging plans and squashing armies.
I know we did what was necessary
To end his reign of terror,
But could there have been another way?"

"If such a means exists," Evoric answered,
"I'm afraid we mortals have no power
To wield it for ourselves, trapped as we are
In a world of violence, so with violence
Are we so compelled to answer back.
But something separates you from him

RAZING HELL

And that is guilt- guilt and understanding.
Perhaps it's that which prevents you
From becoming like the Scourge of God.
Despite what racked sentiments may say,
You and he are not the same.
This much you've proved to all today."

Honoria shook her head. "Those people,
All those who died because of me,
They had family and friends back home.
They had stories to tell, heirlooms to cherish.
Surely they loved their own children as fiercely
As any Roman could, but now they are broken.
Can I ever bear the power to turn
All these woes around for the better?"

"Is it in our power?" Evoric asked,
"Or is it instead charged to us
To bear what hope and healing we can
Onto this world beleaguered by pain?
Even if we do not see any fruits,
Still they must be there. Even now
You just released a thousand times
A thousand souls into the world beyond.
You may not have saved living armies,
But for these you have brought deliverance
Which long their spirits ached for."

Honoria looked toward a gloomy stream,
Watching phantasmal waters ripple.
"I know it was stupid, foolish of me,
I know surely that's not the answer,
But over these years I'd often ask myself

BOOK FIFTEEN

If earth would be better off without me,
To leave the world to fend for itself
Lest I inflict any more pain. And yet
That would offer only me freedom.
What good would my death do
To those so charged to gather up
The ashes left by my fires?"

"The world needs you, Honoria,"
Evoric responded to this proposal.
"It needs your resolve and your lament.
Of all the kings and all the conquerers,
None I have met bear both gifts.
It's what separates you from the rest,
From those who just commanded,
For though you've struggled to prove it,
You know might does not define right."

And so Honoria answered him,
"Attila learned the same when he died,
For he could see the error of his ways
Though it was too late to redeem them.
Do you want to know what he said
Just before he passed beyond?
'Go with Evoric, give him my blessing,
And may you at last find your peace.
No one deserves it more than you.'"

"Then," Evoric said, "perhaps it's time
We take off and live out our lives,
Never again calling armies to war.
Will that solve our problems, highness,
I do not know, but it's a start."

RAZING HELL

But Honoria answered back saying,
"I cannot resign just yet, for there is
But a final task I must see to.
It's time I go to Italy for one last time.
I've been proclaimed the imperial heir,
And so Augustus and all the rest
Saw fit to make me as them.
But I do not deem any throne
Is left for me. Goaded by vengeance,
Surely doom awaits Petronius
And those who go with him.
Perhaps, though, I may yet
Muster those wearied by long wars
Among the folk of Rome
And others from far and wide.
A new city I will found, one that
Shall be a haven and not a harbor for war.
I cannot save the world,
But I at least can offer an exodus."

"Then with you will I go," Evoric answered,
"On this road God directs you.
If it is marked your hour to die,
Then so too shall I go with you
Beyond the gates of the life to come."

So they departed from that dark land
The way by which Honoria entered,
Passing once more through Aegaeon's prison.
Again she looked down into the gloom,
Wondering if Dragon-fires still flickered.
There was no flicker, but instead
The flapping of panicked wings

BOOK FIFTEEN

And the roaring of a mighty beast.
Crying with agonizing wails,
The Dragon rose from the dark,
Wearing Anadavarenu on his finger.
Indeed the words of Aegaeon were true,
And from the deep an old ally emerged.

"Ah!" the Dragon reeled. "What fell fate
Is it that you two had a hand in all this!
Have you come then to gloat at my pain
And mock the tortures given to me?"

His huge frame trembled with fear
At the torments he had endured
While held by the monsters of the deep
Until at last he had escaped.
Or was he released? None knew,
Even though the fortuity of this timing
Seemed to be the work of malice.

Honoria stood motionless with wonder.
"Dear Sighlut, is that you? What terrors
Have dealt you these wounds to your spirit?"

"Once I was called he," the Dragon cried,
"As once you were called Honoria,
Before you hurled upon the West
An age of war and gods and monsters.
How are my people, lowly Franks, to endure this
And the countless other evils that wait
To seize us and swallow us whole?
Europe tears itself apart, empires crumble,
Thousands upon thousands have already died.

RAZING HELL

The old world as we know it is over,
And a thousand kingdoms will squabble
Without the alliances offered by empires,
But it was the empires that caused all this.
The empire of the Huns is no more.
But yours? Your cruel empire still remains.
Death knocks at her door. I knock."

At once the Dragon took off,
Propelled by wings of fire and smoke.
Honoria and Evoric worried then
That he meant foul deeds for Rome
And for her people huddled within.
So they resolved once more
To make their way to Rome's heights
And avert the doom that awaited her
And for the upstart emperor there.
But as Petronius sat upon the throne,
Rumors again began to spread.
These whispers focused not on the emperor,
But on the peril he now faced.
Surely they were whispers, ignored
By the imperial guard and the emperor
Despite the peril Italy suffered
For the ignorance of her rulers.
Marcian's fleet from Constantinople
Had been utterly ravaged, annihilated
By a force none knew drew breath,
Torn asunder by a massive beast
Born aloft on wings of shadow and flame.
Hundred-handed Aegaeon spoke true,
Even now the Dragon from far below
Flew in from the clouds above

And dove through the rising waves,
Spewing fire and ruin upon the vessels.
Archers on the decks fired their arrows
Which with a *twang* sped toward it,
But none could pierce its thick hide,
And all were answered in turn
By fiery darts and blasts of doom
Which tore apart Roman vessels
And sent them sinking into the gloom
That awaited them at the bottom
Of those deep seas. The veil
Left in the wake of its smoldering wings
Covered all, blocking out the sun's light,
And naught but woe followed after them,
Woe and one other thing.
A fleet of Vandal ships, headed
By none other than Gaiseric himself,
Whose son Huneric was lately denied
A regal marriage to Eudocia,
Daughter to the late Valentinian.

Petronius himself denied this union.
So Gaiseric went to avenge this slight,
Goaded on by Sighlut's might
And by promises of wealth
And of the chance to deliver Rome
The deathly blow she so sorely dreaded.
Panic seized the West as doom approached,
The final nail in Rome's readied coffin.
Against the shattered fleet they hastened
And tore through Constantinople's hulls,
Ramming through proud Roman ships
And stripping them of their plunder

RAZING HELL

And all the fine treasures to be won.
But a few vessels survived the onslaught,
And those that did only made it
Because in surrender they gave up
The weapons they bore in their arms
And so swore to return at once
To well-walled Constantinople,
Never to hinder the Vandalic fleet
As off it hastened to wearied Rome
And toward her seven ancient hills.
Slowly came the news of this slaughter,
And those who heard it were gripped with fear,
Seeking at once to flee from the Tiber
And so make a living far from Rome.

But on his throne Petronius sat,
Content instead to plan his escape,
To save his own hide and so
Leave the rest of Rome to the fate
That had long awaited her heights.
He was the emperor after all.
Even if Rome itself remained secured,
There could be no empire without an emperor.

BOOK SIXTEEN
FALL OF THE WEST

The emperor is dead,
The second to fall that year alone.
Up and down his body bobbed
As it drifted down the Tiber's course.
First he was stoned by a mob, angered
At seeing him ride off alone to save himself
From the perils awaiting Rome.
So they waylaid him there
And unleashed on him their barrage,
Pelting without end uncounted stones
Like catapults upon city walls.
Then his body was torn to shreds,
Mutilated by knives and swords
As if he were the well-earned kill
Devoured so by a ravenous lion
Lording over its glorious catch.
Then into the Tiber they hoisted him,
And by its cruising current he sailed on,
Conveyed away to whatever fate awaited him.
For a mere seventy-eight days
Was he emperor of the West.

FALL OF THE WEST

Only two days passed then
Since the death of Petronius Maximus
When Gaiseric seized Rome for himself,
Throwing down the lofty aqueducts
Which for ages bore water to the city.
Down into crumbling ruin they fell,
No surer sign could a seer ever see
That at last the end of an age had come.
But as he did before with Attila
So again did Leo ride forth,
Hoping to turn aside Gaiseric's wrath
And spare the people tucked within,
Though he had not his master weapon,
The knowledge of Honoria's ambitions
Which so before turned the Huns aside.
Yet Gaiseric ensured there would be no massacre,
A small consolation for the temples plundered
And for the shiploads of civilians
Hauled off as slaves to African shores.

For fourteen days the Vandals plundered,
Stripping Jupiter's age-old temple
And hauling away Empress Licinia Eudoxia,
Once Valentinian's wife, and his daughters too,
Placidia and Eudocia, the latter who would
Once more be wedded off to Huneric,
To the son of the Vandals' king
As long ago she had been promised.
So off were hauled the heirs to an empire,
Stuffed away in serpent-prowed ships.
As long ago doom-struck Carthaginians
Were taken off as slaves in Roman lands,
So now were folk of faltering Rome

BOOK SIXTEEN

Returned to the city she destroyed
So many ages before.
A just punishment perhaps, but still
The pains would long be felt by all,
And families without number would grieve
For all they lost to that greed
Festering in the hearts of those Vandals
Who so cruelly plucked them away.
But of the Vandals caught in plunder,
Many held themselves in check,
Dragging people away as slaves, yes,
But only occasionally did they resort
To outright murder.
The same, however, cannot be said
For the one who went before their host,
For as mail-clad Vandals looted churches,
Down from the skies swooped in
The same terror that went before them
And shattered the fleet from Constantinople,
A beast that never before had been seen
Within the walls of high-born Rome
Now brought to her lowest low.

It was said he came to Gaiseric
Seated upon his throne off in Carthage
And egged him on the fight the Romans,
To exploit the weakness of the empire
And so haul off for himself
The abundant wealth of the Eternal City.
But Gaiseric had waited, bound by terms
Of a treaty earlier established between
Seafaring Vandals and beleaguered Romans.
But when his son was denied

Eudocia's hand in matrimony,
In that he found the pretext
He needed for such ambitions,
For surely such a promise broken
Was merit enough for invasion.
So across the sea Vandals sailed,
Spied from afar by Roman vessels,
A fleet gone far from Constantinople.
They knew then Gaiseric's motives
And so pressed the advance against him.
But against them came fiery intervention
As the bestial mastermind of it all
Unleashed his ire against the Romans,
Waylaying their fleet and flying off,
Waiting to himself roll around
In the wreck of the Eternal City,
Seated once upon seven ancient hills
Though now lowered into the grave.

Terrible though the form of Fanefiru was,
It is said this new Dragon was even greater,
For where the Elf was so compelled
By secret plots and by trickery,
But one sentiment poured through the veins
Of the beast brought down upon Rome.
Rage, unbridled rage came flooding down
As Sighlut barreled in, crashing through
Ramshackle shacks and putting to the torch
Houses without count, scorching them
With blasts of his infernal breath,
And he basked in the flaming glow
Like lizards content underneath beaming rays
Sent down from sun hanging overhead.

"Come now!" Sighlut cried. "Come you wretches!
Now at long last has Rome been dealt
Those blows she once delivered
Upon the rest of the world. Fire!
Fire and ruin rain upon you!
Arise and flee while you can,
For at long last your judgment comes!"

A clamor stirred from within the wreck
As Palladius, son of Petronius
And appointed Caesar of the Romans,
In haste gathered to his side
All the soldiers that he could afford,
To defy the Dragon as he rampaged
And so in defiance stave off his advance.
Sighlut was met by whistling arrows
Sent against his hide of armored scales.
Feathered fletchings brushed against his teeth,
Some clanking off of horny growths
While others pierced between his armor,
Inflicting pricking pains upon the beast.
Lethal, no, but they bought time yet
For others to flee from the serpent.
But for all the Dragon cared,
Wailing peasants could flee from him.
They offered good sport after all,
He could snatch them as they fled
Or scorch the fields to which they hastened,
Engulfing not their lives but their hopes,
The latter perhaps even a crueler fate
Than the one before.

Down he came upon this contingent,

Trampling Romans underfoot.
Some he snatched and threw upward,
Torching them as they flew through the air.
Others he simply brushed aside
With a sweep of his mighty tail.
But as for Palladius, wretched Palladius,
First Sighlut closed tight his jaws
Around Palladius' right arm
And jerked his fanged snout upward,
Tearing away the Caesar's limb
And leaving there in its wake a trail
Of splattered blood and pulverized bone.
Then upon Palladius he clamped his jaws,
Nearly tearing his foe in half
When through his body serrated teeth tore,
Slicing through his coat of armor
And crunching bone underneath.

In this carnage the Dragon reveled,
Rolling over the buildings he burned
As he sent the Romans into a rout.
On he continued the slaughter
Until he reached the Flavian Amphitheater,
Where of old warriors wrestled
And slew each other all for sport.
Beside this monument of slaughter he stood,
Watching as from afar Vandals took off,
Hastening to board their many ships
And thence sail on back to Carthage.
Sighlut then turned his hateful gaze
Back upon Rome in flames.
His eyes beheld before the Amphitheater
A huge colossus of the old sun-god,

BOOK SIXTEEN

Earlier built into the likeness of Nero.
The statue towered a hundred feet high
And at its form Sighlut marveled.
A fine prize this city would be
Once he had claimed it for himself!
But more slaughter was to be had first,
For all about him ran scattered civilians
Running without aim from his splendor.
So he set himself upon them, plucking up
All those he could ensnare with fanged maw.
A huddled mass he quickly cornered,
Tucked beneath the statue's shadow,
And there they trembled and quivered,
Each one expecting a fiery death.

Through the chaos of the sack,
Honoria hastened through the streets
And clove her way through a group
Of Vandals lost in their plundering and
Poised to run some hapless soul through.
She took aim and drove her sword
Against Sarus at the root of his neck,
Sword-point going clean through his throat
And his armor rattled as he fell dead.
Then against Sindered and Aioulf she went,
With a single stroke slicing both their bellies
As down they fell bedrabbled with blood.
On she fought, lopping off Theodahad's head
As with another stroke she clove through vertebrae.
She brawled with Vithericus too until
Triple-lanced Sophia barreled in,
Snatching him up in her beak
And tossing him through the air

To be hewn by Evoric's sword.
Down to the ground he fell, and others
Of the Vandals rushed upon these foes
Only to be beaten back in full rout,
Either trampled by raging beast
Or cut short by human blades.

But their deeds gripped the attention
Of dread Dragon poised to slay
Those who cowered from his might.
His sights shifted, focused on a prey
That might offer him greater sport
Than peasants caught in a full out.
Infernal furnaces began to broil
From deep within the Dragon's breast,
But still the three stood there,
Honoria, Evoric and Sophia
Before the civilians made their stand.
Sophia wagged her fearsome phalanx
Huffing and puffing as from her snout
Arose an inflated air sac, and blaring cries
Issued from her dreadful honks.
Evoric threw in the air a sphere of light
That warded off draconic breath
As on the cacophonous sirens continued,
The sac dilating and contracting
Each and every time Sophia cried.
As flames like waves beat down upon him
Evoric trembled, drenched in sweat
And a wall of fire rose before him.
But still he strived to hold off the attack.
So as he contended with blasts of fire,
Sophia rushed into the fray,

Fearsome Triceratops throwing up her spears,
And driving them deep into the Dragon's hide.
Then from afar came another combatant
From the wreck of high-borne Rome,
Jiggles lunging with jaws opened wide
And rushing with hot lust for battle
As he wrapped his fangs around serpentine neck.
Twisting and jerking a mouth filled with knives,
The mighty Tyrannosaurus threw his foe aside,
Sending the Dragon crashing
Against the ancient form of Nero
Who cracked and nearly fell then and there.
Together ancient animals tore at their foe,
Pushing him through crumbled dwellings
And slamming him against the amphitheater.
His neck held in place by Jiggles' jaws,
Sighlut could do little to stave them off.
Wildly his head twisted about, spewing small volleys
Of jumping flames with each gaseous gasp.

From a safe distance awestruck peasants
Looked on at the dread clash before them,
Watching Sighlut's spastic movements.
On their protectors pressed the attack.
As Evoric probed about for weaknesses
The Dragon twisted and turned,
Tossed about by prehistoric assailants.
But as Honoria timed her blows
And watched the Dragon writhe,
Consumed by an agonizing pain,
She saw a richly engraved band
Wrapped around his scaled forefinger,
Even now it fueled his rage.

Again and again, Sophia drove on
Keen-edged horns against the Dragon's hide,
Sometimes stabbing, other times driving
Him deeper into Jiggle's biting grasp,
Now poised to tear apart the windpipe.
But as two strove with the one,
Again and again they hurled him
Against Nero's looming colossus,
And with each bash that statue cracked
And began to falter to their blows.
At last Sighlut came hurling through,
Blasting apart the sun god's legs,
And down the hundred-foot titan fell,
The rays that crowned his head
Piercing through the Dragon's nape
As he fell trapped beneath a fallen monument.
Even now he hissed most pitifully,
And pulpy blood began to surge forth
From uncounted grievous wounds.
And as Sighlut struggled to stir
And push aside Sol's overbearing weight,
Honoria scrambled toward his writhing claws
And tried at once to remove the ring.

But Sighlut pushed her aside
And heaved to overturn fallen statue.
So again Honoria pressed after him,
Raising aloft her keen-edged blade
And bearing it down upon his finger.
At once the ring was removed
And the Dragon reared and cried out.
His hide hardened and grew black with ash
As like an insect's shell it cracked,

BOOK SIXTEEN

Foul magics of ancient Elves oozing out
As a wind bore aloft his molted hide
And carried it away to oblivion.

Beastly warriors drew themselves back,
And at once their foe's form was changed,
Cracked shell revealing former human shape.
There on the ground, cold and naked,
Sighlut huddled up, nursing lacerations
Lined up and down his battered body.
Yet though his form survived,
The once mighty warrior seemed so frail
Quivering against the fallen colossus.
His mangled body was still quite large,
Though long sapped of its strength
And of its heroic vigor.
His spirits were utterly broken,
Shattered at built up rage
Against she who hurled his people to war.

And Sighlut cried out, "I only wanted
"To do right by my people. That is all.
To find that you hurled us all to war,
That you brought upon us so much death
And yet were free to go as you please-
How else can I answer that?
So I have broken your world
As you once broke mine. Justice,
No longer will justice cry out to silence."
Then Sighlut searched for a blade,
Weeping and crying out, "Begone!
Where's my sword? I'll kill you all!
We'll see who's the hero then!"

FALL OF THE WEST

But as Honoria and Evoric
Planned to approach Sighlut
And offer him their clemency,
The War-Sky came to them and spoke.
"So now falls the Eternal City.
This is incredible, is it not?
Still you continue to fight, hoping
That by violence you may ward it off.
When will you learn, girl?
When will you at last understand
That by this double standard
You shall be so soon consumed?"

"We are not you," Honoria answered.
"Nor shall we ever become like you.
There is a difference between you and I.
No longer do I care to kill my foe,
To catch the villain at all cost.
All that has done is break me
And a myriad souls I never knew.
But saving the innocent and
Healing the harmed? Watch and see.
That is a far greater purpose."

Honoria knelt down before Sighlut
And Evoric followed her example.
Extending her hand toward his,
She offered the fallen Frank
Some help in getting on his feet.
"You are more than this," she said.
"You need not writhe like this.
Rise up and come with us."

BOOK SIXTEEN

"I would sooner die," he answered,
His hands clasped tight around
A small sword he eyed, discarded
During the thick of Palladius'
Failed attack against his draconic form.
Rising up until he rested on his knees,
Sighlut swung the blade at them,
And quickly they leapt backward.
"May I perish before I so dishonor
The legacy of my brothers-in-arms.
A curse then on both your houses!
May you live long and in misery,
Doomed to forever watch
As all before you falls apart."

He continued to swing, twisting
In vain as they slowly backed away,
Watching the miserable wreck of a man
Fight off swarms of thin air.
So again the War-Sky spoke to them..
"Your mercy has done nothing.
It never will. Surely you've seen enough
To know this shall always be. This world's too bitter,
Too racked with pain to forget
The uncounted slights she has endured.
Always will this fight be in vain."

Honoria answered him, "Then
Through this vanity I will walk,
And it hasn't been harder than today,
When at last both empires crumble
Despite the better part of my efforts,
All of my labors discarded like refuse.

FALL OF THE WEST

I know the road ahead will be hard,
Filled with suffering and anguish.
We may struggle a thousand years in vain,
For has not all of human history
Been one fell deed after another?
You might say so, but I won't;
I refuse to validate you even now.
I do not care where this path may lead,
For I will go down it nonetheless.
I will fight whenever I must,
And always will I take the chance
To extend a hand of pardon,
No matter how it will be answered.
In the face of all telling us to turn back,
We will persevere, we will endure,
And- by God- triumph will come,
If not in my time, then in an age to be."

"Though God already knows," Evoric said,
"History will see which of us is right.
But as for me, and Honoria too,
We will strive to be better
Than our predecessors taught us.
Above all, we will have hope."

"This will I watch," the War-Sky answered.
"Though still I am doubtful you will succeed,
Your optimism has impressed me.
Once I would have called it young naiveté,
But no. You two have seen too much
To be considered naïve. Foolish?
I do not know. Perhaps that's so.
But your averted sacrifice in Panhušu

BOOK SIXTEEN

And your demeanor here have stirred me.
I will be watching, though no longer scheming.
History will see which of us is right.
This is not the last you'll see of me."

Then the War-Sky left them there
And Honoria turned again to Sighlut,
Though she dared not approach him,
Still swinging about with rage.
But even as he cried out curses
And so longed for Honoria's doom,
She took pity on his wretched fate,
And she seized some salves Evoric found,
Some bandages too, and tossed them
Down toward Sighlut's injured self.
And as they walked away,
At last he ceased his screaming,
His wearied arms dropped the sword
As downcast gaze beheld the offering,
A gracious boon given him,
Though he brought Rome to her knees.

Evoric and Honoria then went off,
Standing before the old imperial palace.
And as they gazed upon ancient spectacle,
Evoric solemnly broke the silence.
"The Western Roman Empire is gone
She may still live in name, yes,
Even if only for a little while,
But she is a dying animal caught
Alongside the edge of the road.
Come the next generation,
She will not live even in name,

FALL OF THE WEST

Succeeded only by the Roman Church.
Take a moment, your highness,
And bask in the warmth of the fire
And in the glow of the rising sun.
Though all the powers of the earth
Have tried to destroy you, still you stand.
You have outlived them all."

"And still you call me *highness*,"
Honoria sighed as she smirked.

"I know you miss those days of splendor,"
Evoric answered. "You miss
The splendor and the regal architecture.
I picked up on that even before
We came into Karoputaru,
But were you not proclaimed
By your brother to be his successor?
Besides, it's not as if the smirk
You throw my way whenever
I say it isn't obvious, your highness."

Looking out at the charred buildings
All around them and then at
The emptied palace, Honoria said,
"You know, there was a time
When that dwelling could have been mine.
Oh, those were different days.
All this time I've strived for peace,
Peace and to thwart Attila.
But there was something else,
Another thing I wanted:
Through sleepless nights I dreamed

That I might see my family smile again
And to be counted among them.
But that will never happen.
My nieces go now to Carthage,
And my mother's been long dead.
My entire family I bury now
With but a single goodbye
To my dear Valentinian.
Is it emptiness I feel now,
Or is it relief to know that
The weight of the world hangs
On me no more? Of my house
I am all that remains. I am alone,
Never will I be as a queen
Nor share power again with my kin.
There is no place here for an empress,
Though my predecessors proclaimed it.
But in solitude have I been freed.
No matter what, I accept my fate."

Evoric smirked, "I do think
You may have a kingdom of your own,
That city you so lately proposed to me.
I've not so soon forgotten the words
We shared ere Attila drove us apart.
As those who love and who avenge
May we from this hidden throne
Continue to aid this land and others still."

He knelt on one knee, holding
His sword in his hand so that
The tip of the blade dug into the earth.
Honoria saw his gesture and she smiled,

FALL OF THE WEST

Gently tapping his shoulders
With the flat edge of her blade.
"If you're to be my co-regent,"
She said, "you must bear a token,
A symbol of our shared domain
As masters of the wild and lords
Of labors in this age of turmoil."

She lowered herself, and placed
On Evoric's finger a ring.
He recognized that band as
The same one sent to Attila long ago,
Returned to its owner with his final breath.
Gladly he met her embrace, and
Looking into her eyes he said,
"What do you think should be
Your first decree, your highness?"

"Soon we may yet be joined formally,
But there are other duties to see to first.
There are people gathered round,
Their homes burnt to the ground,
Loved ones hauled away to Carthage.
Let us dig them from the rubble,
Use the mighty beasts brought for war
And with them save what we can.
Tend to the wounded and mourn
With those who have lost."

So they did, and long they labored,
Using the strength of their allies
Called forth from Karoputaru
To push aside toppled towers

BOOK SIXTEEN

And clear out collapsed churches.
Those they found were promptly
Reunited with what relatives remained
In this shattered city on seven hills.
Out from hiding came the children,
Amazed by the animals before them.
Taking turns they offered gentle scratches
To these gargantuan animals, laughing
Whenever one of them sneezed,
Giggling for the first time in ages.

When he saw this Leo joined them,
Rome's bishop calling those who could
To join them in their labor,
Yoking together horses and mules,
Teams driven on through the city
Carrying away piles of rubble
And the slain to be buried.
Clothed in robes of mournful black, Leo
Caught sight of those too weak to help,
Offering them food and drink
To nourish their aching limbs.
Then he took his seat and watched
As massive beasts gave them aid,
Huge Jiggles sifting through rubble
And lumbering Sophia hauling away
Burdens of loaded goods and heaps
Of debris hoisted upon her back.
When the time presented itself,
Honoria and Evoric left Rome's heights
For but a brief while, at once casting
Anadavarenu into the sea where
Never again it would sit upon

FALL OF THE WEST

The fingers of any mortal. Yet tidings
Of all that happened would soon spread,
Reaching the ears of one Avitus
Seated in the court of Theodoric,
Son of his namesake and a brother
To Thorismund, whom he slew, seizing for himself
Dominion over the Visigoths.
In his embassy Avitus had lingered,
And when news of the sack reached him
He would come to Italy as an emperor
Accepted by both the Visigoths and the Senate.
Perhaps he would try to bring Rome back
To her elder days of glory, though it was clear
That her time had come and it had gone.

But still those in ransacked Rome labored,
Not to empower themselves,
But to nurse their wounds
And to ensure their own survival,
The efforts spearheaded by Leo,
Clergy serving in the place of kings.
There was no man or woman in Rome
Now who idled without labor,
For even those who had not the strength
To haul away piles of withered stone
Or carry off their fallen friends
Were weighed down by their sorrow
And lamented all that had been lost.
Through the gates they bore the dead,
Holding a funeral in their honor,
Not that of kings and conquerers
But of the common folk lost
To the terrors of this awful war.

They flew toward the wagons
And laid their hands on the dead,
Weeping round a thousand corpses.

"Ah, high-born Rome," Leo spoke,
"Long have you stood as the peak
Of Italy's power, and though still
You may stand for a while longer,
Your supremacy has come and gone.
Once more shall you be overthrown,
And the generation after us will live
In a world where you are not master.
You are not the Eternal City
As our ancestors once believed.
So now we heed blessed Augustine
Who years ago so wrote
That earthly rule could never last,
It could never gain ultimate triumph.
But still I will weep for you
And for those you have lost.
Even now as you lay dying
We will give you warm embrace,
Bidding to you our final words
Addressed to an age now gone,
Overcome by tears for sorrow,
And lightened with hope for days to come.
Sorrow may last through the night,
But with dawn may joy yet come."

Bitterly then did Pope Leo weep,
And Roman folk joined in his lament.
But as they wailed and mourned
Away from them Honoria walked

Once more to speak with Evoric.
But as she went she looked back,
Her eyes fixed on those mournful throngs
Gathered in lament for the dead.
They seemed so cold and stiff, even
Those still in the height of youthful vigor.
As at Jalaŋgül before, there was little joy
To be found among the Romans.
So Honoria saw, and so she continued
And spoke once more to Evoric saying,
"Long ago you whisked me away,
Off to a land old and wonderful,
And watching these majestic animals
I found both awe and joy. Then too
Did you also say to me guilt alone
Could not compel me to my full purpose,
And finally I see the truth in your speech.
Let's do for those all around us as you
Once did for me and found a city there."

Evoric answered, "Then you may yet
Do as you so lately declared, for off
Karoputaru sits an island unclaimed
By any city of the Swart Elves, huge
And rich with resources. There perhaps
You might build your city for those
Who so would like to start anew.
Rome and Jalaŋgül may be lost to us,
But a nobler proper city may rise in their place."

Honoria nodded and turned herself
Toward those who long had mourned.
"What sorrow grips your hearts!

Come with me, those who will,
For Evoric and I may show to you
A land ancient beyond all reckoning,
And across its plains migrate forms
Such as those that came with us,
Wondrous creatures them all.
Take some time away from sorrow,
Lost in awe and in wonder,
Overcome by adventure.
See for yourself a Land of Dragons.
Older than human empires.
For as Aeneas led his Trojans long ago,
In lands far off can we again start anew."

Most among the folk refused, hesitant
To venture off into wild unknowns.
But many among them consented.
Three thousand followed Honoria,
Eager to see more than dreary gloom
And share in such wondrous sights.
So they went after Honoria and Evoric,
But she was not content only
To offer aid to her Roman kin.
Far away she went with her host,
Joined in turn by Goths and Gepids
And others so wearied by the battles
That long had ravaged Europe
Until at last she came upon Jalaŋgül
Lorded over by Attila's sons Ernak
And distant Dengizich, who abroad
Sought to punish those who had plundered
The riches from this wretched city.
Already had her heights fallen

FALL OF THE WEST

And her people caught in disarray,
Gripped in lament even as before
Gepids and Goths plundered their dwellings.
Rumors had already reached the Huns
Of what fate befell Rome itself.
Angrily, Huns gathered from their yurts
Hooting against Honoria as they seized
Their arms, grieved at the sight
Of hated Romans gathered round.

Before them rose Ernak, and he spoke.
"You were a friend to my brother
And a spouse to my father, Honoria,
Though you came under another name.
Have you now come to usurp my throne
And guarantee my own downfall?"

"I have no need to," Honoria answered.
"Already has your strength fallen.
Jalaŋgül's withered palisades attest well
To the sad plight of your people.
You are already lost to history's annals,
Ernak; your name and mine also
Shall only be known to learned scholars
With no better use of their time.
In Europe, we are lost to history.
But I offer your kin and mine
A chance at a new beginning
Far off in distant Karoputaru,
On the shores of pristine Talalit.
No finer island- Evoric says-
Could house this nation of refugees."

BOOK SIXTEEN

And Ernak answered her, "What honor
Could be held for the fathers of my host
If we mingle with those we swore to slay?
Away with you! May you and
Any worthless traitors who run off
And clasp hands with your host rot!"

With a shout he left the assembly,
Holding fast hatred to his heart.
But others saw the folly of his speech,
And a chieftain called Öktar spoke for them.
"Children of the steppe, the blame
For the troubles of this age lie upon
The Romans' shoulders and our own.
Folly among our bickering nations
Led us to this crumbling of empires,
And already other factions wait to rise
And fill the void left by our demise.
Fools would we be if we ignored
The chance offered by Honoria
To build for us a newborn city
Like those famed Trojans ages ago."

Many Huns returned to the rubble
And to make one last concerted effort
To leave their footprint on the affairs
Of tumultuous Europe. Yet others,
Several thousands from their ranks,
Saw the wisdom of Öktar's speech
And with him followed Honoria
And Evoric, whom long they had seen
In the company of the late Attila.
But now he led them far across the earth

FALL OF THE WEST

Until at last they saw Karoputaru,
Unfettered by the weight of faltering Rome
And by withered Jalaŋgül, and across
The seas they sailed until at last
They reached the isle of Talalit.

Up above shone the sunless sky,
Overcome by celestial clouds
Ablaze with radiant bands of color.
Upon the shores of that far-flung island
They began to work upon a city,
A new Rome for those who so wished
To continue her legacy even as Europe
Continued to break into fractious nations.
There they built a city called Elpis,
Hope in the tongue of the Greeks.
Often groups of Romans, Goths, and Huns
Would go out and, following after
The lead of Honoria and of Evoric,
See before their very eyes all of
The vast expanses of Karoputaru.
Through stampeding herds they weaved
And they trekked through dense woodlands
As they walked beneath colossal beasts.
They were even borne aloft on wings,
Seated upon aerial steeds soaring far
Over mountains and across seaways.

Down below the cloud-frothed waves
They could see creatures slither below,
Monsters of the primordial deep
Breaching for air or snatching fish
With draconic jaws lined with teeth.

BOOK SIXTEEN

Even as, like huge sea serpents,
Predators leapt from rising waves
And from blasts of salty sea water,
Tried in vain to clamp their jaws
Around Honoria's winged steed,
She could only laugh as she rode off,
Heart pumping with adventure's thrills.
She looked on at Evoric, who too laughed,
And off they rode beyond the horizon.

Seated upon their winged beasts,
Those gathered round understood
That Honoria found what she
And all of them had long craved.
Though still she bore her many scars,
No longer did they weigh her down.
The heavens shone in her starlit eyes
And she proclaimed, "No power
On the earth or in hell below
Can ever bring me down.
Flying with you, I fly freely,
Saved by God's good favors
And by the will to endure.
No longer can I despair,
Battered though the world and I
May be. Hope is my cloak,
And wearing it I can embrace
All the turmoils of the age.
Continue this flight with me, Evoric.
The sun has set and risen again.
After every end comes a new beginning."

At long last, Honoria is content.

APPENDICES

ON THE LANGUAGES
AND PEOPLES OF KAROPUTARU

Wešikeriaya

The language of the Swart Elves, Wešikeriaya is written using a syllabic script, rather than an actual alphabet, and consists of approximately 100 syllabic signs, though there is some slight dialectical variation. The script is read from left to right and much of Wešikeriaya vocabulary seems to bear some distant relationship to words from a number of Bronze Age languages, particularly Linear B, Cypriot, and Hittite, and it may be that their language developed into a form ancestral to its present incarnation as they interacted via maritime trade with the peoples that spoke these languages.

The oldest historical evidence of this language dates back to the Middle Bronze Age (c. 1900 B.C.E.) in tablets recovered by the Swart Elves during the collapse of the island of Sikeria, and the vocabulary is admittedly quite different from even tablets just a few centuries younger, indicative of the reality that Wešikeriaya did not always have the Bronze Age Mediterranean touch it currently bears.

Of the historic influence of the Swart Elves beyond the bounds of their realm in Karoputaru, there is little that can be said with much confidence, though it seems that they are synonymous with the

APPENDICES

Phaeacians of Homer's *Odyssey*. The narration of
their history in Book Four bears many elements similar to Odysseus' encounter the Phaeacians, and their
names bear a distant similarity (Oruseu=Odysseus,
Arikenou =Alcinous, Sikeria=Scheria, *et cetera*). Although Homer never describes the Phaeacians as being grey-skinned, it should be noted that the Greek
word *phaios* (φαιός) does in fact mean 'grey,' perhaps a
preservation of some faint memory of the grey-
skinned seafarers.

The narration of Book Six and the backstory
given by the War-Sky in Book Fourteen also seem to
suggest that a number of Swart Elves joined the infamous Sea Peoples, a confederation of seafaring
folk known to have attacked Egypt and several other
notable empires around the time of the Late Bronze
Age collapse. This might mean that the Wešekeriasi/
Swart Elves are synonymous with those Weshesh Sea
Peoples mentioned as going against Rameses III,
known from an inscription in the mortary temple of
Rameses III at Medinet Habu, or the Swart Elves
may be another group unmentioned in the pharaonic
records.

Stangaz

Stangaz is the language of the Thurs, who call
themselves the Gromangaz. The language has no
written script, and as such there is little archaeological
evidence detailing the morphology and syntax of
Stangaz. It can only be learned by communication
with either the Thurs or an outsider who has taken
up their language. The phonology of Stangaz clearly

resembles Proto-Germanic, and many of the words seem to draw back to Proto-Germanic origins. It is said by the Thurs that they first learned to speak when *mannazun nurdzra* ('folk of the North') came to their crags and gave them the gift of speech, and it may be that those who came to them were originally from northern Europe during the latter half of the first millennium B.C.E.

A large, troll-like people standing four meters high with hides thick like moss-green scales, the Thurs live in a region called Dawwo-Hanhilaz, a plateau surrounded by a series of volcanic peaks near Karoputaru's southern borders. The Swart Elves rarely venture this far south, usually only a small band of adventurers or some warmonger seeking mercenaries to bolster his or her army. The majority of the interior of their domain is a semi-arid plateau populated by strange mammals including brontotheres, uintatheres, indricotheres, and entelodonts.

Due to their remoteness, little is known about Thurs culture. The Thurs live in tribal communities headed by two separate leaders, the Guðandun and the Werzleith, the shaman and the chieftain. The Guðandun serves as a religious figurehead for the tribe and prays to the gods on behalf of the Thurs. The Werzleith is in control of the political and the militaristic side of things. The role of Guðandun is hereditary, while each new Werzleith is selected by the Guðandun.

APPENDICES

The Guðandun usually choses the strongest Thurs of the tribe and performs upon the Werzleith a ceremony called the Aitizguð, "Possession by the gods." The Guðandun carves off the flesh covering the incoming Werzleith's heart and, being blessed with magic, is said to send a surge of energy- the blessing of the gods- into the Werzleith's heart. The wound is not healed after this, but simply covered up with an adamantine guard which covers up the left pectoral, forever a sign of the Werzleith's prestige and position.

Little else is known about the Thurs, for the Swart Elves have historically made minimal effort to document their ways. It is curious indeed that the Huns seemed more inclined to come upon the Thurs during their brief excursion into the Karoputaru than the Swart Elves have in the entire 3,000-year span of their occupation of the region. The people of Elpis have tried to engage with the Thurs from time to time, but the great folk of Dawwo-Hanhilaz showed little interests in the material goods or the religion offered by the Elpians.

Elpian

The Elpian tongue is one spoken by those who travelled with Honoria and founded the city of Elpis. It is written using the Latin script, and the modern variant of this language is a clear descendant of a combination of the Latin, Gothic, and Hunnic languages spoken by those people who first raised up the city. However, Latin remains the language used for official documents and the inscriptions on monumental architecture.

Under the Augustan Dynasty, the Elpians have thrived as a multi-ethnic population, living on relatively friendly terms with the Swart Elves with whom they frequently exchange goods and art. The dominant religion by far is Christianity, and an elite theological academy was built in Elpis c. 1050, one which even those most prestigious from among the scholars of the Swart Elves have come to revere.

Arhkvun

Arhkvun is said by the Swart Elves to be the inborn language of all primordial creatures-the Šaliyanka- though few among them ever learn to speak it. Among these few is Nildahgiiv, warden of the World Tree Artaru. As such, there is little written information on Arhkvun, and those Elves versed in the language tend to be reclusive scholars living out on the edge of the wild or in the hollows of Temekuš. All attempts to tie Arhkvun down to some linguistic origin, both by myself and by the Swart Elves, have been unsuccessful.

ON THE AUTHORSHIP
OF *AUGUSTA*

The author of *Augusta* is never explicitly mentioned by name in any of the earliest known manuscripts, which have been dated via palaeography to approximately the beginning of the tenth century, although some would push this date back to the latter half of the ninth century. Regardless, there are several scholarly traditions dealing with the matter of authorship that can be explored to some capacity, even if a definitive answer cannot at this moment be reached.

Late Anonymous Authorship

The first, and by far the youngest of these traditions, is that the epic was written at least three centuries *ex post facto* by an anonymous author who shall likely never be identified. It was first put forth by the scholar Wedanu in his edition of *Augusta* published in 1643. Perhaps the strongest argument for this case is the quasi-prophecy in Book One foretelling the rise of Charlemagne (see page 14).

> *Yet one day shall from the Franks*
> *Emerge a mighty kingdom*
> *And among their number shall be named*
> *An emperor of the West,*
> *The first since the fall of high-born Rome.*

APPENDICES

Criticisms of this argument usually fall under one of two categories, the first being that this semi-cryptic foretelling of the Holy Roman Empire was an addition made by a scribe transcribing an earlier manuscript. Others argue that the author of the text had some sort of interaction with Nildahgiiv, and it is known that the *Duanrok Mahtviiri* ('Warden of the World Tree') has come to perceive time differently in her long years at Artaru.

Nildahgiiv herself has seemed to deny the validity of this perhaps more cynical tradition of authorship, although when I spoke with her she remained cryptic on the identity of *Augusta*'s true author, saying it is better the scholars learn to wrestle with the issues themselves rather than use her seeming omniscience on the matter as a crutch. To be fair, I will admit that the mystery of the matter makes the question all the more enticing for me, though my opinion may not be shared by all.

Authorship by Evoric

None of the Swart Elf scholars to date would assert that *Augusta* was an autobiographical text, although many have argued that the oldest forms of the epic were actually written by none other than Evoric himself. Those who adhere to this tradition typically hold the opinion that Evoric sought to preserve the memory of Honoria as he knew her to counteract the legacy he reckoned would be instilled by the works of Roman historians. If this is the case, then it seems that finally his gamble has paid off, albeit fifteen hundred years after he first penned these words.

Authorship by Harmonia

By far the most popular tradition would contest that *Augusta* was written by Harmonia, the sole child born c.458 to Honoria and Evoric, just three years after the Vandals' sack of Rome. She is known most strongly for boosting amicable relationships between the people of Elpis and the Elves of Newa Sikeria. Christianity, while not the majority religion of Karoputaru, has also claimed a substantial foothold as a result of this. It should be noted that while most Christian Swart Elves do recognize the existence of their ancestral gods, they regard these beings as either spirits or powerful entities lower in might to the Christian God. The monolatry vs. monotheism debate is a common subject of discourse for Swart Elf and Elpian theologians.

It was Harmonia who introduced the study of Latin to the Swart Elves, a study which has survived in Karoputaru to this day, and it was through this shared understanding of the Latin language that I first came to learn Wešikeriaya when I explored Karoputaru. Writing an epic concerning her Roman-born mother would certainly seem consistent with her apparent goal of preserving the memories of late Roman Antiquity in Karoputaru, and I admittedly am also of the opinion that Harmonia is the author of *Augusta's* earliest manuscripts.

APPENDICES

One of the libraries at Kunasa has preserved a small sampling of a fragmentary text dating as far back as the middle of the sixth century, perhaps only a hundred years after the events narrated by *Augusta*. This parchment bears a single Latin phrase:

ATRO ARCE EBURATA SUBLIMA ZARSUMOT

This phrase is remarkably similar to one that appears in *Augusta*:

DEMUSO ZARŠUMOT INE GURATA LAHAŠA
MUKARA

"... *[by] Dread Zaršu-Mot in [his] lofty ivory citadel.*"
(Book Fourteen, see page 312)

Some Swart Elf scholars have suggested that this phrase may be the sole surviving remnant of earlier Latin manuscripts, and they have even gone so far as to suggest that the original author- Harmonia or another- first wrote *Augusta* in Latin before it was rendered in its longer-lived Wešikeriaya counterpart. Given the scarcity of evidence one way or another, any conclusions made from this data must no doubt be considered speculative. However, the argument made by these scholars would hardly be inconsistent for those who do insist on having Harmonia as the author of *Augusta*. Perhaps more early manuscripts will yet be uncovered so as to allow for a more definitive conclusion.

ON ANADAVARA
AND HIS DRAGON-RING

The Germanic peoples of the north once told tales of a magic ring, a band imbued with the power to multiply the wealth of its bearer. This ring, however, was both blessed and cursed, for it would cast upon its bearer the shape and form of a terrible dragon. This ring was Andvaranaut, forged by the dwarf Andvari, and it is known to modern scholars in texts such as the Völsunga Saga. The story of this ring helped to shape Richard Wagner's famous *Der Ring des Nibelungen*, and it would also an inspiration for J.R.R. Tolkien's own ring of power. Before there was Andvaranaut, however, there was Anadavarenu. Before there was Andvari, there was Anadavara.

Over four thousand years ago (c. late 22nd century B.C.E.), the Swart Elves had yet to come to their jungle home of Karoputaru. Indeed, they had not even settled the island of Sikeria. In those distant days they lived as disparate nomads wandering the wide wastes of the world. Rarely they stayed in one place for long, save for those who lived in small cultic sanctuaries tucked within deep forests.

Among those was the cult of Apatiyo- the Master Artificer, who no longer holds cultic significance among the Elves. In those days he did, and his chiefest sanctuary was hidden somewhere in what would one day become Roman Gaul. His high priest was Anadavara, who by forge-craft fashioned many mighty gifts and bestowed them upon the surrounding tribes and communities.

His benevolence was not unending, and the historical record does not record why he betrayed the god to whom he was so devoted. Poets and novelists are wont to create their own explanations for the sake of constructing a more complete narrative. Some of these are truly quite compelling, even if they are all mere speculation.

But Anadavara forsook the smith-god, seizing for himself the riches stored up by Apatiyo's priesthood. Having claimed these goods as his own, the disillusioned Swart Elf hid them in mountainous caverns I dare not reveal. He heaped up the gold and riches in a mound that has since then been named Gold Tor, and in the heart of Gallic mountains he forged his final gift for the world. As he began the creation of this deadly ring, it is said he sang a chorus which still can be heard whispered into the ears of those who would wear it:

Apatiyo pašau gei metu
Keredai toa dolu ema
Medaso hanoši galaï
Baï karuke huša karuke
Šapeï didosi enaku
Šumaku gei he'eu anapu
Kešo abumo seko eme
Eruno hapaïma ema
Zeü pašau, teu eme.

Ine deuvu keïri epi
Kuropabizo belušaï
Ša'abari 'ne razau daako
Anabomuši Wazezoši
Pa'aïrore tešu uše
Pa'aïrore razau daaku
Anepu wanakuši zeu
Arezamoši 'paparusu
Gei banako baarusu

APPENDICES

Translation: *"I renounce [you] Apatiyo, and with your art I will forge my gift. To the damned it calls- a herald of fire, a herald of death. To its bearer it will grant power unmatched and woes unending. Hate [is] my only friend. Vengeance [is] my wergild. I defy you, my god. In the deep, it lies upon Gold Tor, adding to [its] splendor in the dark of the world, [where dwell?] the Unnamed Things, older than our gods, older than the world, [and] lords of the endless dark. The unformed shapes will seize and swallow [you] whole."*

This ring, Anadavarenu, he bestowed with a blessing and a curse. When one wore it, always would it add to the wealth of the treasure hoard, and this promise of assured abundance no doubt tempted many more adventurous types to seek out the ring for themselves. This gift came at a cost, however, and whoever bore it would take on the form of one of Sikeria's dreaded Erepši- the dread fire-breathing Dragons. For most, this was truly a dire curse, for surely it guaranteed exile from society at large. For the militaristic opportunist, however, it presented an opportunity, one that was pursued even two-and-a-half millennia later when Europe stood poised to tear itself apart at the end of Antiquity.

GLOSSARY OF
SWART ELF NAMES AND TITLES

Throughout the entirety of *Augusta,* there is an immense number of names referring to people, places, and other such things which will likely not be known to the average reader. I have decided to limit this glossary to simply words used by the Swart Elves for two reasons. Firstly, a complete glossary would be dreadfully long and thus consume an absurdly unnecessary number of pages. Secondly, those other entries can easily be looked up either via the internet or some other source, whereas Wešikeriaya and co. and are virtually unknown languages and therefore no English-based sources exist to define or clarify these names and terms. I hope the justifications listed are sufficient for the reader and that this prepared list of entries serves as an accessible resource for those readers so inclined to utilize it.

Aïasa- A large male Suiayo apparently known for his fierce temperament, Aïasa was a participant at the battles of Catalaunian Plains and at the mountainous Bones of Arana.

Aikaza- An animal indigenous to Karoputaru known for the bony dome atop its skull, the Aikaza is otherwise called *Pachycephalosaurus wyomingensis.* They are aggressive animals and sometimes hunted by Swart Elves for their hides or for sport rather than the quality of their meat.

APPENDICES

Aïšti- An Orokeruša-jumper of Puaita, Aïšti was an accomplished athlete whose prowess was unmatched. The heyday of her athleticism was during the fifth century, between 445 and 460.

Akareu- Known nowhere else in the historical record, Akareu was a Swart Elf slain by Ellac in Keradoru.

Akeru- A host-leader (*lawakutaso*) of unknown history, Akeru is attested only in a commemorative inscription at Parahu-Ku. He appears to have been regarded in ancient some sort of demigod-like figure, although his historicity is not verifiable.

Anadavara- Known in Norse mythology as Andvari, Anadavara was a Swart Elf who forged the ring Anadavarenu (Norse Andvaranaut), said to multiply the abundance of his treasure hoard. He placed a curse on it when his treasure was robbed from him, condemning its wearers to take on the shape and characteristics of a Dragon. Beyond forging the ring, he was a priest of Apatiyo and lived circa 2150 B.C.E.

Anadavarenu- The ring forged by Anadavara, Anadavarenu multiplies his abundance of gold, though at the cost of turning its bearer into a deadly Dragon.

Apatiyo- The Master Artificer, Apatiyo was the craftsman god of the Swart Elves, born to the goddess Ara. He has many forges, all of them tucked inside volcanos. Though acknowledged by the residents of Karoputaru, he is not actively worshipped and has no existing cults or temples dedicated to him.

APPENDICES

Ara- The queen of heaven, Ara is the consort of Dewo and feared for her temper. She appears to be a rather generalist deity, not specializing in one particular sphere of influence, though she is said to watch over childbirth a bit more frequently than other gods. The center of her cult is at the temple in Puaita, and the Orokeruša is often regarded as her herald.

Araksadra- A native to Puaita born in 425, Araksadra was the twin sister to Kuanipou and a member of the Forest-Walkers.

Arana- An ancient goddess of the sea, Arana seems to have embodied the chaos of primordial creation. She is said to be the mother of all monsters, and she was slain by Dewo shortly after he assumed kingship over all the other gods. She appears typologically comparable to the Mesopotamian Tiamat.

Artaru- Attested in Norse mythology as Yggdrasil, Artaru connects the many worlds of Germanic/ Swart Elf cosmology, along with realms not included in either mythos. Though depicted as an ash tree in Norse Myth, Artaru appears to have been a stone tree far underground in Toratanatu. It is known in Arhkvun as Mahtviir.

Arikenou- King of the Elves when they still lived on the island of Sikeria, Arikenou was slain when the sea god bore his wrath against the island to appease him. Arikenou was the first king of the Swart Elves after dissolving the assembly predating his rule, and he was succeeded by his son Laodame.

APPENDICES

Atana- Goddess born to Dewo, Atana is most often associated with tactics. She is a virgin goddess and fiercely defends women who are taken advantage of. The center of her cult is Kunasa, though her worship is found throughout Karoputaru. She often carries a shield and her favored animal is the Toraku.

Demodoko- Unmentioned elsewhere in historical records, Demodoko was slain by Ellac in Keradoru.

Dewo- King of the gods and consort to Ara, Dewo's cult is 'universal' in that he has a temple in every city in Karoputaru and all Swart Elves acknowledging their traditional pantheon offer some sort of tribute or prayers his way, even if he is not the chief god to which each individual pays homage. As king of the gods, he is chiefly associated with storms, hospitality, and ambition.

Dola- A god of trickery and guile, Dola is a deity of unknown origins and is relatively obscure compared to the majority of Swart Elf deities. He has no official cults, though is often referred by crime organizations and those proficient in the art of thievery and espionage.

Dunosulu- A large pterosaur found in Karoputaru, Dunosulu is scientifically referred to as *Hatzegopteryx thambena*. When standing on the they are nearly tall enough to look a giraffe in the eye, and thus are popular display animals, though they are difficult to contain given their volational nature. The Huns managed to control some of their kind for use in warfare.

APPENDICES

Duworekoro- A ribbon-tailed bird known today as *Changchengornis hengdaoziensis*. They are popular pets among Swart Elf aristocracy.

Erepši- Called 'Fire-Waurms' by Franks and Ōtebren by the Huns, the Erepši is a huge creature that served as the basis for later dragon legends. This term is more specific than Šaliyanka, the generic Swart Elf word for dragon-like beasts, and it refers specifically to fire-breathing dragons that appeared in form not unlike the mušḫuššu of Babylonian art, although the Erepši also bore wings of fire and smoke.

Erinuša- (sg. Erinuwa) Female spirits associated with impending doom, the Erinuša were said to hover about the battlefield, marking out those among the wounded whose lot would be to die, though few Elves have seriously regarded this aspect of their nature for the last millennium. They are handmaidens to Zaršu-Mot.

Fanefiru- Known in Norse mythology as Fafnir, Fanefiru was the Swart Elf who slew his father Rhedemaru and seized claimed the Anadavarenu, transforming into a fire-breathing Dragon.

Gamaru- A gregarious herbivore indigenous to Karoputaru, the Gamaru may also be referred to as the dinosaur *Ouranosaurus nigeriensis*. They are striped similarly to zebras, a natural defense which disorients predators seeing hundreds of them clumped up together. Their tender meat is prized by the Swart Elves of Kunasa for its rich flavor.

APPENDICES

Gaopato- Known today as *Istiodactylus latidens*, the Gaopato is a pterosaur that makes its living off of carrion. They are not highly regarded by the Swart Elves and are often associated with the Erinuša.

Gaotalu- Known also as *Pteranodon longiceps*, the Gaotalu is a common marine pterosaur that is a popular motif in Swart Elf mosaics. They can be found anywhere near Karoputaru's seas.

Hatuwiyo- Contending with Oratu for the Swart Elf throne after Rhedemaru's death, Hatuwiyo withdrew after suffering several minor defeats, relinquishing his claim and serving instead as host-leader.

Hudaru- Situated in the thick of eastern Karoputaru, Hudaru is a lone mountain whose subterranean springs serve as the source for Kupasiyo.

Karoputaru- The mysterious land ruled by dinosaurs and Swart Elves, Karoputaru was supposedly created by Karotu as a last-ditch attempt to preserve the wildlife he so cherished, knowing such wondrous creatures would become extinct during his son's supremacy, regardless of whether or not Dewo would personally instigate their extinction.

Karotu- Father to Dewo, Karotu was the leader of the generation of gods that ruled prior to the current pantheon. He was defeated in a rebellion instigated by Dewo and has since been shackled far from the rest of the world.

APPENDICES

Kenateyo- The infamous *Tyrannosaurus rex*, Kenateyo is an animal that needs little describing. While not presently endangered, they are neither especially common and were said to be beloved of Karotu.

Keradoru- A gorge running approximately 73 miles through northeastern Karoputaru, the easily accessible Keradoru serves as a common passageway for trading caravans or armies on the march. It was here that the Huns under Ellac were ambushed by the Swart Elves and Honoria tamed her Kenateyo.

Kuanipou- A native of Puaita born in 425, Kuanipou was the twin brother of Araksadra and a member of the Forest-Walkers.

Kunasa- Famed for its artisans, Kunasa is a city tucked beneath the flows of Karoputaru's northwestern volcanoes.

Kupasiyo- Flowing approximately two hundred miles from its source in Hudaru to the sea, the Kupasiyo is a river dividing northeastern Karoputaru into nearly two evenly sized halves. Small boats are occasionally used to quickly travel this distance, though dense forests and shallow riverbeds bar larger vessels.

Laodame- Son of the ancient king Arikenou, Laodame served as king over the Swart Elves during their migration from the island of Sikeria into Karoputaru. Newa Sikeria was the first of many cities founded by Laodame when he settled his people down in central/northeastern Karoputaru.

APPENDICES

Makarosola- Identifiable as *Deinocheirus mirificus*, the Makarosola is an unusual herbivorous dinosaur known for its large arms, humped back, and billed snout. They hold no cultic significance, but are popular among explorers.

Meša- (sg. Mena) Classified as *Tawa hallae*, the Meša are small dinosaurs that wield saliva laced with mildly narcotic venom which disorients their prey. These animals once lived in Karoputaru with the other dinosaurs, but were supposedly called away to Toratanatu by a former member of the Torapaï upon abandoning their order to pursue other ambitions.

Newa Sikeria- Established in approximately 1150 B.C.E. amid subterranean ruins previously constructed and abandoned by an unknown civilization, Newa Sikeria was the first city erected by Laodame when the Swart Elves inhabited Karoputaru. It remains their capital and the center Posedawone's cult.

Nildahgiiv- Warden of the World Tree Artaru, Nildahgiiv seems to be an incredibly large member of the genus *Scutosaurus* who acquired sentience long ago by some currently undescribed method. Though she is not the founder of the Torapaï, she is by far its oldest member.

Nukera- Also known as the ant *Ceratomyrmex ellenbergeri*, the Nukera is known for its unusual hornlike structures. Some of these ants were brought to Ravenna by Hunnic diplomats.

APPENDICES

Oratu- Upon the death of Rhedemaru, host-leader (*lawakutaso*) Oratu claimed kingship (450-476) after a brief interregnum, prevailing after a few skirmishes against his rival Hatuwiyo.

Oretera- A ring of standing stones encircling a tower of unknown origins, Oretera is where the Torapaï first summoned the Host of Dragons and have since then used the site as a rally point for further beckons. The ruins are empty, and there is little of archaeological interest beyond the architecture.

Orokaraü- A game popular among the Swart Elves though, given its danger, few actively participate in it, Orokaraü consists of an acrobat leaping over a charging Orokeruša by grabbing the animal's brow horns and somersaulting over its massive head. Fatalities are common, as many less-skilled athletes are gored on the horns that adorn the Orokeruša's frill.

Orokeruša- Also known as *Diabloceratops eatoni*, the Orokeruša is a dinosaur bearing two pairs of curved horns, one above the eyes and the other atop the bony frill that protects the animal's neck. They are fiercely aggressive and popular obstacles for athletic games, most especially Orokaraü.

Oropukonu- An animal for its unique array of natural body armor, the Oropukonu is identifiable as *Dacentrurus armatus*. These dinosaurs have no cultic significance and, given their small brains, bear little capacity for training for warfare. They are, however, a popular motif for tapestries, particularly those in temples for Dewo, though this phenomenon seems to be originally an odd coincidence that later became tradition rather than being symbolic of any religious significance.

Oruseu-An ancient wanderer from far off lands, Oruseu was offered shelter and safe passage home by the Swart Elves after being washed onto their ancestral island home. His parallel to the Greek figure Odysseus as written in *The Odyssey* is obvious.

Oturu- Preserved in Norse myth as the dwarf Otr, Oturu was the third son of Rhedemaru, slain by the god Dola while fishing because he was somehow mistaken for some wild animal. Later Norse stories say he took on the form of an otter before he was killed by Loki.

Pahkvaas- Steed of Veydaalfar, Pahkvaas is identifiable as a large *Thalassodromeus sethi*, who carries his rider as he brings supplies and tidings of the outside world to Nildahgiiv and Tosarkhaan.

Panhušu- Stronghold of Zaršu-Mot, Panhušu sits at the heart of the Mist-Crags of the Netherworld.

Paotopuga- Classified as *Sharovipteryx mirabilis*, the Paotopuga is an unusual reptile known for its elongated hind limbs that support membraneous wings, allowing it to glide from tree to tree. They are popular among the Swart Elves as pets, though they have not historically adjusted well to the stresses of captivity.

APPENDICES

Panuko- Identifiable as *Shuvuuia deserti*, the Panuko is a small dinosaur known for its enlarged claw and at first glance might be mistaken as having only one finger on each hand. One was brought to the Frankish king Merovech by Hunnic diplomats.

Parahu-Ku- An ancient underground viewing space tucked beneath a commemorative mound, Parahu-Ku allows travelers to look through a glass wall at the giant sea creatures that live off Karoputaru's eastern shore. It is a popular location for travelers, though not often frequented due to its relative remoteness.

Peteyopuga- Identified as *Diplocaulus magnicornis*, the Peteyopuga is a meter-long amphibian known for its boomerang-shaped head. Though now extinct in Karoputaru, a number of their population was once imported to the subterranean waterways surrounding Gold Tor, and they have flourished in this ecological isolation.

Poliwu- The First-Elder (*poropaai*) of Puaita (448-470), Poliwu is most known for the massive expansion of the city undergone during his twenty-two years of holding office.

Posedawone- The god of seas and earthquakes, Posedawone is the older brother of Dewo. His cult center is at Newa Sikeria, though he has temples in every coastal settlement, and he is highly revered by all seafaring Elves.

Puaita- Situated on the northeastern coast of Karoputaru, Puaita is a maritime city famed for the immensity of its harbor. It also serves as the center of the cult to Ara and has a bustling athletic culture, Orokaraü being the favored sport.

Rega- Known in Norse mythology as Reginn, Rega was the son of Rhedemaru who went into self-imposed exile after his brother Fanefiru seized Anadavarenu and slew their father.

Reputorewa- The monkey puzzle tree (*Araucaria araucana*), Reputorewa is a tree common in Karoputaru's less densely forested areas, though a thick forest of them also welcomes travelers who enter Karoputaru through Artaru.

Rhedemaru- Known in Norse mythology as the dwarf Hreidmar, Rhedemaru reigned as king over the Swart Elves 413-450 until he was slain by his son Fanefiru. After a brief interregnum he was succeeded by Oratu. His reign was marked by relative peace until the coming of the Huns.

Salorana- A huge *Shastasaurus*-like ichthyosaur, the Salorana is an enormous marine reptile known for its placid demeanor. They frequent the eastern coast of Karoputaru and thus are popular objects of observation for those who visit Parahu-Ku.

Šaliyanka- A generic term translated as 'dragon', Šaliyanka refers not only to fire-breathing monsters of legend, but to any creature of at least semi-reptilian appearance indigenous to Karoputaru, especially dinosaurs and other such creatures.

Sikeria- The ancient homeland of the Swart Elves, Sikeria was a remote island in an unknown area of the Atlantic Ocean first settled in circa 2000 B.C.E., and the island is said to have been sunk by Posedawone eight hundred years later, forcing the Elves to migrate until finding Karoputaru. Its strange fauna, including beasts like winged man-bulls and other hybrid forms, was boasted to be the inspiration for the myths and artistic designs of various civilizations in the Ancient Near East

Suiayo- A huge dinosaur, the Suiayo is identifiable as none other than the massive titanosaur *Patagotitan mayorum.*

Talalit- A large island located a hundred kilometers off the eastern coast of Karoputaru, Talalit is the fertile island where Honoria established her city Elpis with Roman and Hunnic fugitives.

Talhuit- Identifiable as a large member of the marine genus *Pliosaurus*, Talhuit is a great marine predator common throughout the seas of Karoputaru.

Taumazo- The Swart Elf term for the iconic fight between famed rivals *Tyrannosaurus rex* and *Triceratops prorsus*, the Taumazo is an occasion rarely witnessed, though it is understandably a popular motif for Elven art and epic mythological tales.

APPENDICES

Temekuš- A small moon measuring nearly thirty kilometers in diameter, Temekuš is treated in Swart Elf literature as a low-lying moon or some other such satellite. Legend says that Temekuš was lifted from the earth at Karotu's command when he first made Karoputaru. Its internal springs are said to be the life-force of the land, providing nourishment to the Land of Dragons. The floating rock has often served as a study for the scholars and sorcerers of Karoputaru.

Terikeruša- Known also as *Triceratops prorsus*, the Terikeruša has attained a near-legendary status among the Swart Elves for its power and willingness to fight a Kenateyo. They hold no cultic significance, but are greatly revered by Karoputaru's residents for their imposing appearance.

Tiwokeru- Referred to by the scientific community as *Guanlong wucaii*, the Tiwokeru are small carnivorous dinosaurs known for the hollow crests on their heads. They are rarely seen by most Swart Elves and hold a place of high regard among the Torapaï, going forth as their heralds whenever the Torapaï summon the dinosaurs of Karoputaru to war.

Toradaaku- The "Dark Forest", Toradaaku appears nowhere else in the historical record beyond *Augusta*, thus its actual geographic location is difficult to pin down. However, it seems like it might be related to the Myrkviðr (anglicized as Mirkwood) which in tradition separated the Goths from the Huns.

APPENDICES

Toraku- Also called *Desmatosuchus spurensis*, the Toraku is a herbivorous reptile known for its thick armor and shoulder spikes. Its kind is most frequently found in Karoputaru's densest jungles. Due to an association with the goddess Atana, some are trained to carry libations and ritual elements to her altars.

Torapaï- Translated as 'Forest-Walkers' the Torapaï are a multiethnic order originally founded to preserve Karoputaru's fauna from outside corruption, though they have stepped beyond these bounds, either summoning those very same creatures to war when so needed or seeking out and banishing primordial threats to other realms. Their members are well-versed in powers often described as magical and have an innate gift of communicating with, or even controlling, the animals of Karoputaru.

Toratanatu- A subterranean city built by an unknown people, Toratanatu was said by legend to be the center of a significant battle in Dewo's rebellion against the older generation of gods. It was the first defeat for those who served Karotu and the older generation, and those who allied themselves with him were cursed by Dewo to endless wandering as idle shades.

Tosarkhaan- A *Drepanosaurus unguicaudatus*, Tosarkhaan, like Nildahgiiv, gained sentience some time deep in immemorial antiquity. He is a member of the Torapaï with a reputation for his alcoholic tendencies and an affinity for absurd questions.

APPENDICES

Tuwinono- Known nowhere else in the historical record, Tuwinono was a Swart Elf slain by Ellac in Keradoru.

Veydaalfar- The *Yi qi* Veydaalfar rides upon Pahkvaas, serving as a courier for Nildahgiiv and Tosarkhaan.

Wanaku- The *Wešikeriaya* word meaning 'king', Wanaku typically takes the place of any king's name while he rules. The king is again referred to by his birth name only after he has stepped down or died. Wanaka- the feminine equivalent- rarely replaces the queen's name, even if she is sole monarch. Although the Wanaku's seat of power has occasionally be moved, it is most often centered at Newa Sikeria.

Zamaro- A large, herbivorous animal known for its bombastic, trumpeting sounds, the Zamaro is easily identifiable as the hadrosaurid dinosaur *Parasaurolophus tubicen*. They are popular for their deep, bellowing songs and thus are often held on display by the Swart Elves, though only the Torapaï have successfully made choruses featuring these creatures.

Zaršu-Mot- Swart Elf god of the dead, Zaršu-Mot rules the Mist-Crags of the Netherworld. He is said to create phantoms of those near their hour of death and house them in his halls, although he will occasionally snatch actual mortals, 'saving' them and thereby keeping them in his domain as either eternal servants or as prisoners.